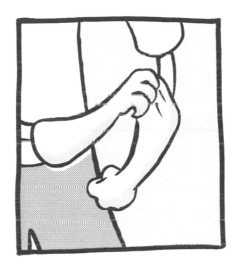

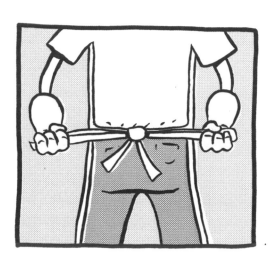

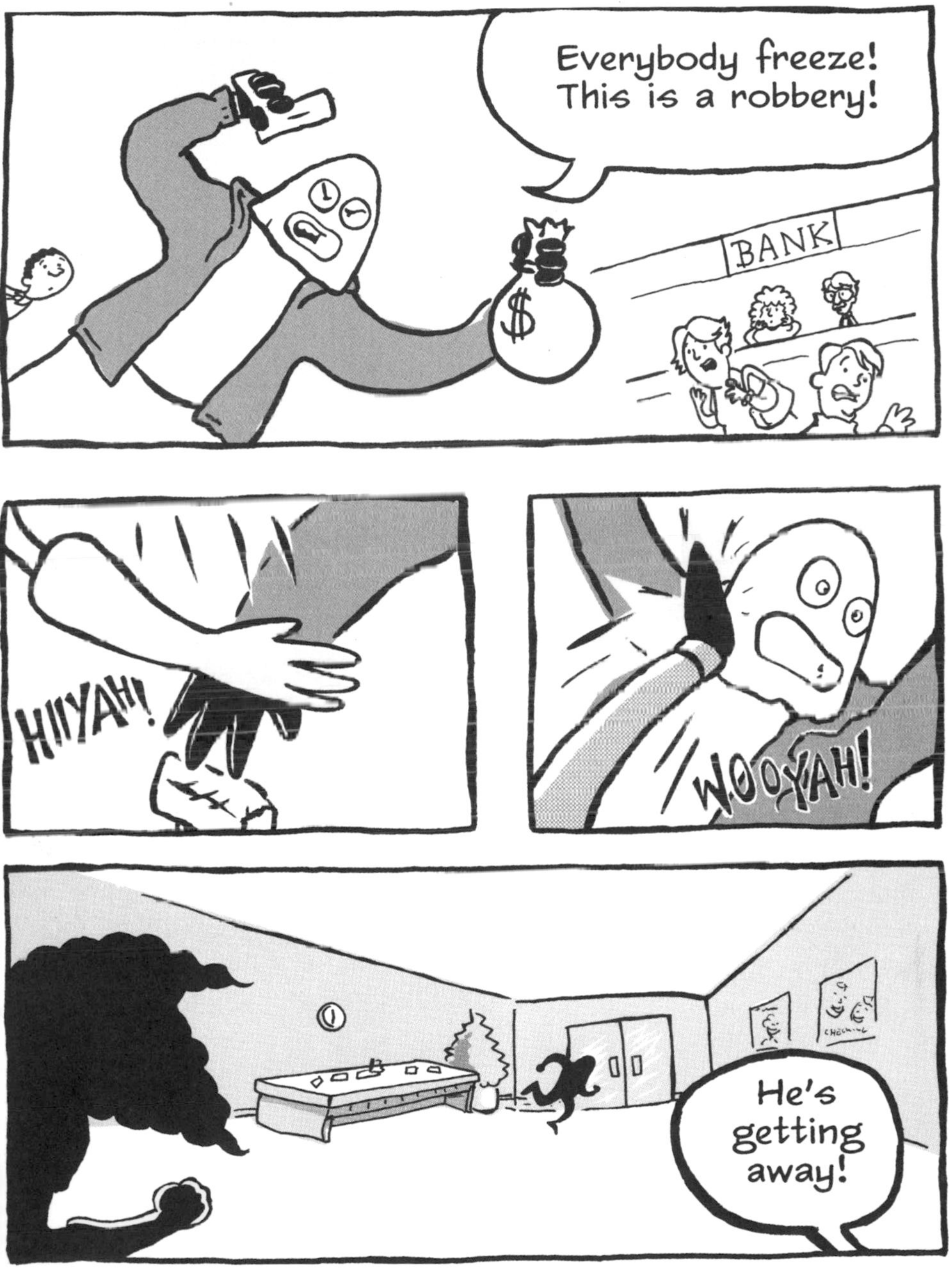
Everybody freeze! This is a robbery!
BANK
HIIYAH!
WOOYAH!
He's getting away!

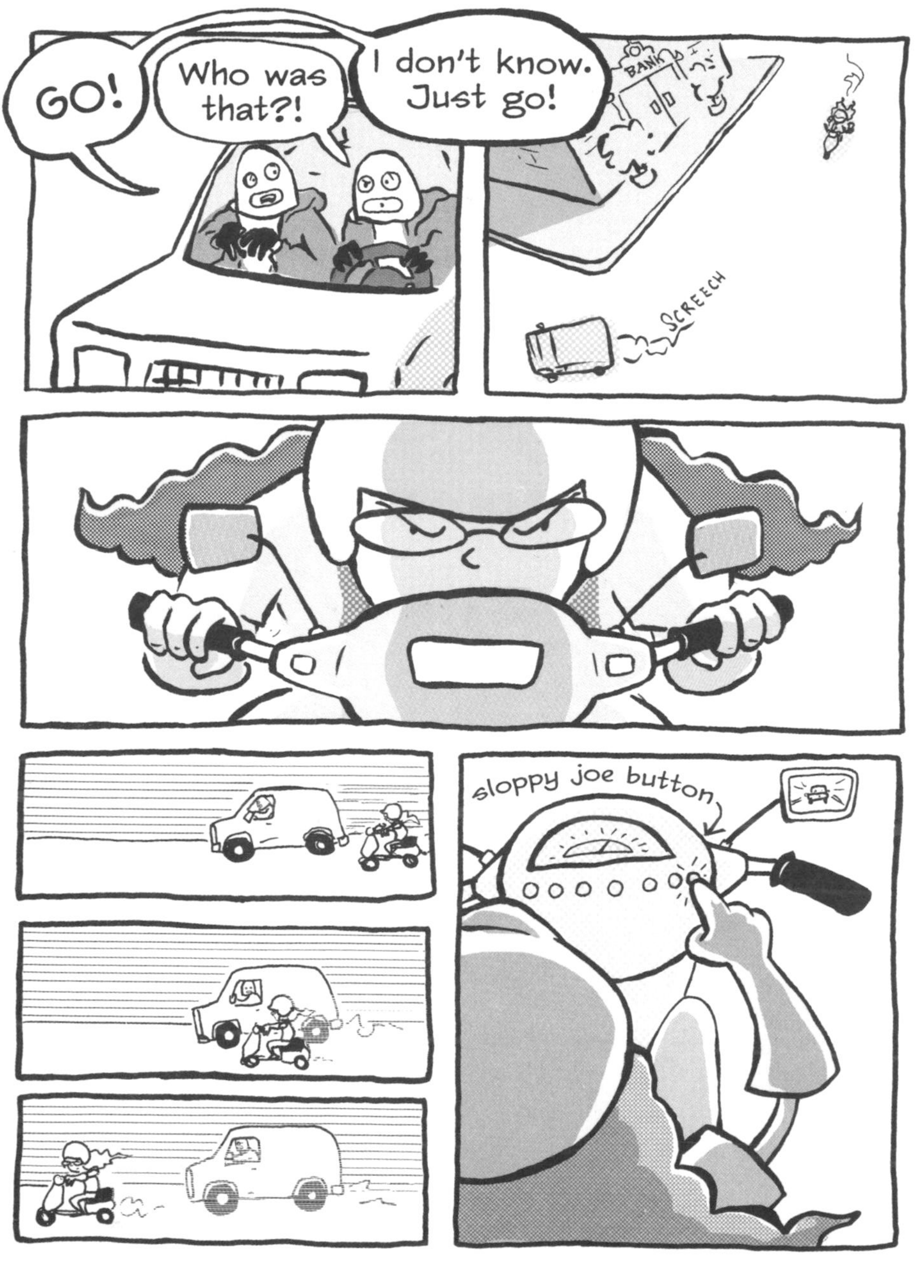
GO!
Who was that?!
I don't know. Just go!
BANK
SCREECH
sloppy joe button

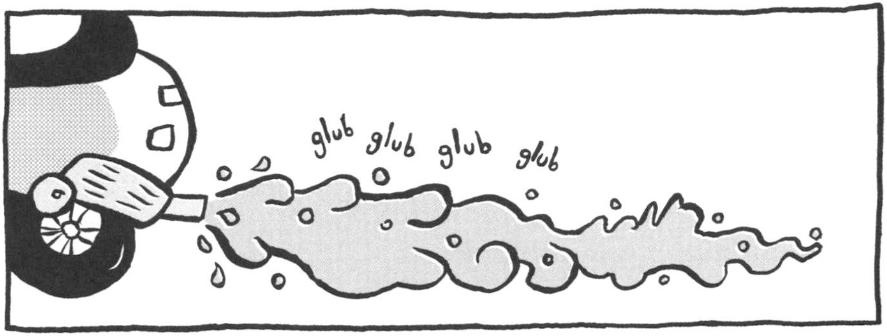
glub glub glub glub

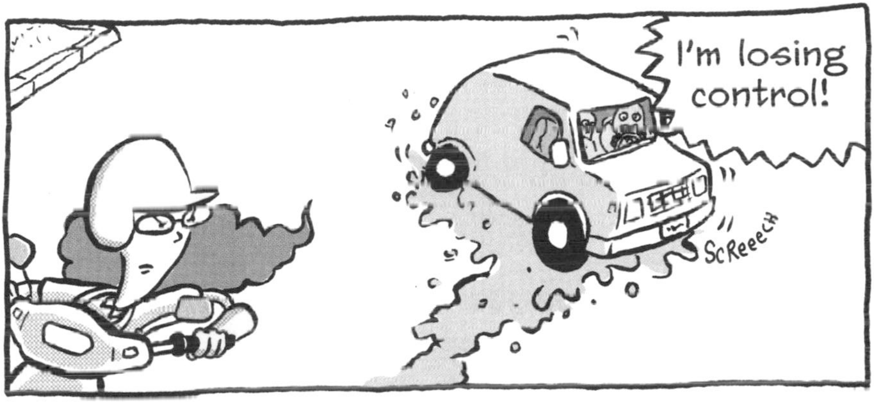
I'm losing control!
SCREEECH

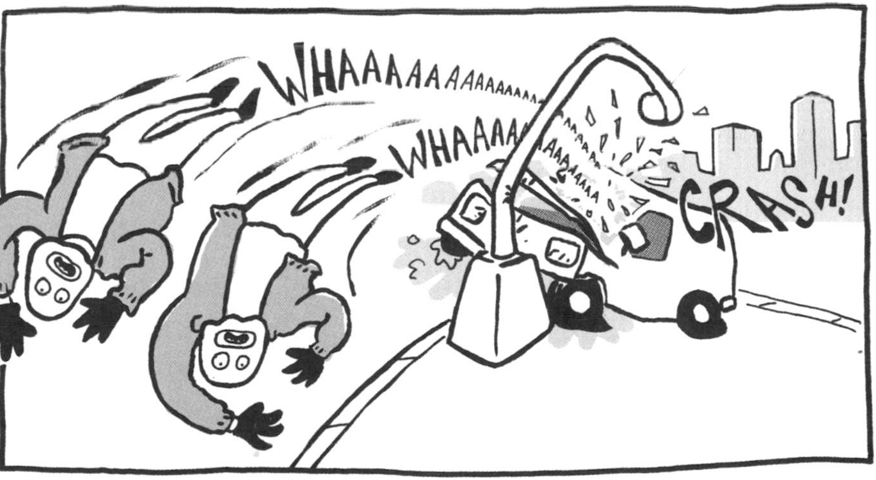
WHAAAAAAAAAAAAAA
WHAAAAAAAAAAAAA
CRASH!

LUNCH

Jarrett J. Krosoczka

LADY

and the Cyborg Substitute

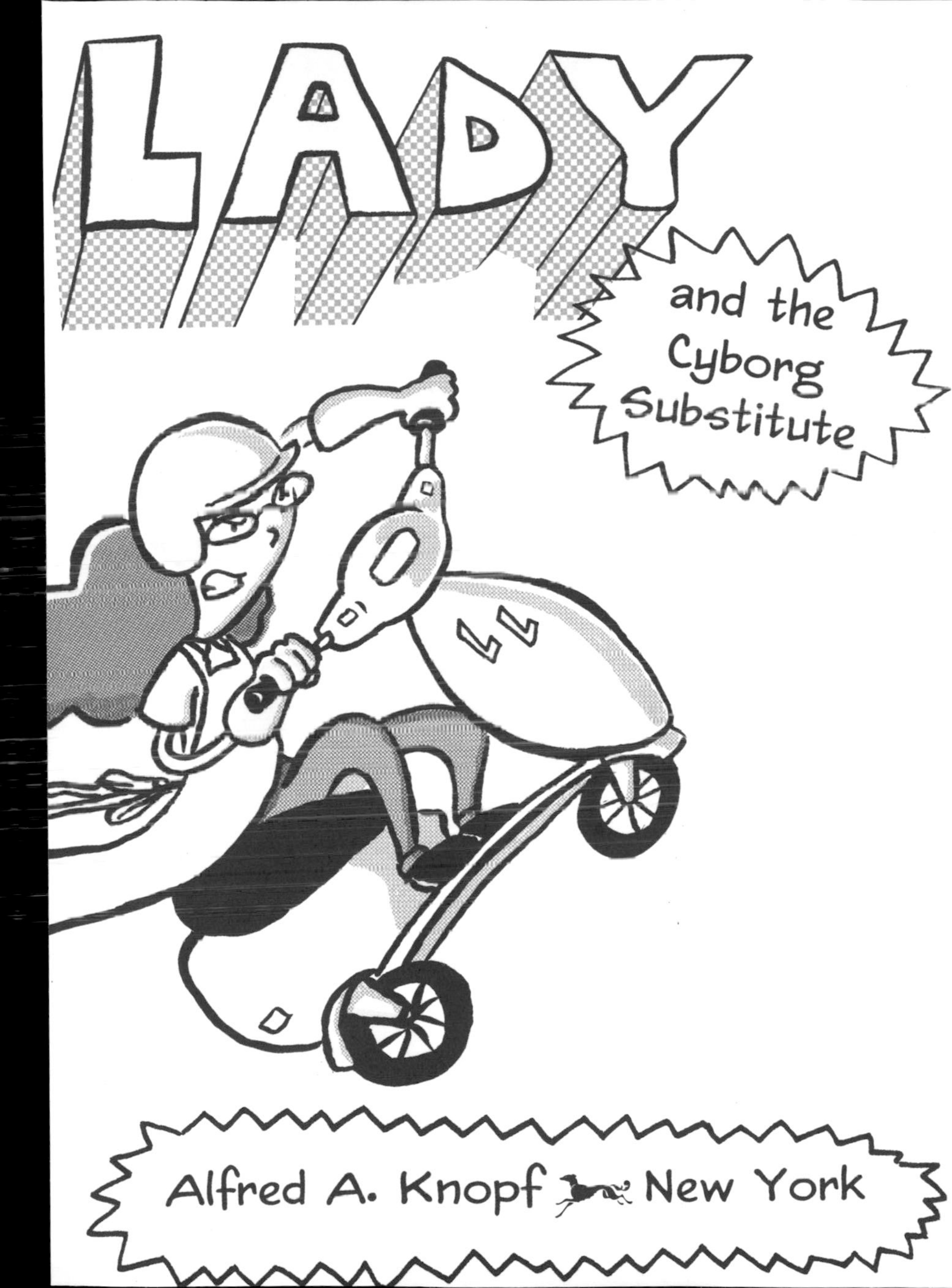

Alfred A. Knopf New York

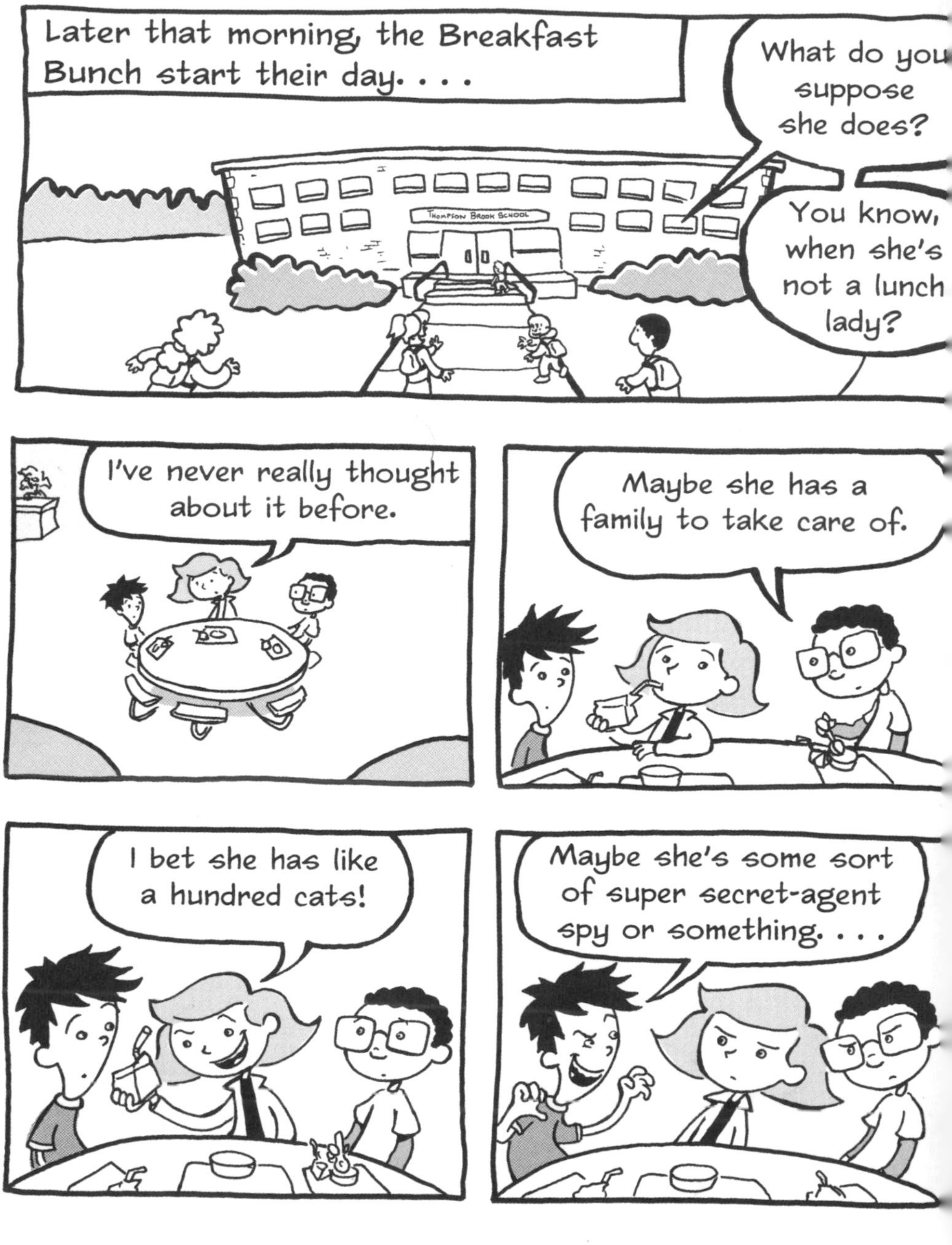

Later that morning, the Breakfast Bunch start their day. . . .
What do you suppose she does?
You know, when she's not a lunch lady?
THOMPSON BROOK SCHOOL
I've never really thought about it before.
Maybe she has a family to take care of.
I bet she has like a hundred cats!
Maybe she's some sort of super secret-agent spy or something. . . .

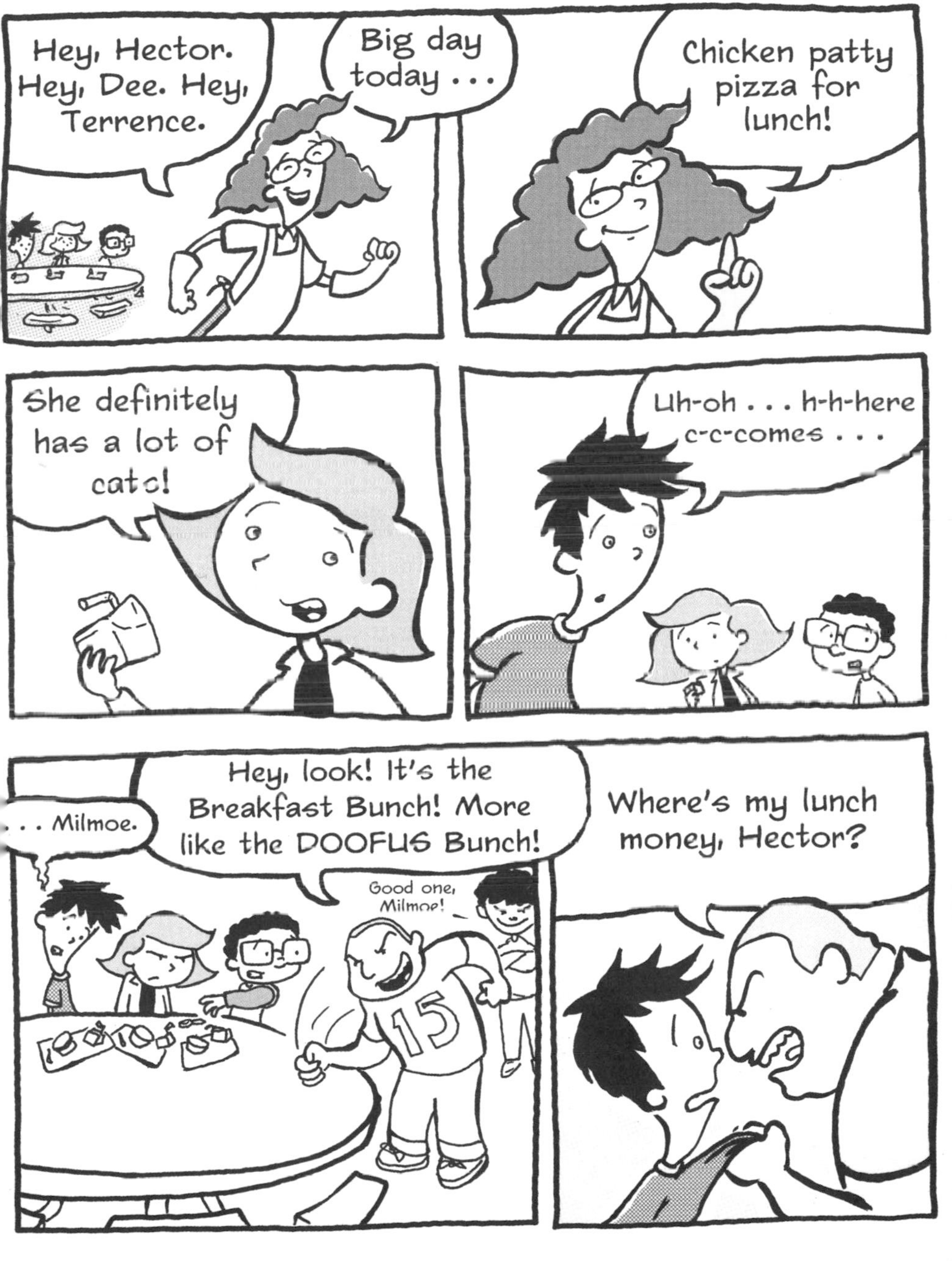
Hey, Hector. Hey, Dee. Hey, Terrence.
Big day today . . .
Chicken patty pizza for lunch!
She definitely has a lot of cats!
Uh-oh . . . h-h-here c-c-comes . . .
. . . Milmoe.
Hey, look! It's the Breakfast Bunch! More like the DOOFUS Bunch!
Good one, Milmoe!
15
Where's my lunch money, Hector?

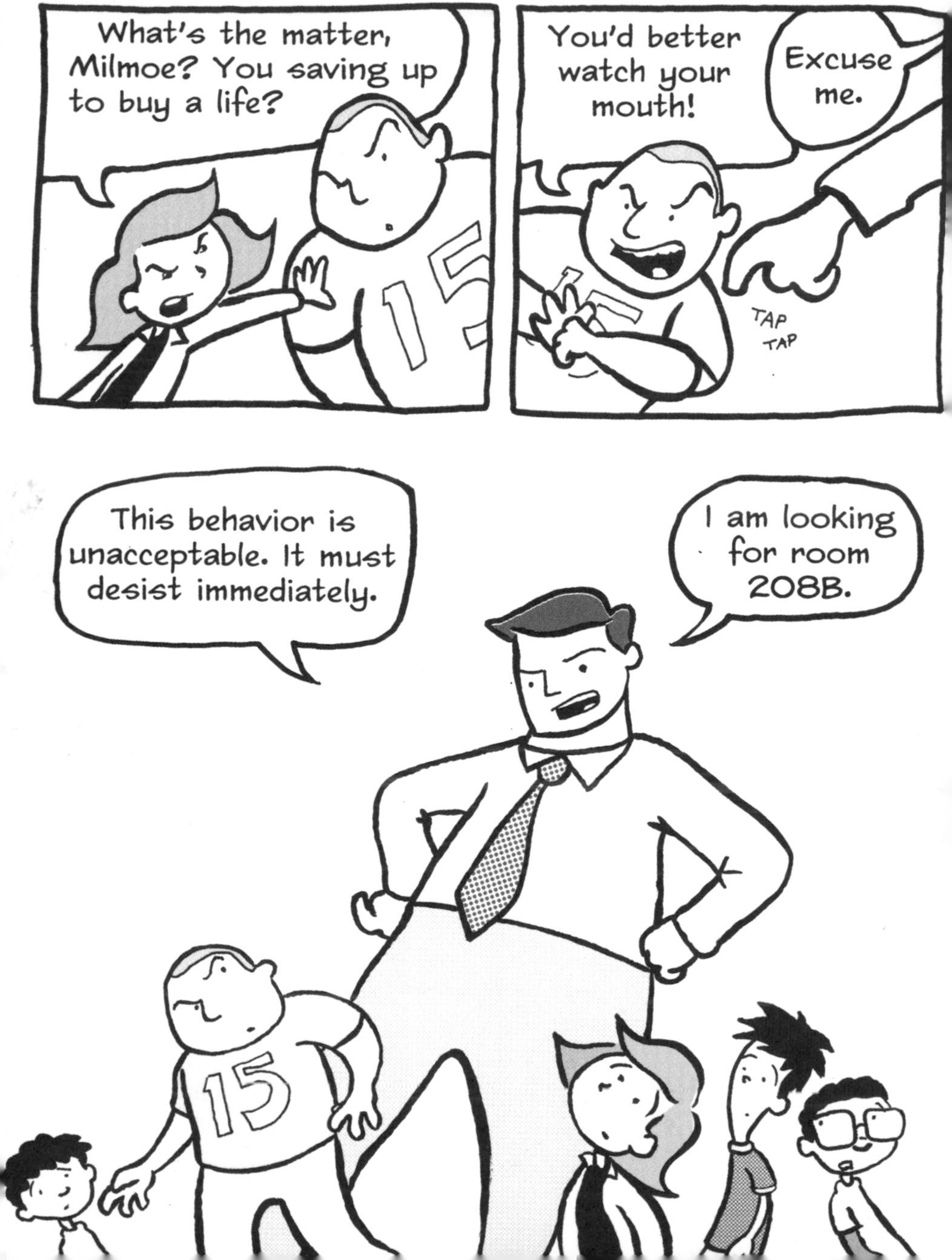
What's the matter, Milmoe? You saving up to buy a life?
You'd better watch your mouth!
Excuse me.
TAP TAP
This behavior is unacceptable. It must desist immediately.
I am looking for room 208B.
15

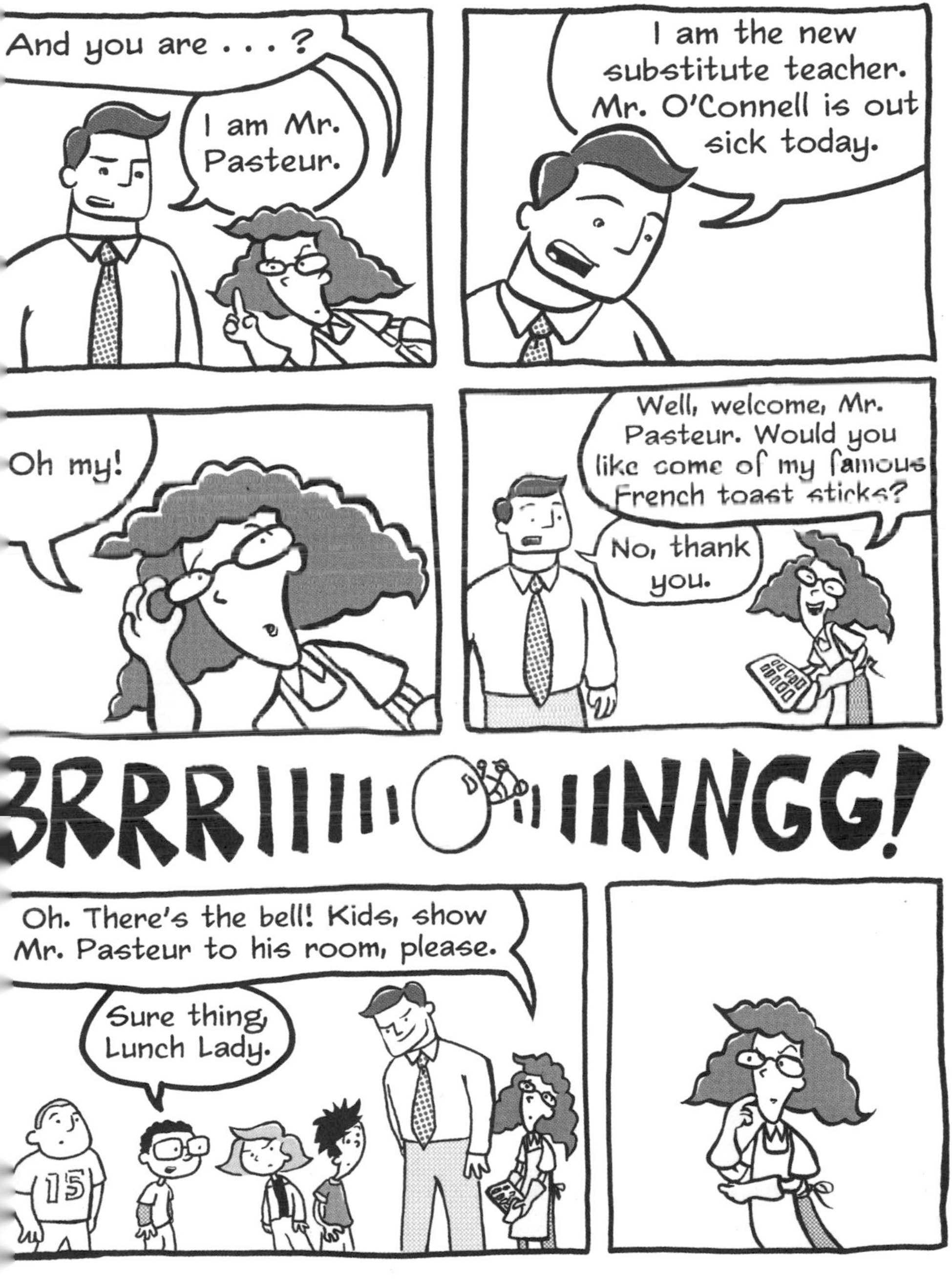
And you are . . . ?
I am Mr. Pasteur.
I am the new substitute teacher. Mr. O'Connell is out sick today.
Oh my!
Well, welcome, Mr. Pasteur. Would you like some of my famous French toast sticks?
No, thank you.
BRRRIIIIIIIIINNGG!
Oh. There's the bell! Kids, show Mr. Pasteur to his room, please.
Sure thing, Lunch Lady.
15

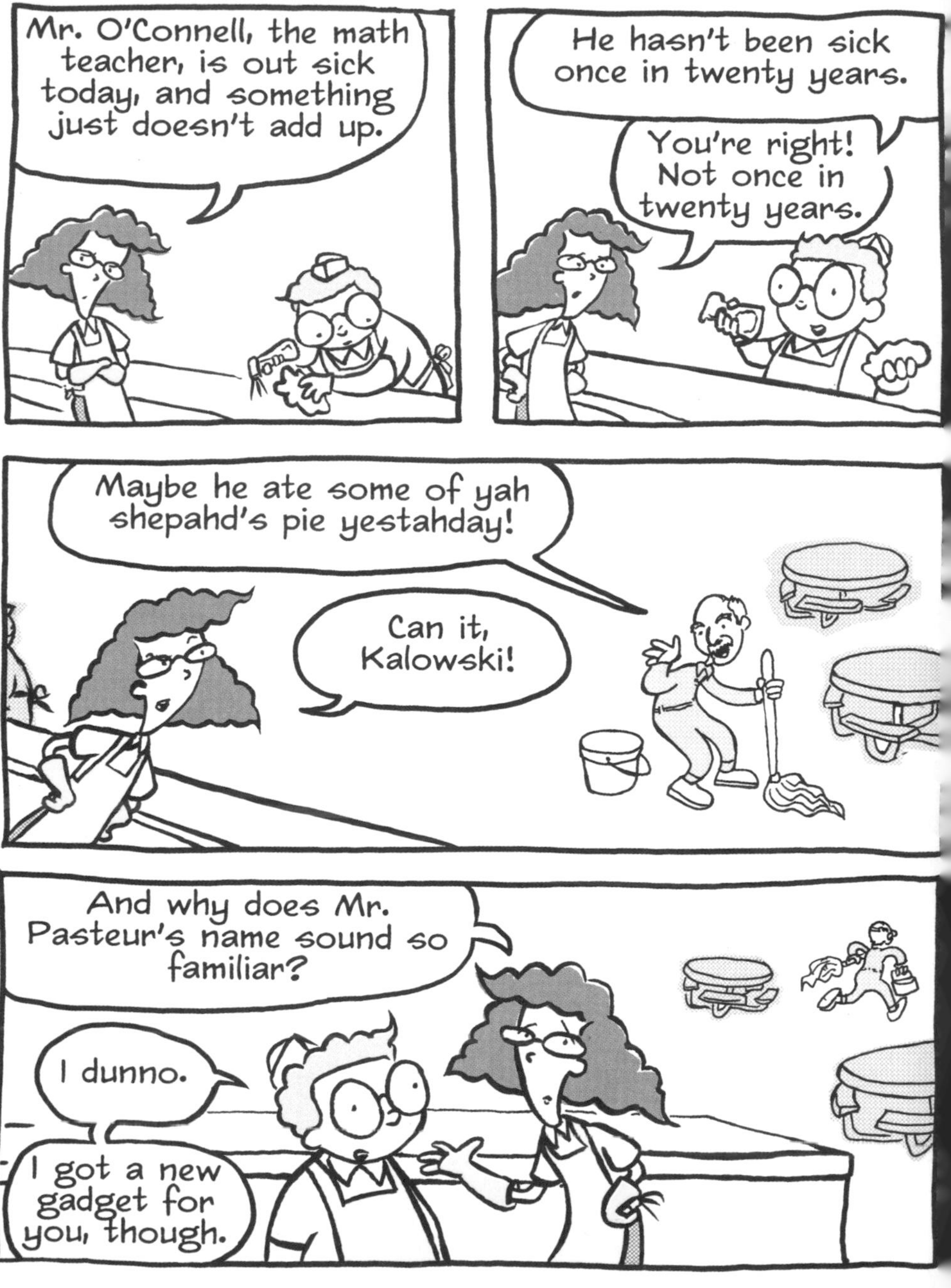
Mr. O'Connell, the math teacher, is out sick today, and something just doesn't add up.
He hasn't been sick once in twenty years.
You're right! Not once in twenty years.
Maybe he ate some of yah shepahd's pie yestahday!
Can it, Kalowski!
And why does Mr. Pasteur's name sound so familiar?
I dunno.
I got a new gadget for you, though.

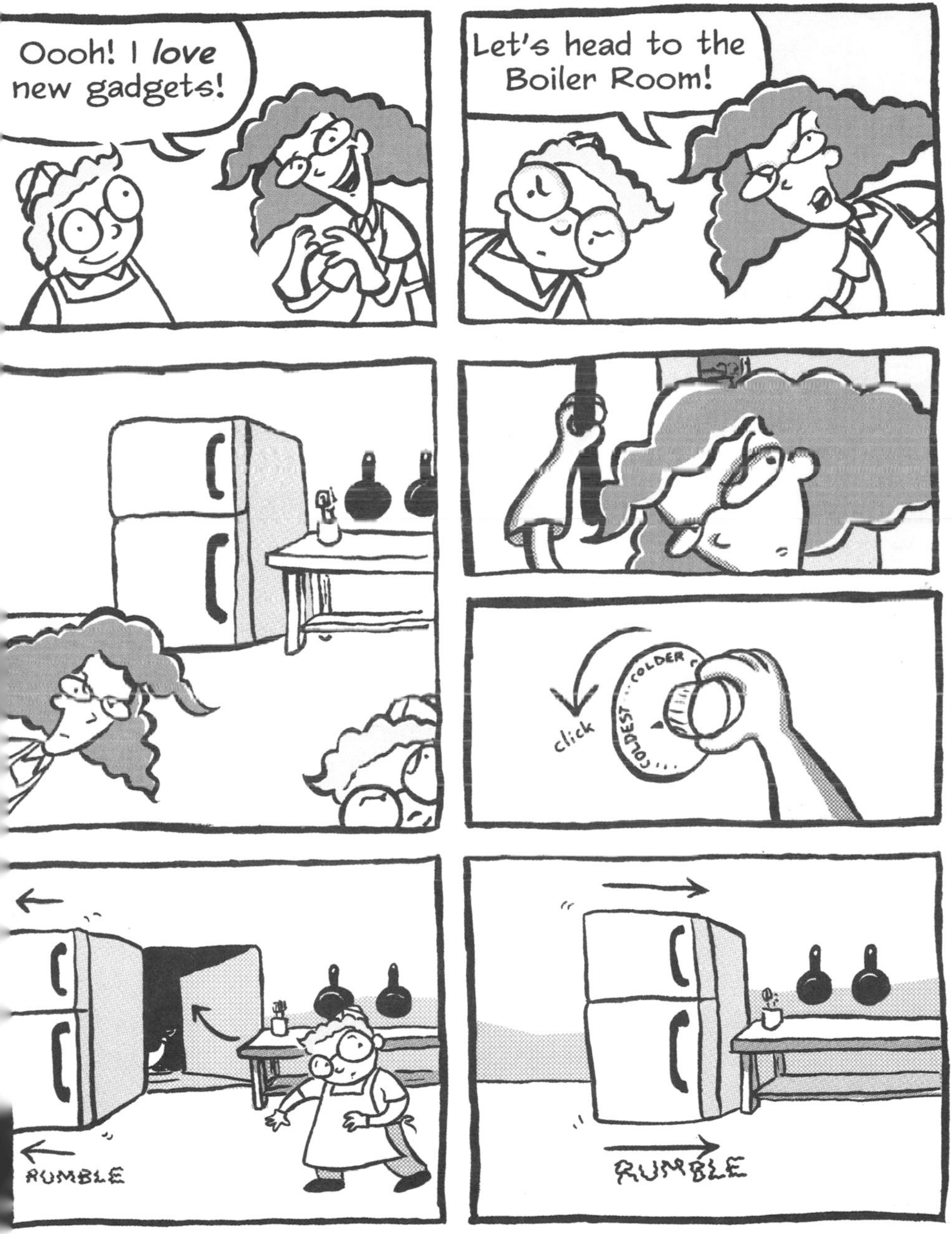
Oooh! I *love* new gadgets!
Let's head to the Boiler Room!
COLDER
COLDEST
click
RUMBLE
RUMBLE

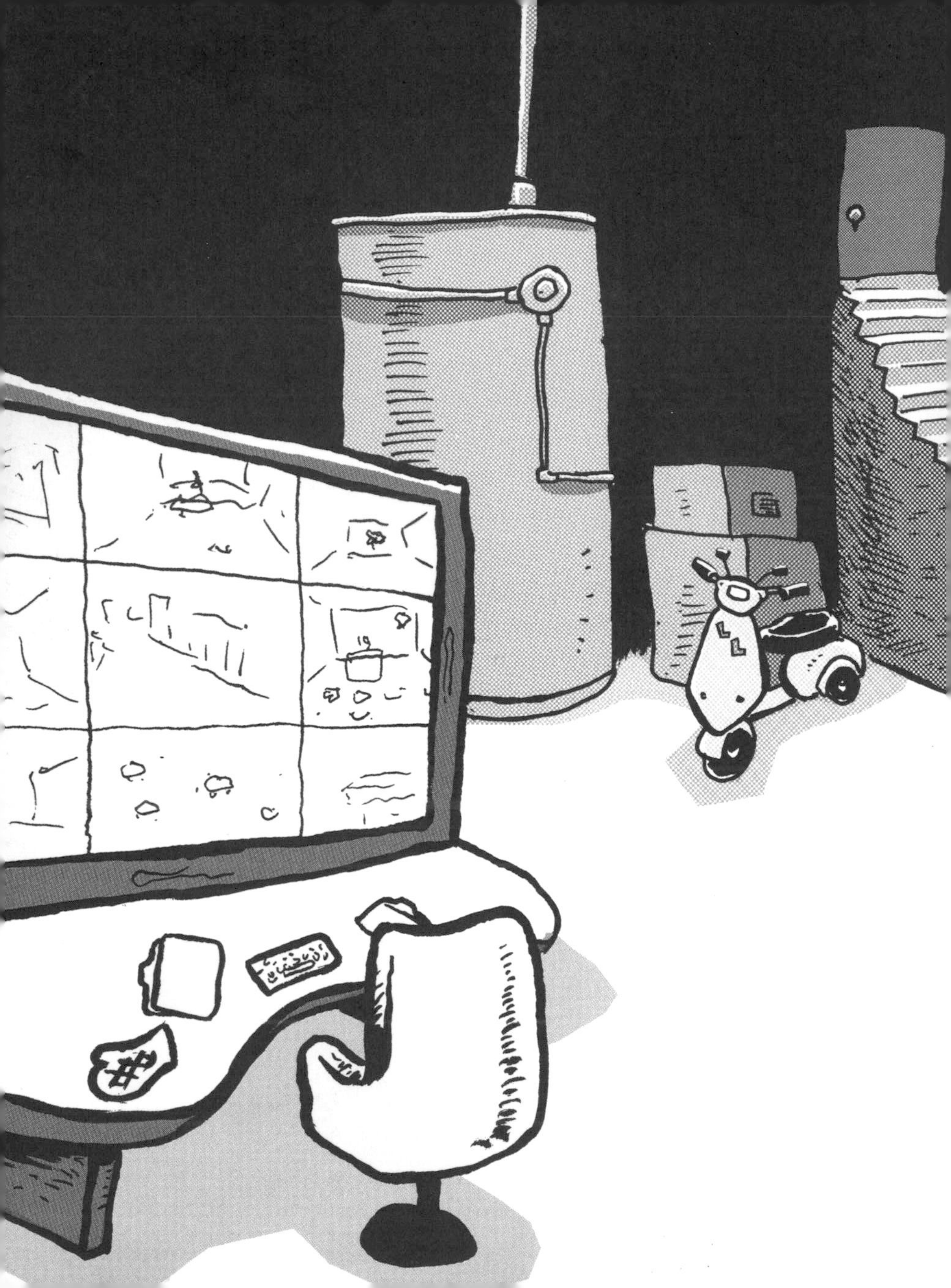

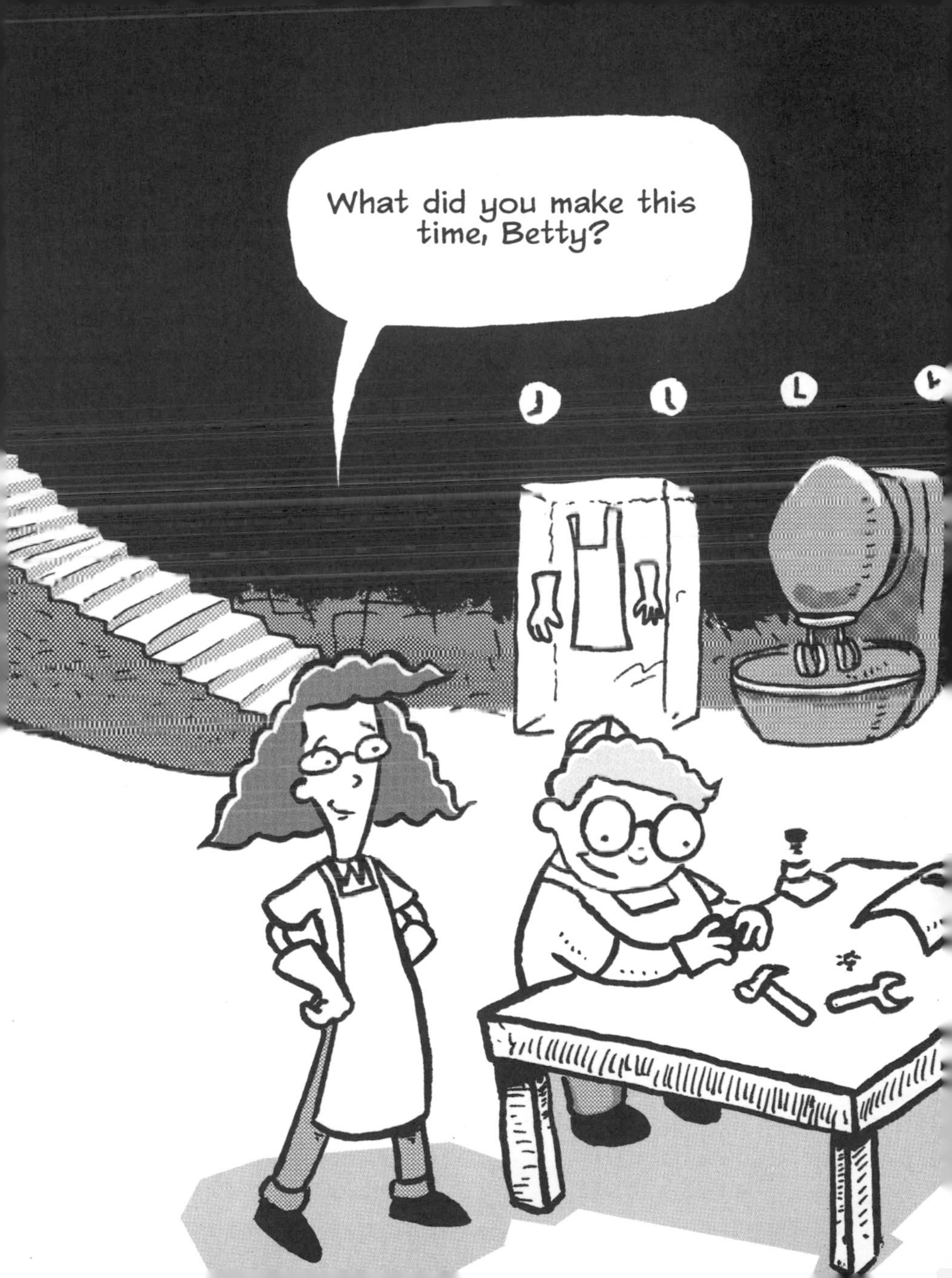
What did you make this time, Betty?

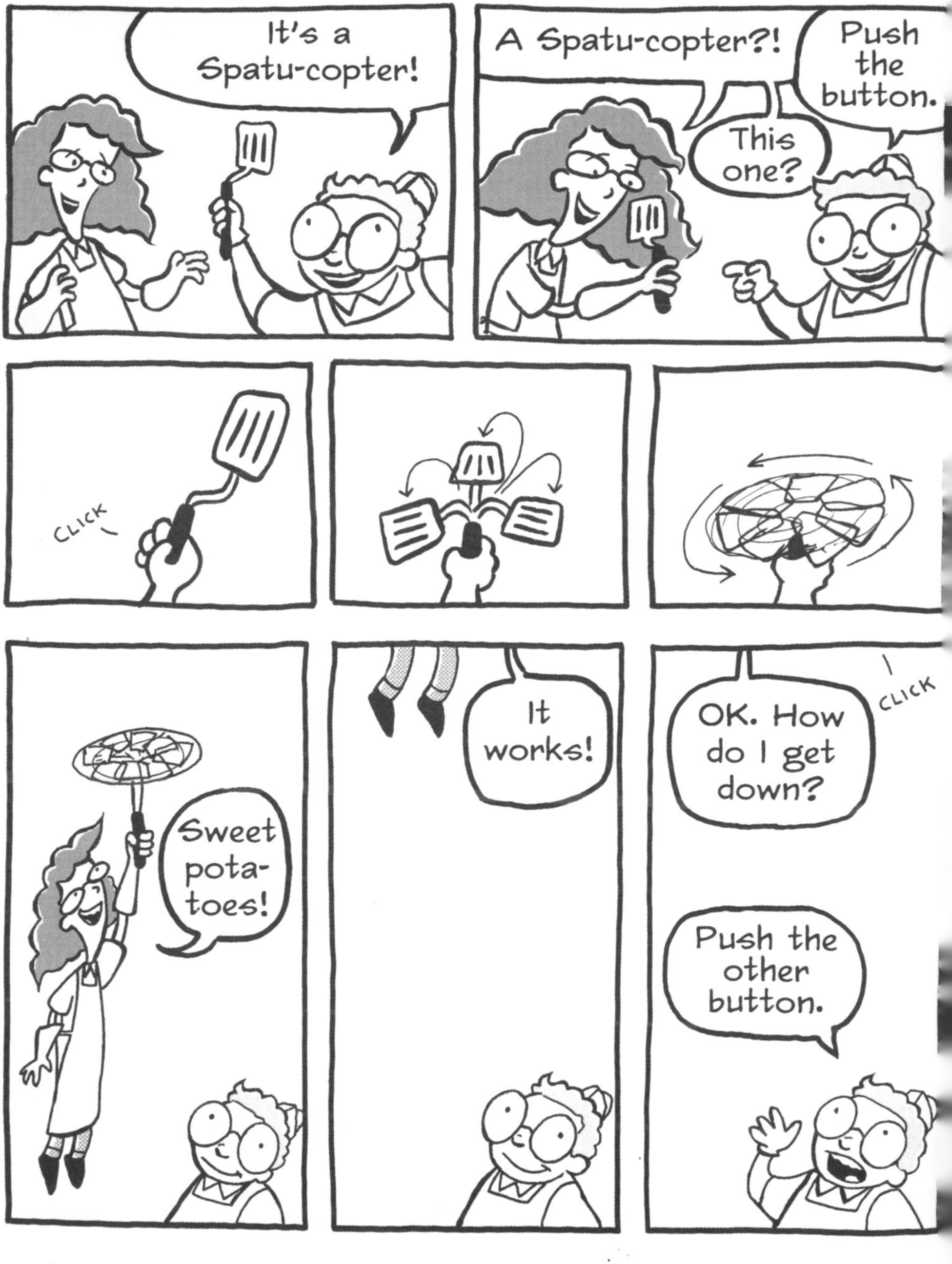

It's a Spatu-copter!
A Spatu-copter?!
This one?
Push the button.
CLICK
Sweet pota-toes!
It works!
OK. How do I get down?
CLICK
Push the other button.

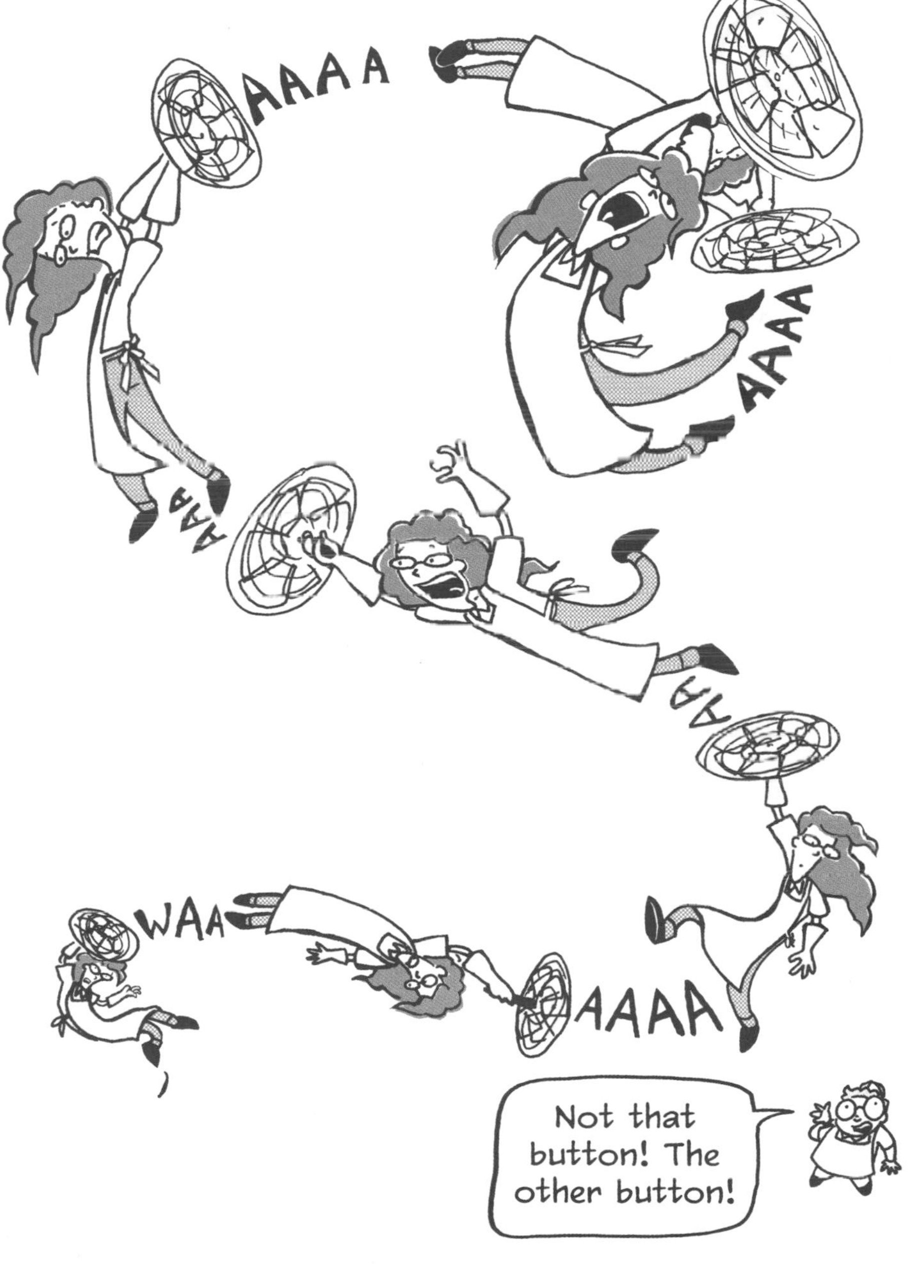
AAAA
AAAA
AAA
AA
WAA
AAAA
Not that button! The other button!

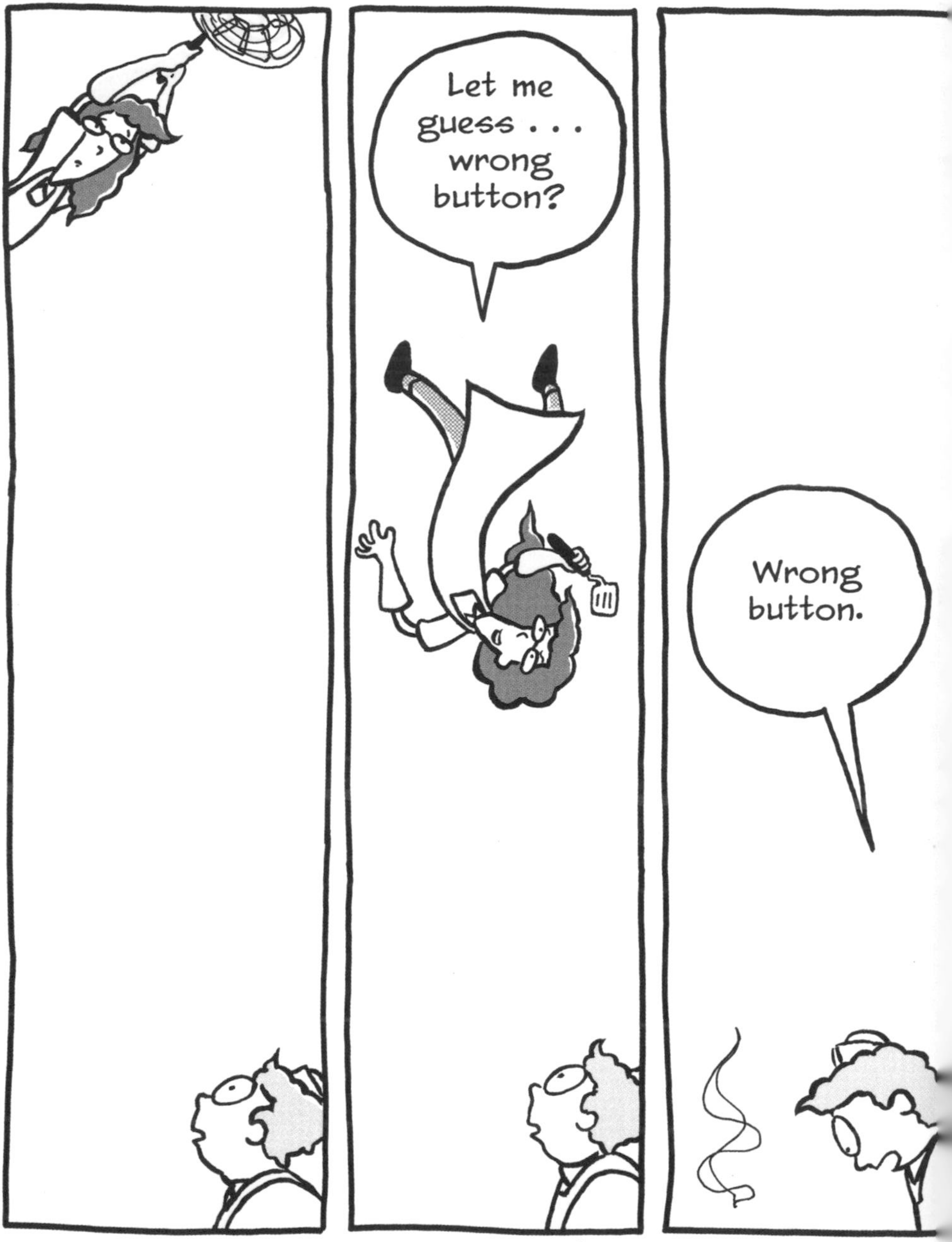
Let me guess . . . wrong button?
Wrong button.

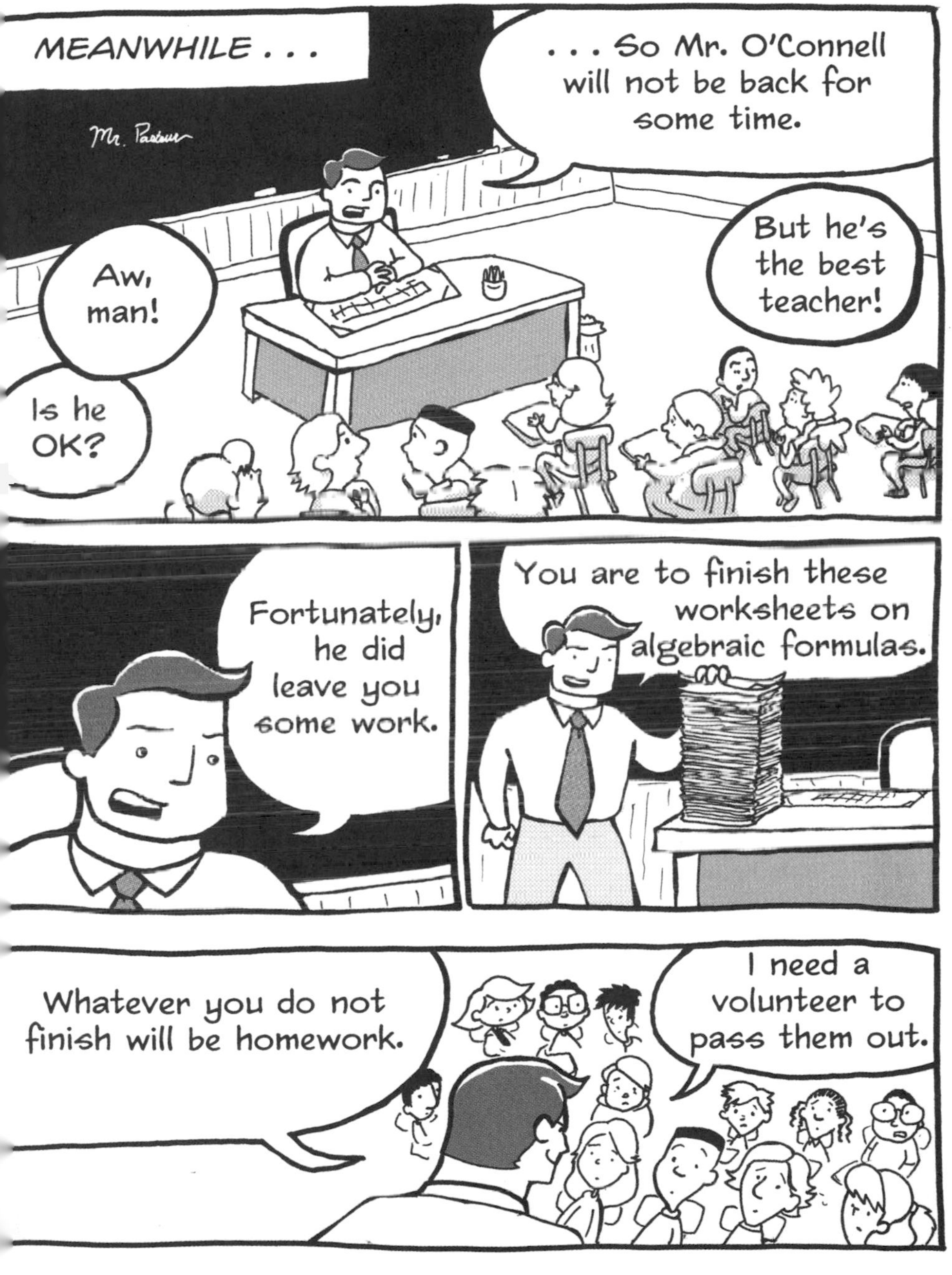
MEANWHILE . . .
Mr. Pastore
. . . So Mr. O'Connell will not be back for some time.
Aw, man!
But he's the best teacher!
Is he OK?
Fortunately, he did leave you some work.
You are to finish these worksheets on algebraic formulas.
Whatever you do not finish will be homework.
I need a volunteer to pass them out.

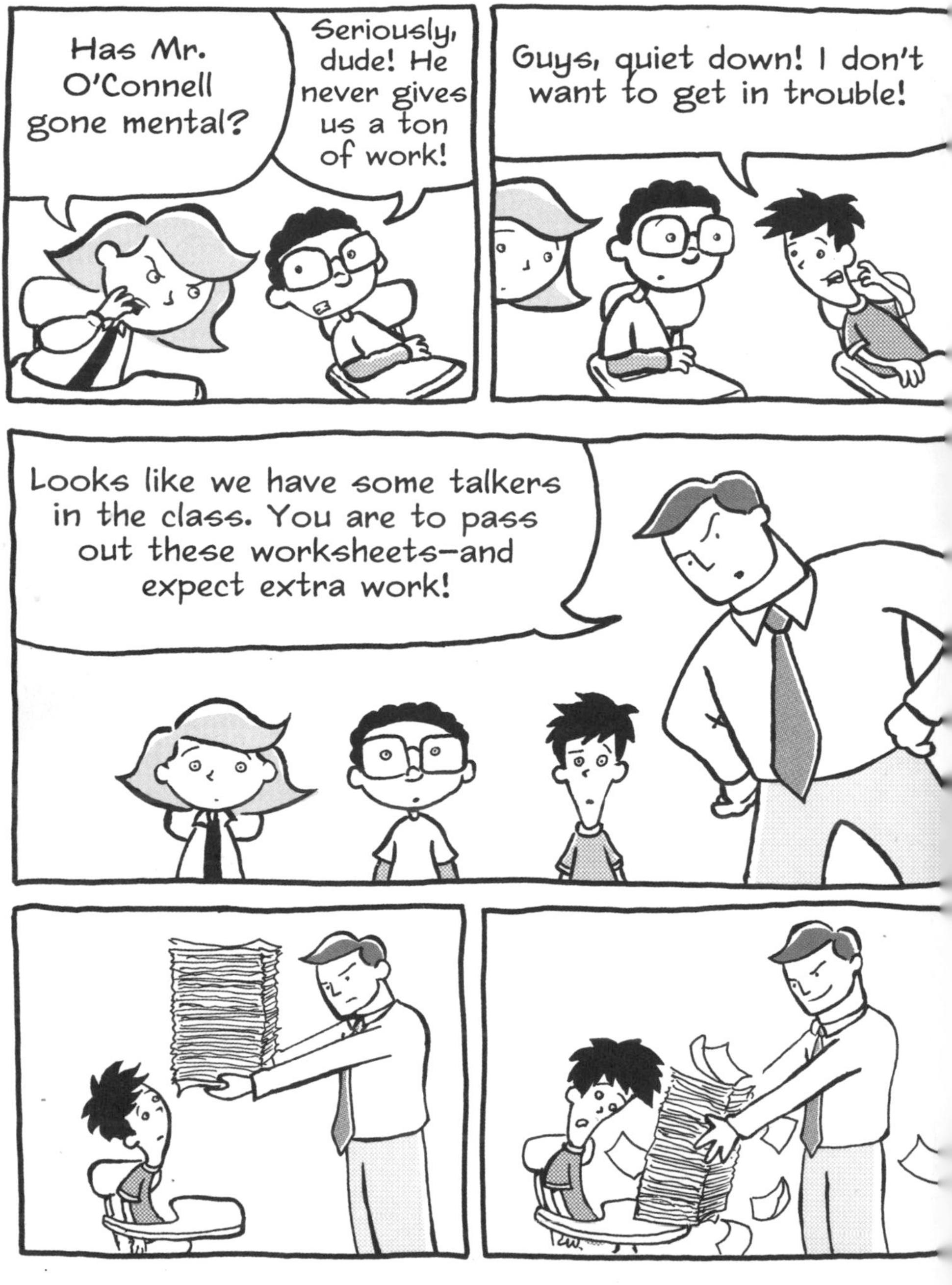
Has Mr. O'Connell gone mental?
Seriously, dude! He never gives us a ton of work!
Guys, quiet down! I don't want to get in trouble!
Looks like we have some talkers in the class. You are to pass out these worksheets—and expect extra work!

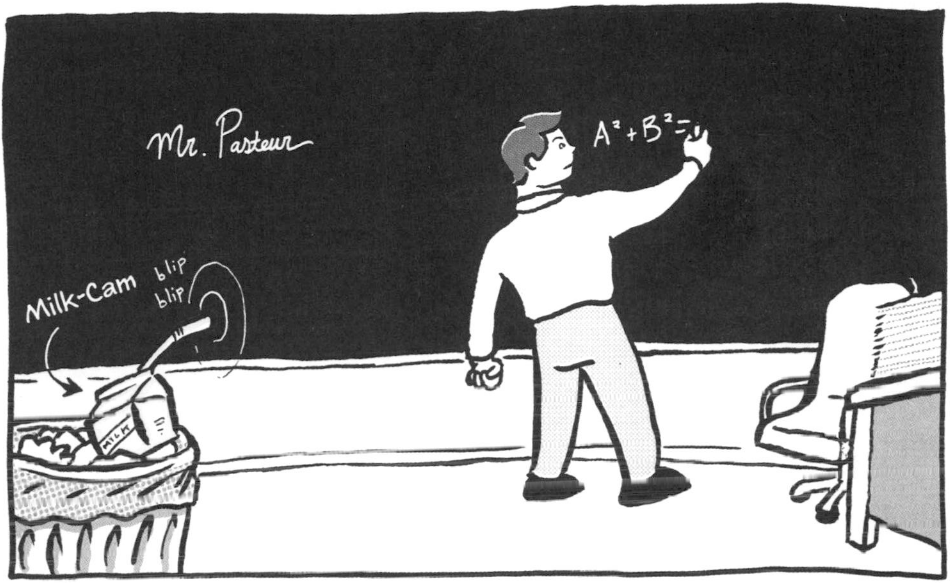
Mr. Pasteur
A² + B² =
Milk-Cam
blip
blip
MILK

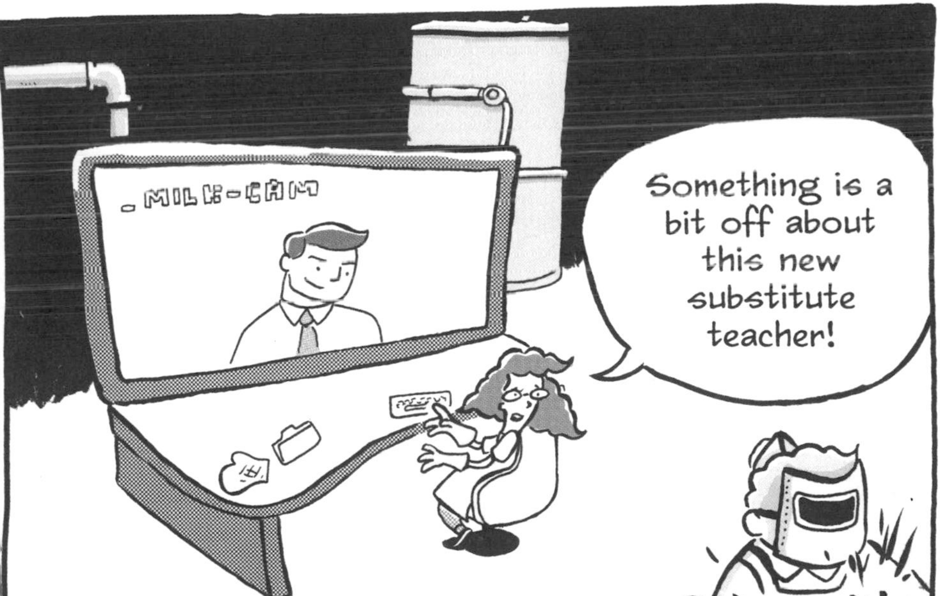
MILK-CAM
Something is a bit off about this new substitute teacher!

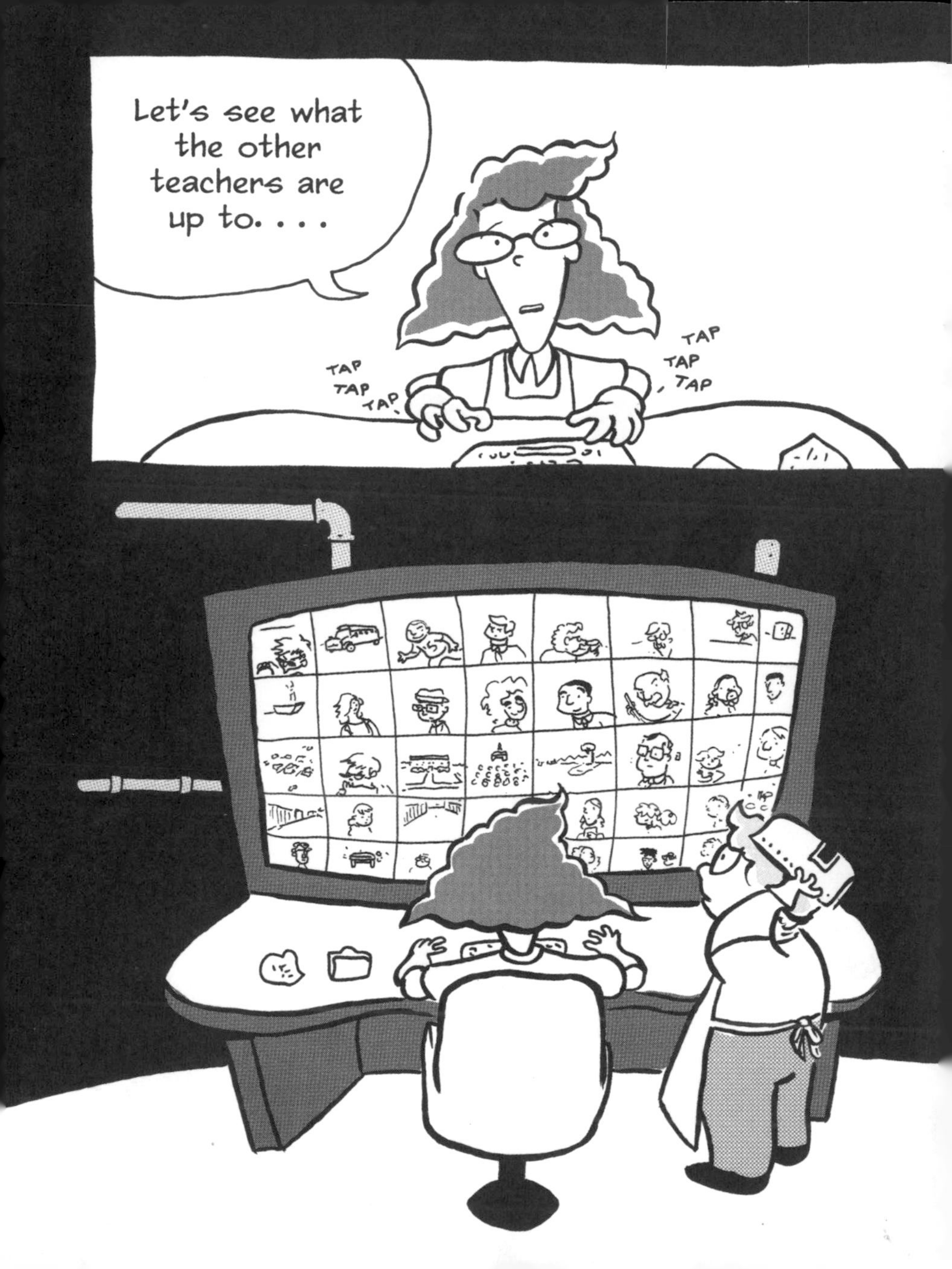

Let's see what the other teachers are up to. . . .
TAP TAP TAP
TAP TAP TAP

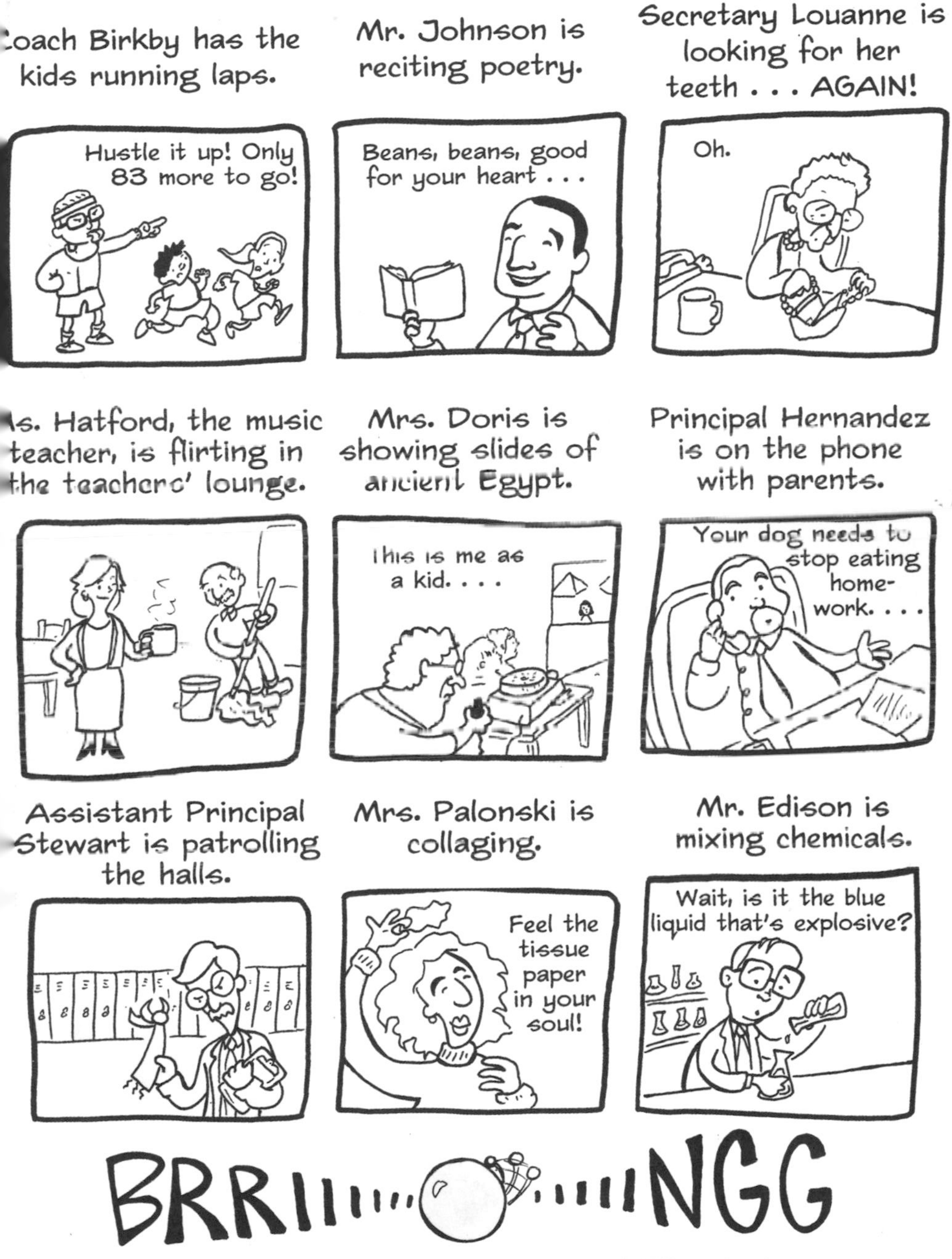
Coach Birkby has the kids running laps.
Hustle it up! Only 83 more to go!
Mr. Johnson is reciting poetry.
Beans, beans, good for your heart . . .
Secretary Louanne is looking for her teeth . . . AGAIN!
Oh.
Ms. Hatford, the music teacher, is flirting in the teachers' lounge.
Mrs. Doris is showing slides of ancient Egypt.
This is me as a kid. . . .
Principal Hernandez is on the phone with parents.
Your dog needs to stop eating home-work. . . .
Assistant Principal Stewart is patrolling the halls.
Mrs. Palonski is collaging.
Feel the tissue paper in your soul!
Mr. Edison is mixing chemicals.
Wait, is it the blue liquid that's explosive?
BRRIIIIIIIIIIIIIINGG

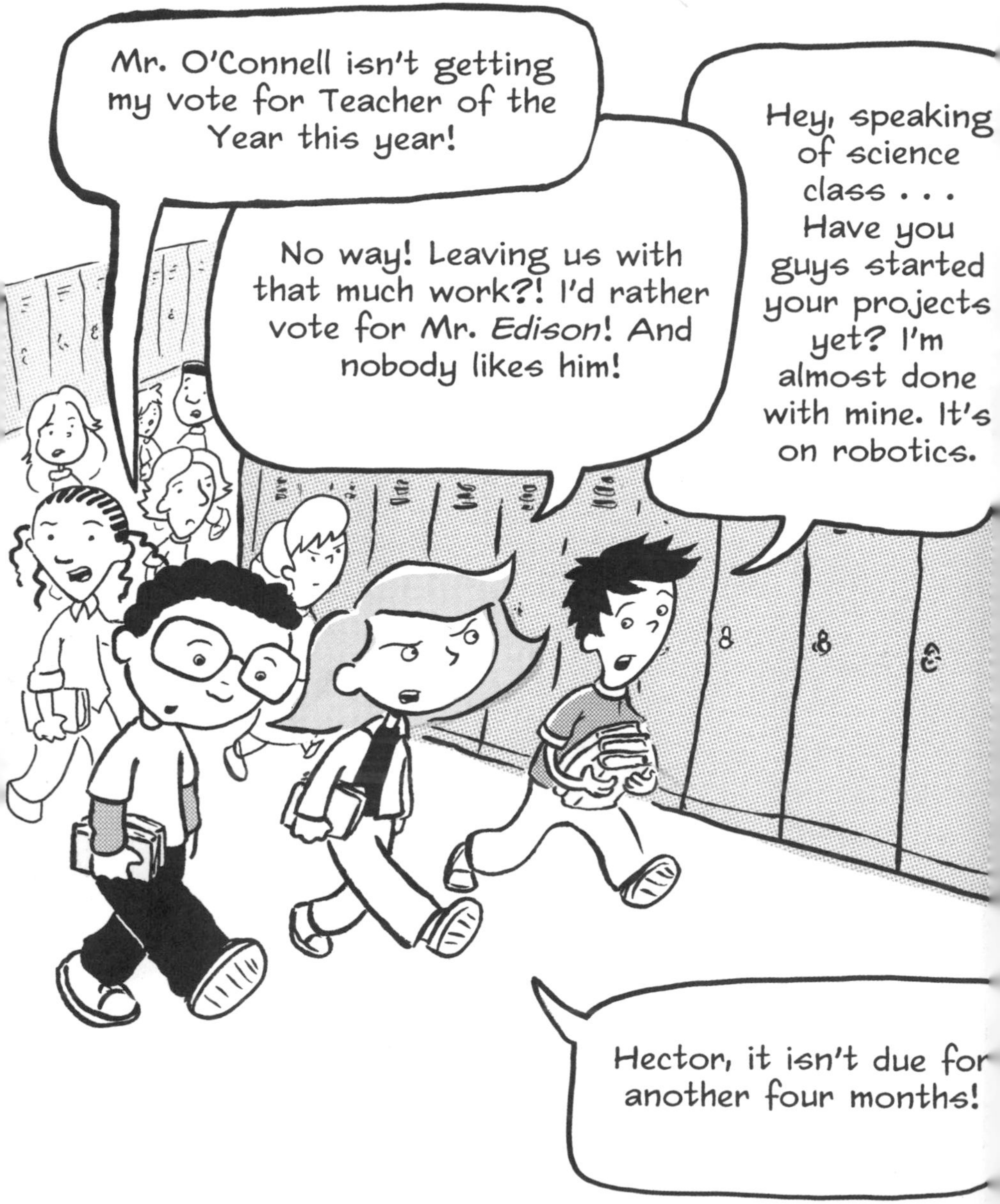
Mr. O'Connell isn't getting my vote for Teacher of the Year this year!
No way! Leaving us with that much work?! I'd rather vote for Mr. *Edison*! And nobody likes him!
Hey, speaking of science class . . . Have you guys started your projects yet? I'm almost done with mine. It's on robotics.
Hector, it isn't due for another four months!

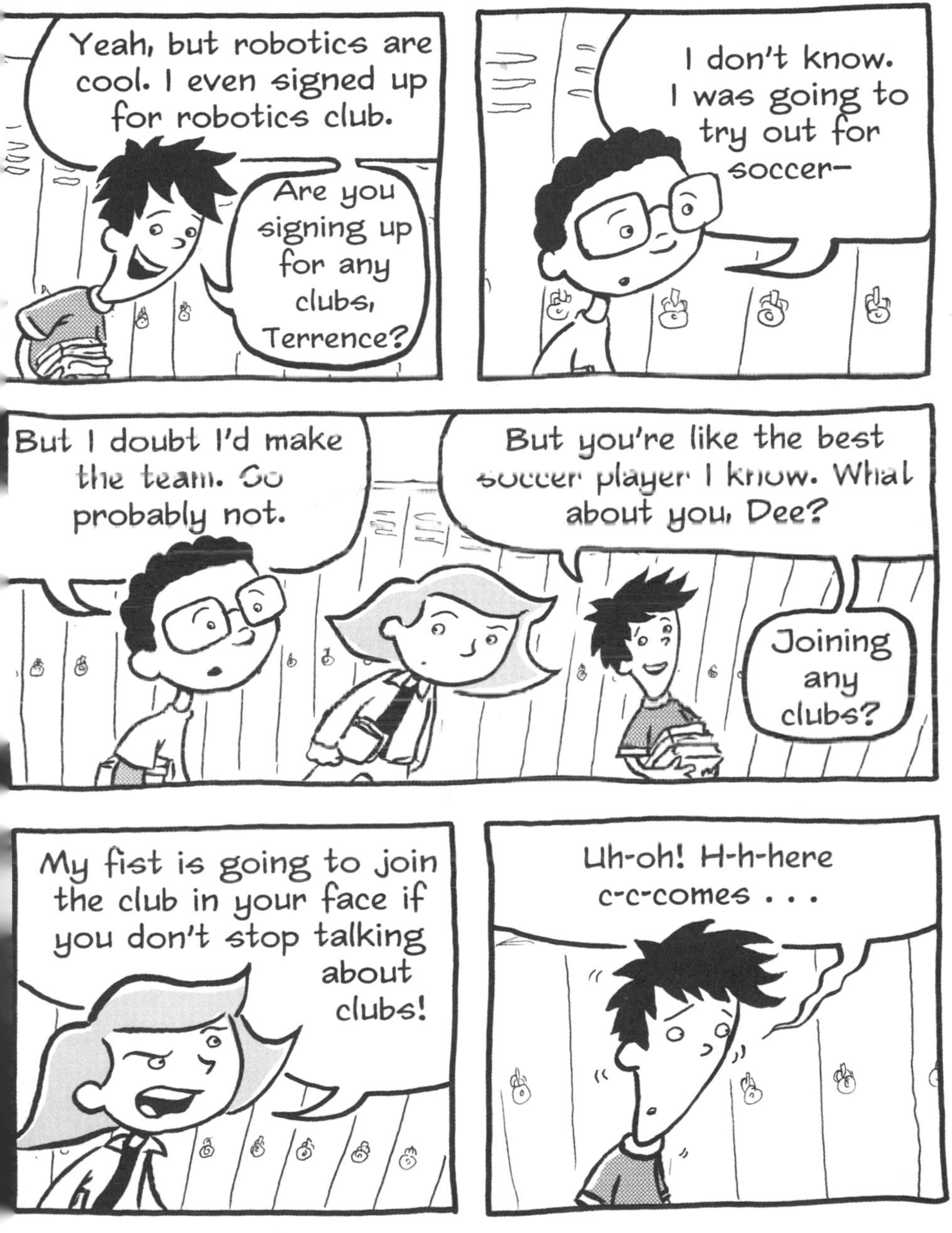
Yeah, but robotics are cool. I even signed up for robotics club.
Are you signing up for any clubs, Terrence?
I don't know. I was going to try out for soccer—
But I doubt I'd make the team. So probably not.
But you're like the best soccer player I know. What about you, Dee?
Joining any clubs?
My fist is going to join the club in your face if you don't stop talking about clubs!
Uh-oh! H-h-here c-c-comes . . .

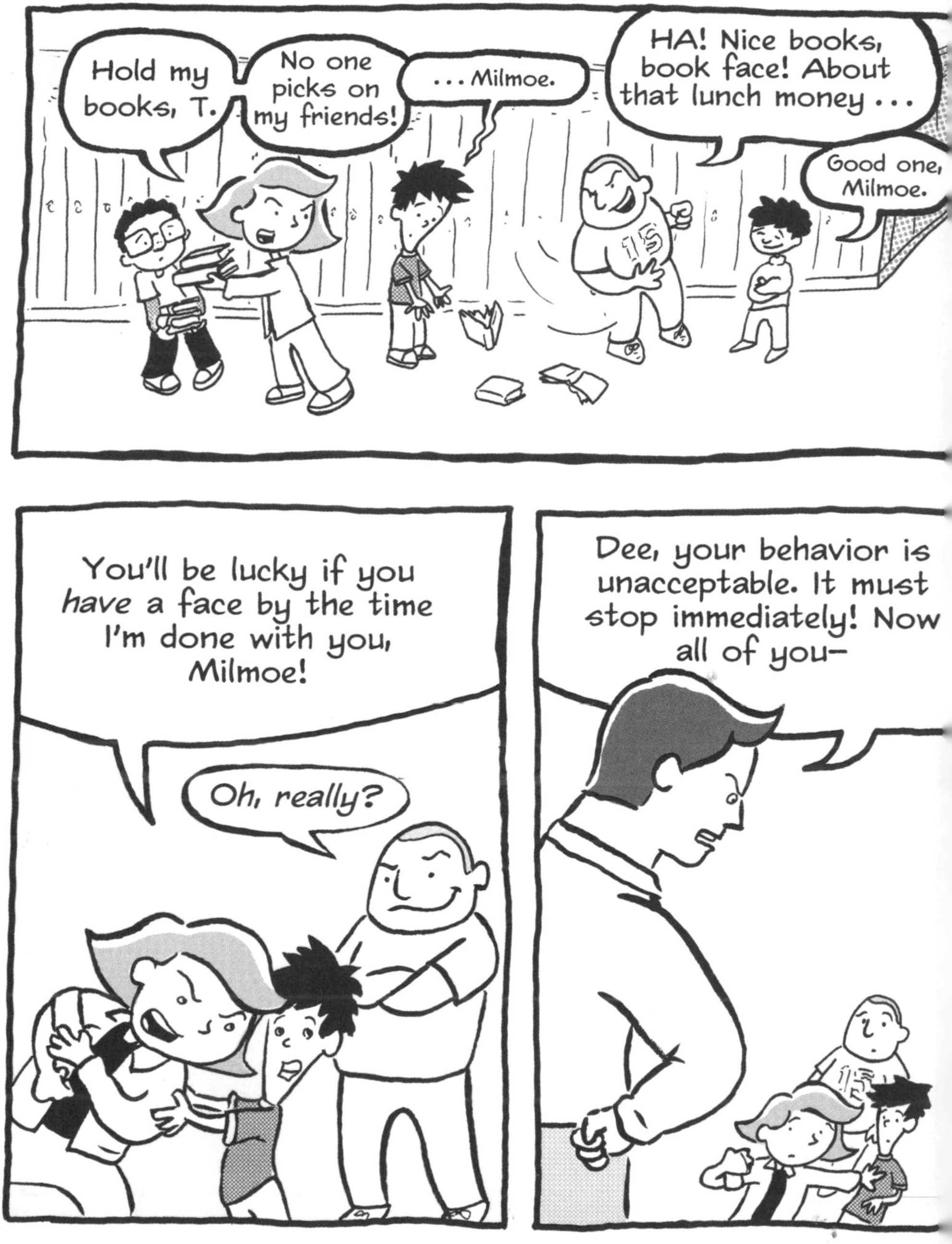
Hold my books, T.
No one picks on my friends!
. . . Milmoe.
HA! Nice books, book face! About that lunch money . . .
Good one, Milmoe.
You'll be lucky if you *have* a face by the time I'm done with you, Milmoe!
Oh, really?
Dee, your behavior is unacceptable. It must stop immediately! Now all of you–

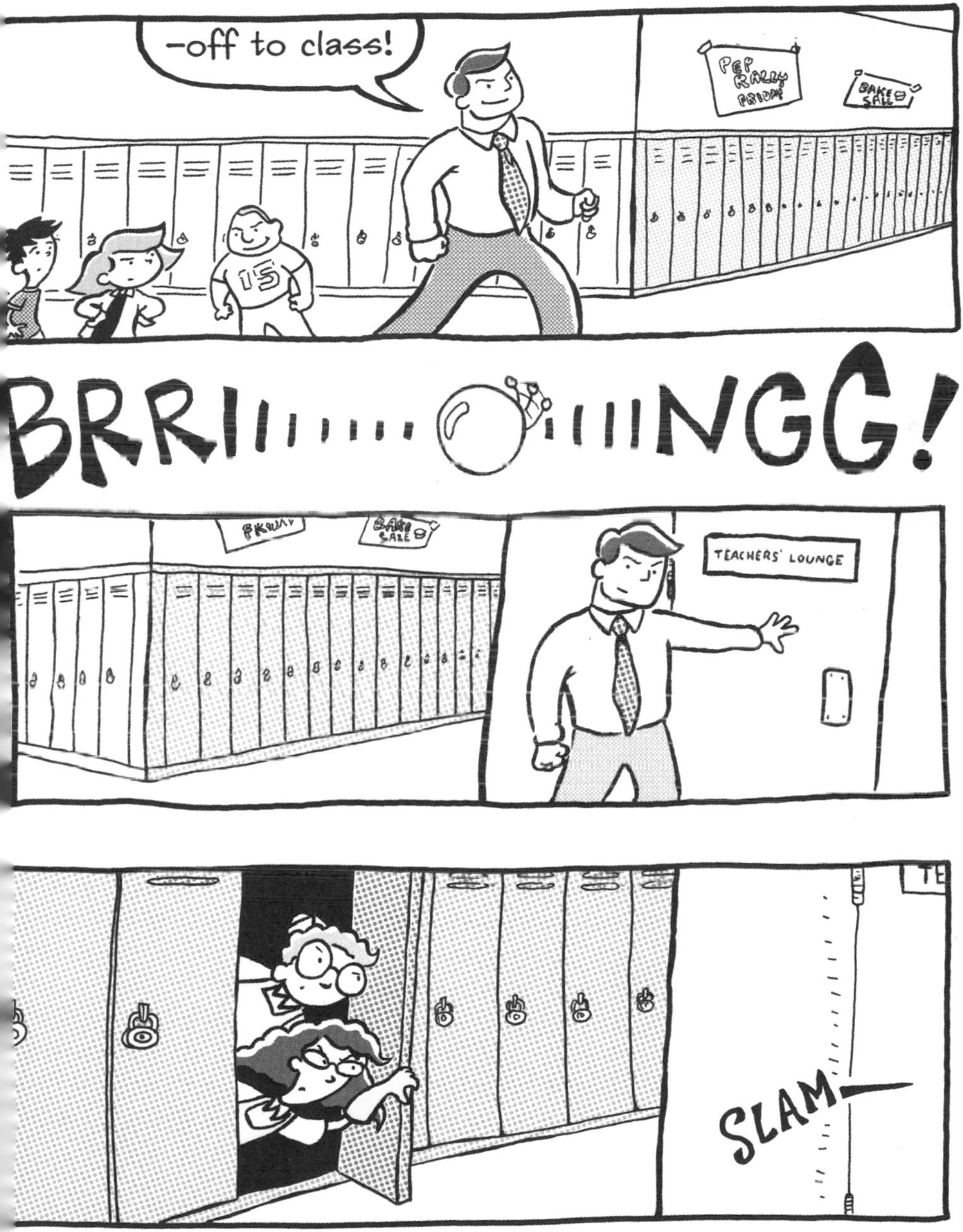

-off to class!
PEP RALLY FRIDAY
BAKE SALE
BRRI..........NGG!
BAKE SALE
TEACHERS' LOUNGE
SLAM

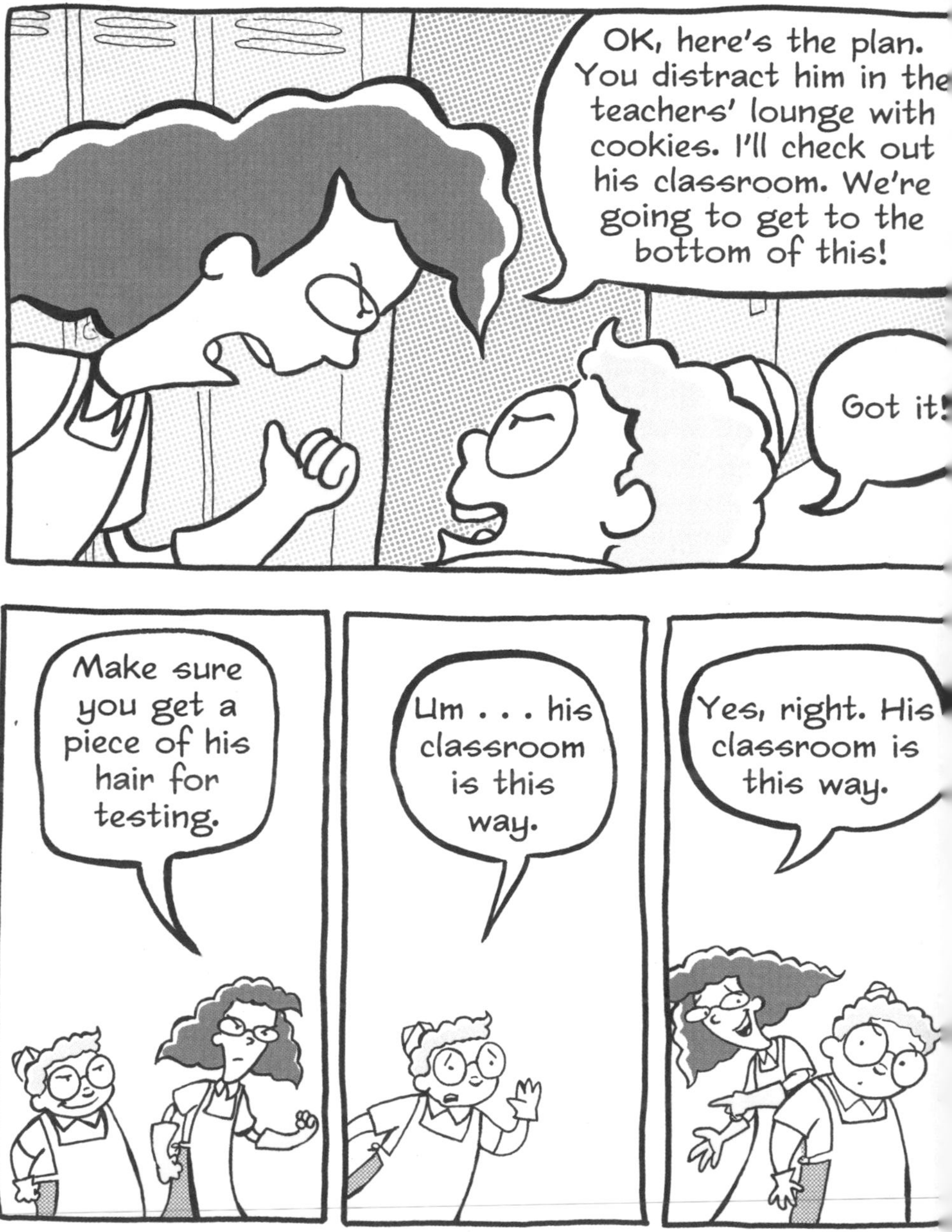
OK, here's the plan. You distract him in the teachers' lounge with cookies. I'll check out his classroom. We're going to get to the bottom of this!
Got it!
Make sure you get a piece of his hair for testing.
Um . . . his classroom is this way.
Yes, right. His classroom is this way.

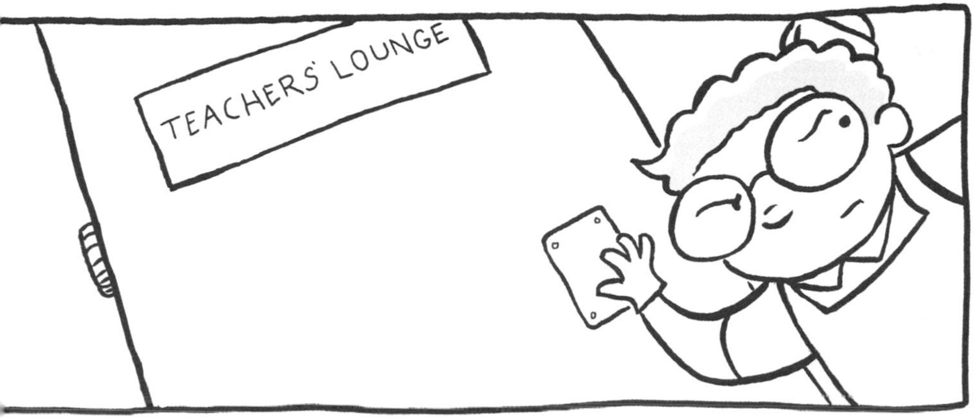
TEACHERS' LOUNGE

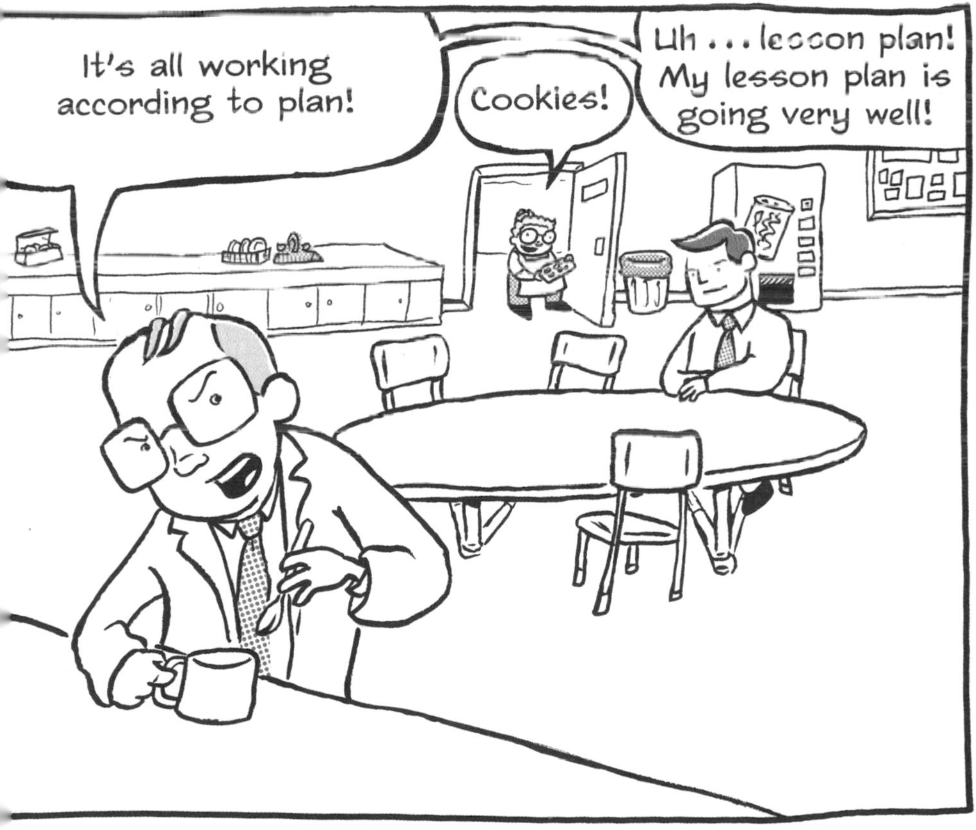
It's all working according to plan!
Cookies!
Uh . . . lesson plan! My lesson plan is going very well!

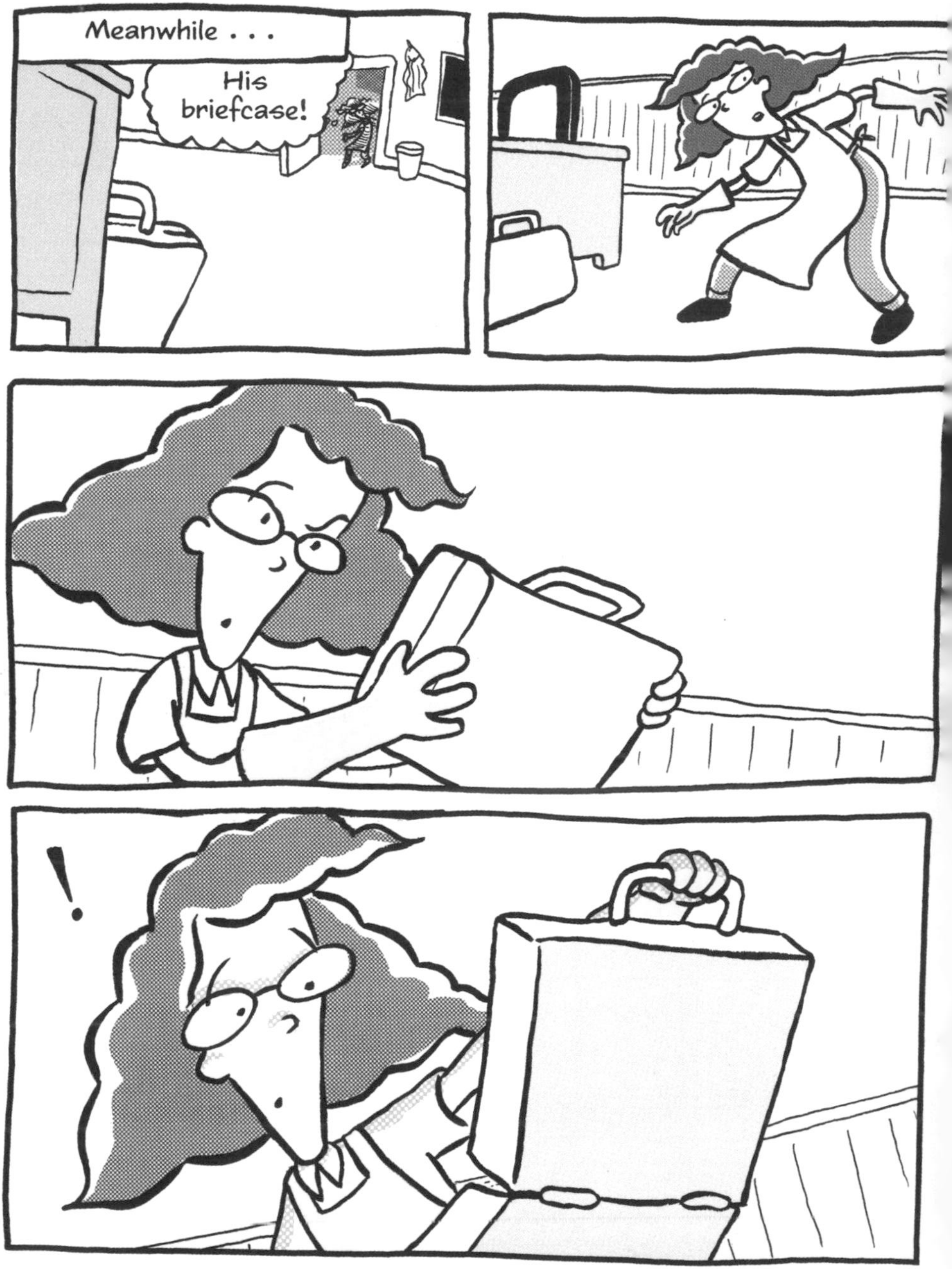
Meanwhile . . .
His briefcase!
!

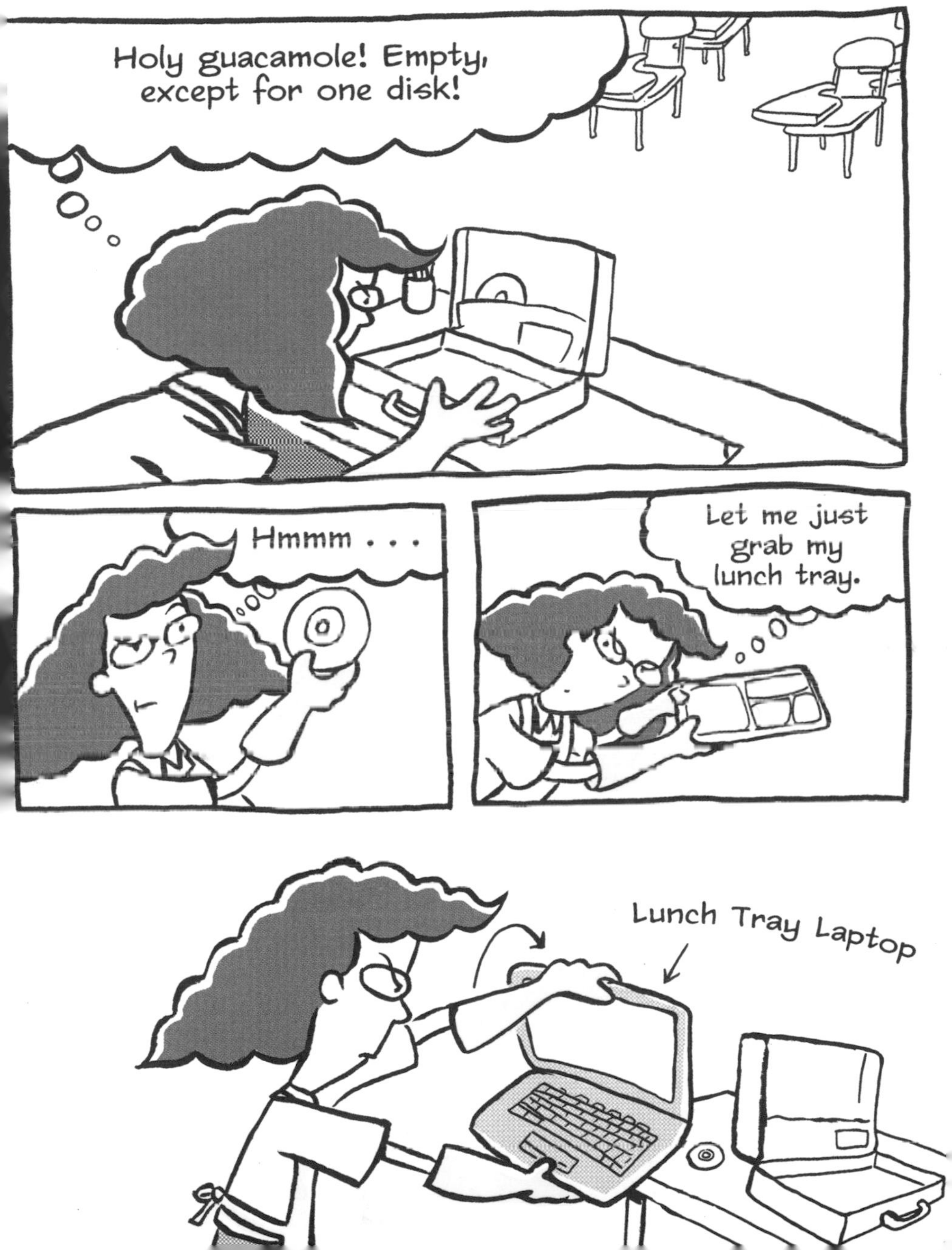
Holy guacamole! Empty, except for one disk!
Hmmm . . .
Let me just grab my lunch tray.
Lunch Tray Laptop

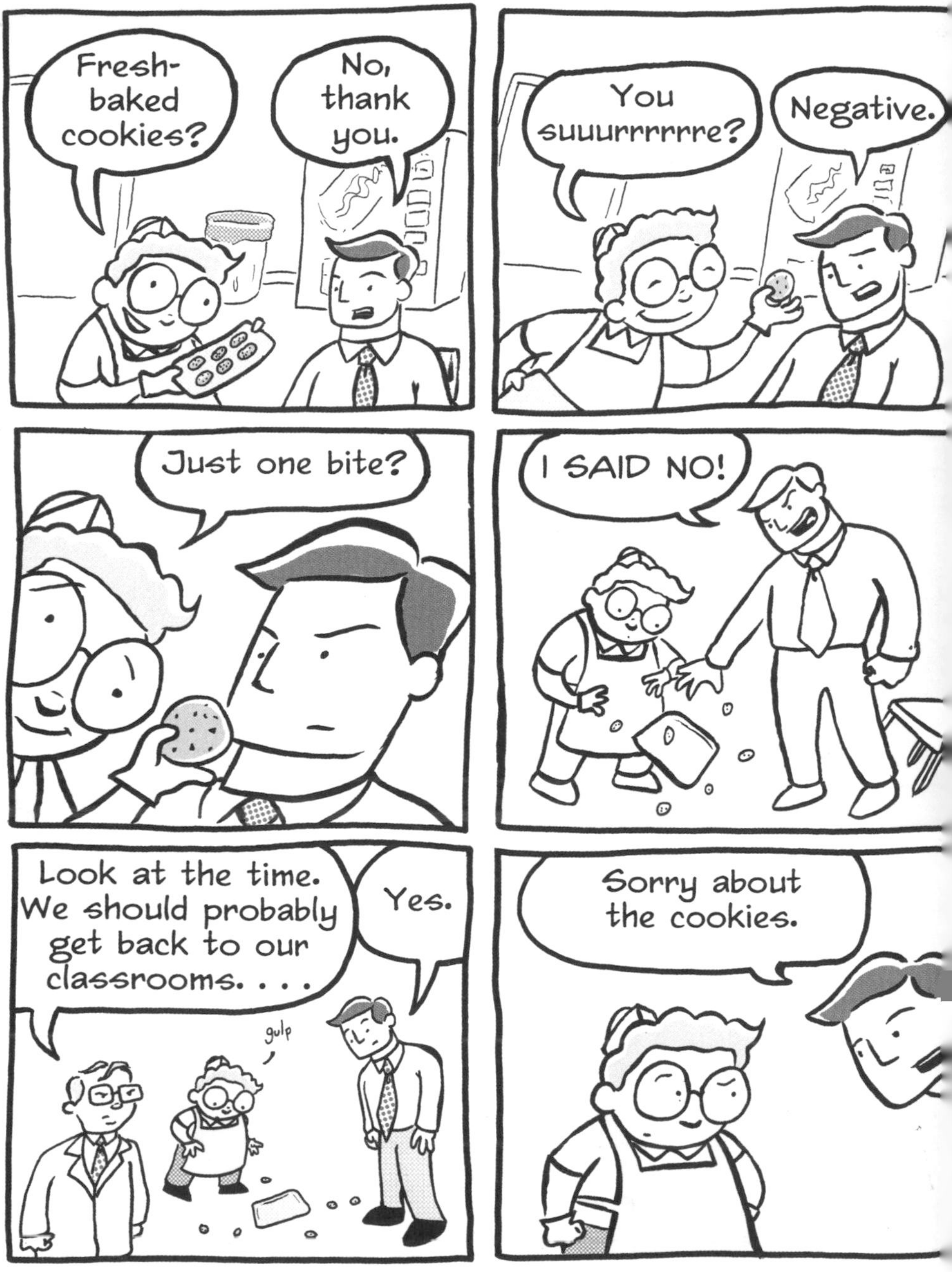
Fresh-baked cookies?
No, thank you.
You suuurrrrrre?
Negative.
Just one bite?
I SAID NO!
Look at the time. We should probably get back to our classrooms. . . .
Yes.
gulp
Sorry about the cookies.

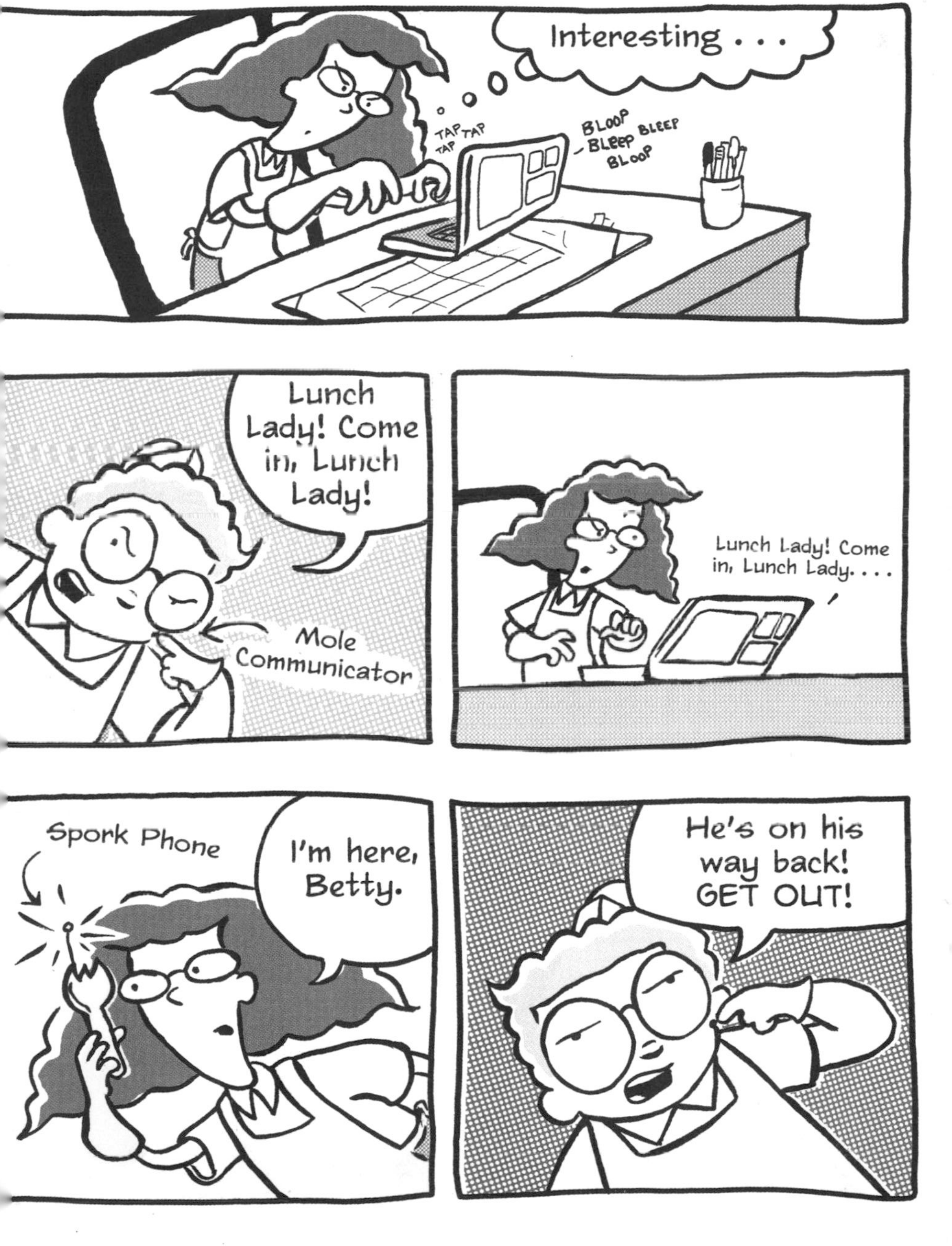
Interesting . . .
TAP TAP TAP
BLOOP BLEEP BLEEP BLOOP
Lunch Lady! Come in, Lunch Lady!
Mole Communicator
Lunch Lady! Come in, Lunch Lady. . . .
Spork Phone
I'm here, Betty.
He's on his way back! GET OUT!

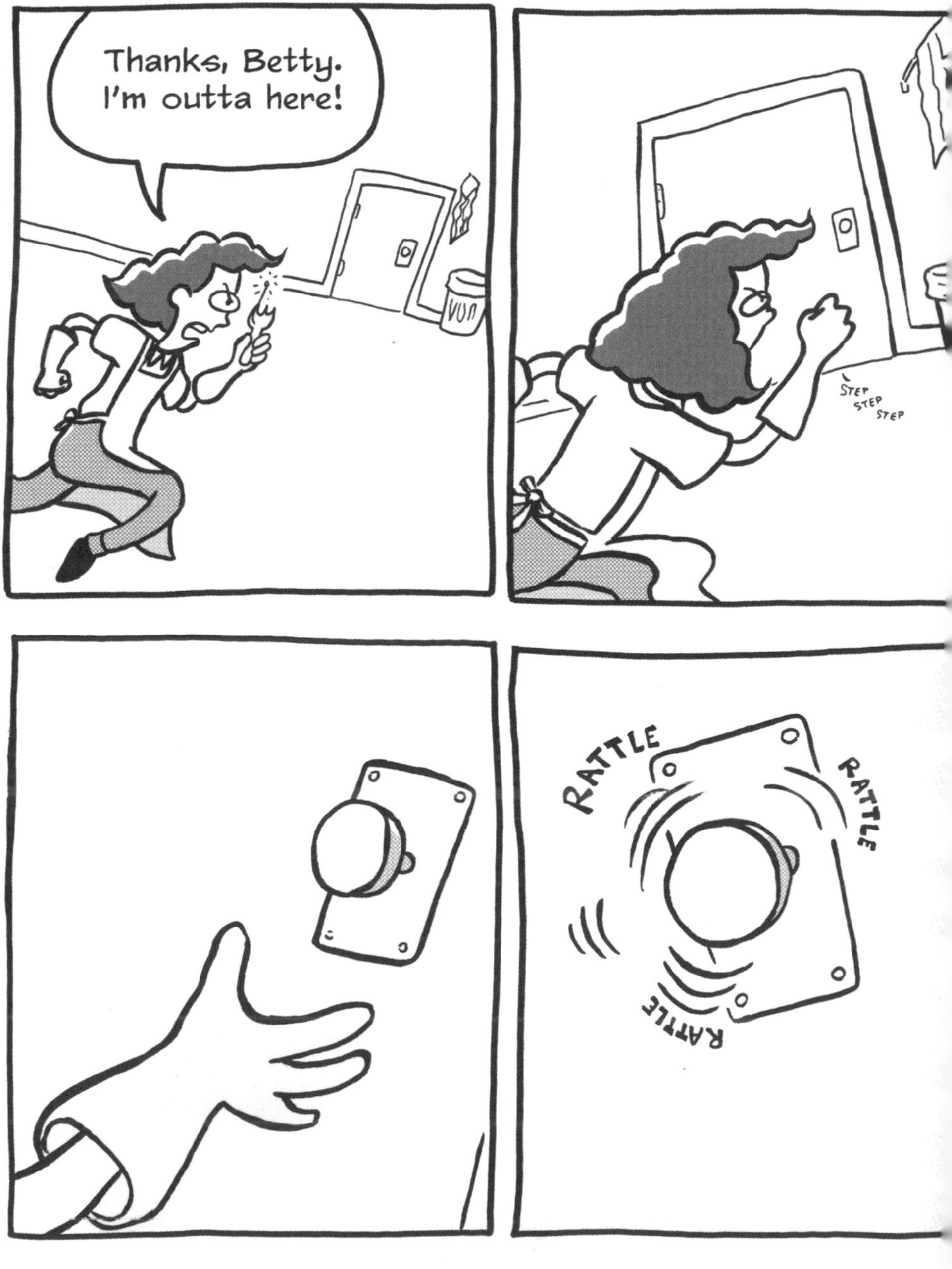
Thanks, Betty. I'm outta here!
STEP STEP STEP
RATTLE
RATTLE
RATTLE

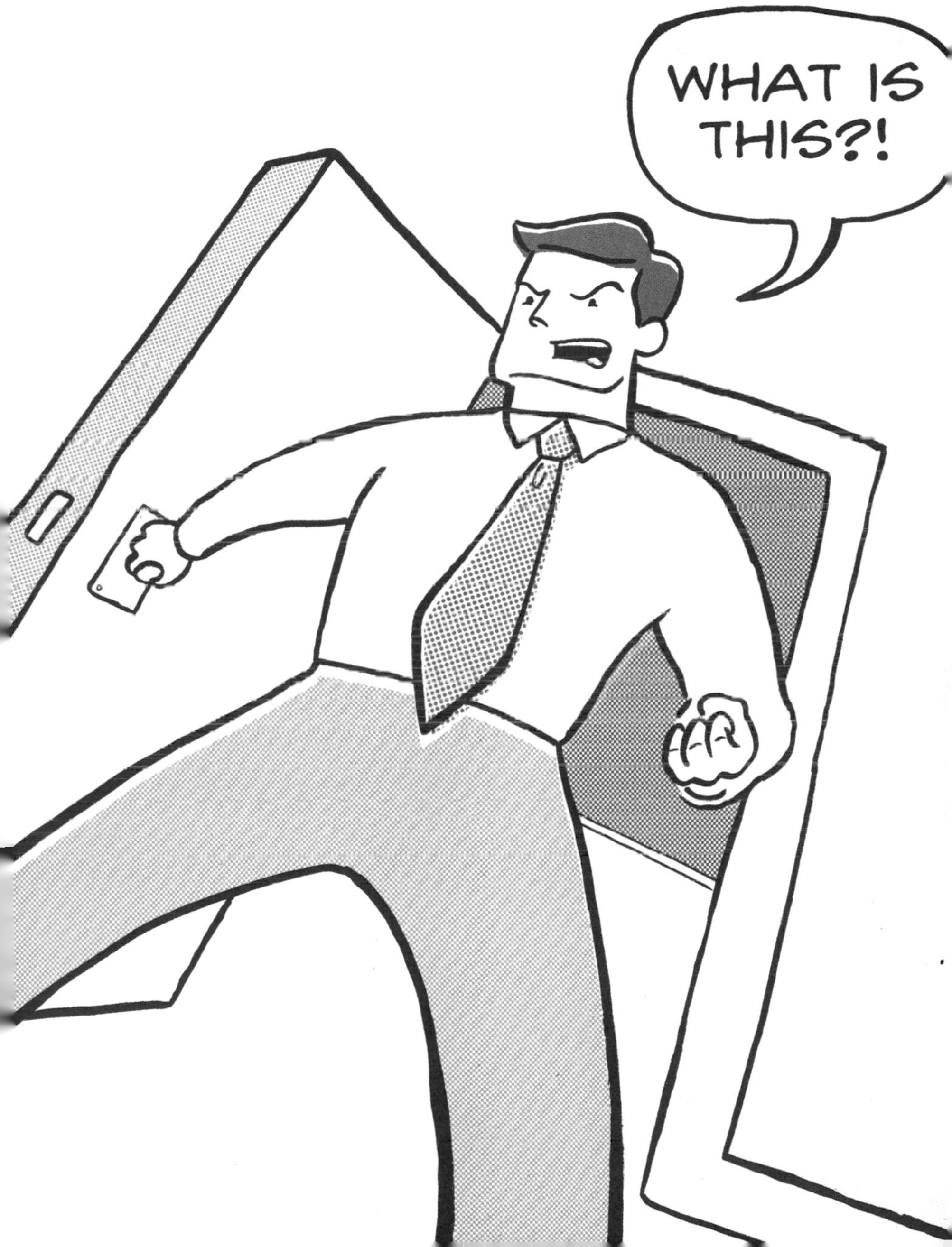
WHAT IS THIS?!

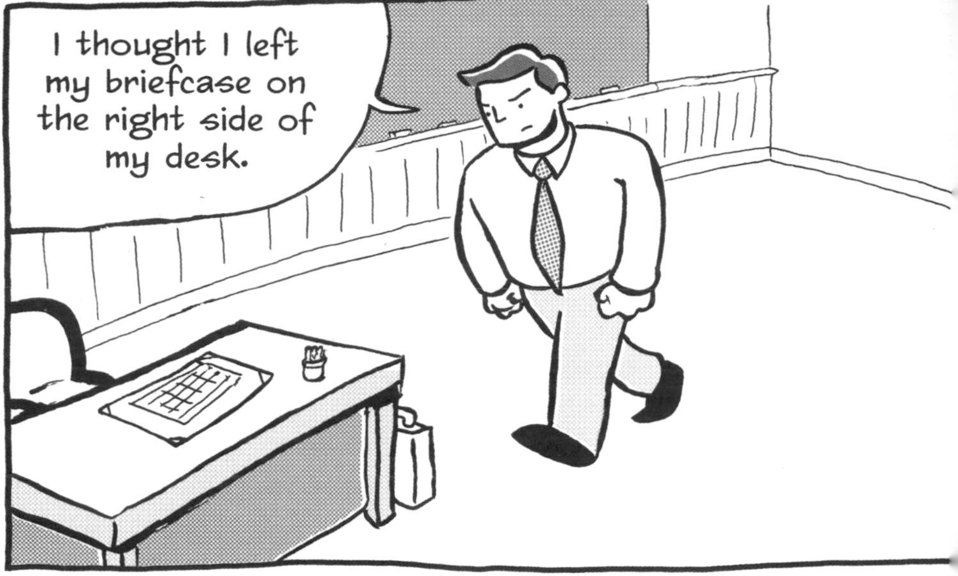
I thought I left my briefcase on the right side of my desk.

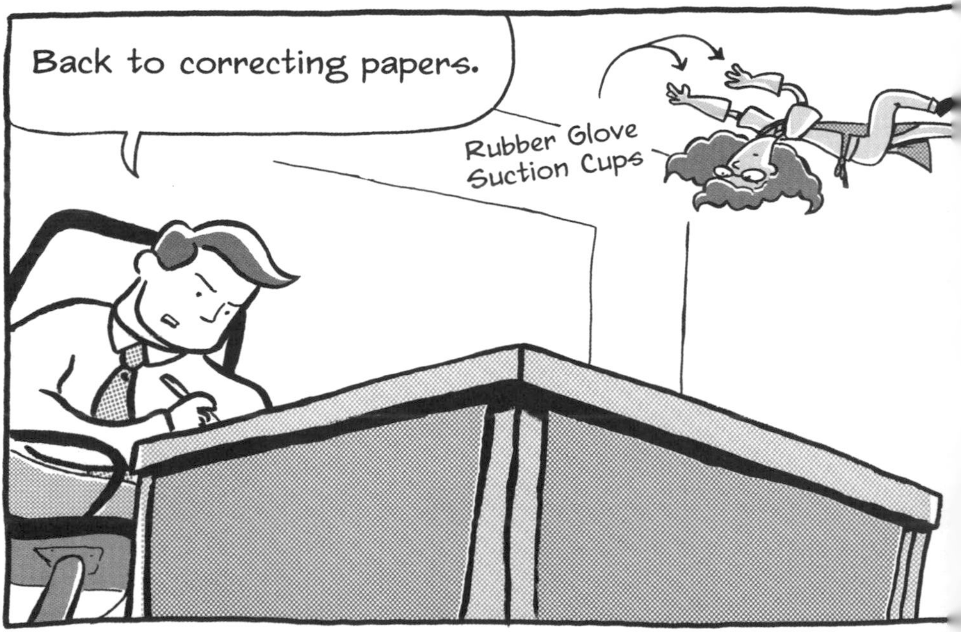
Back to correcting papers.
Rubber Glove Suction Cups

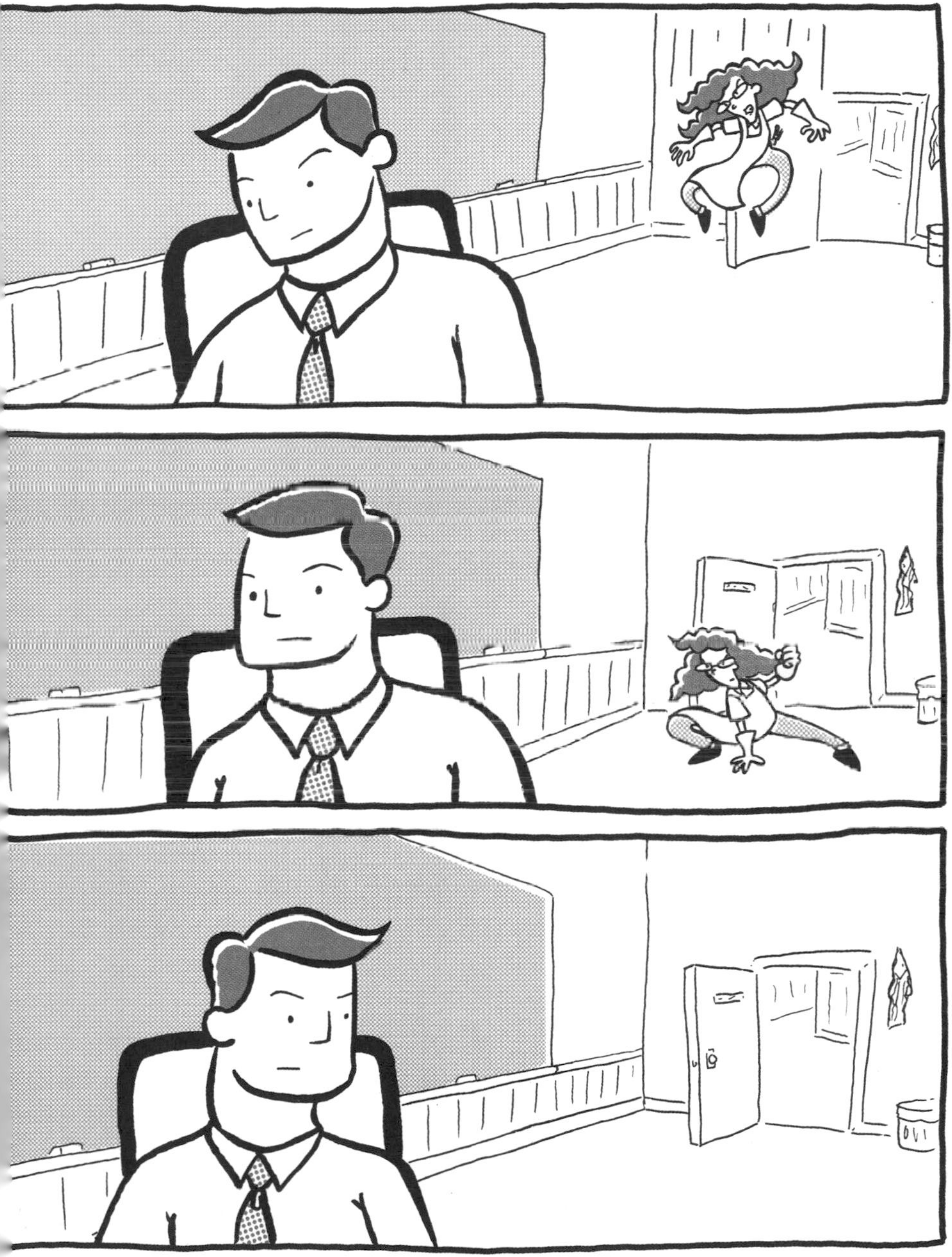

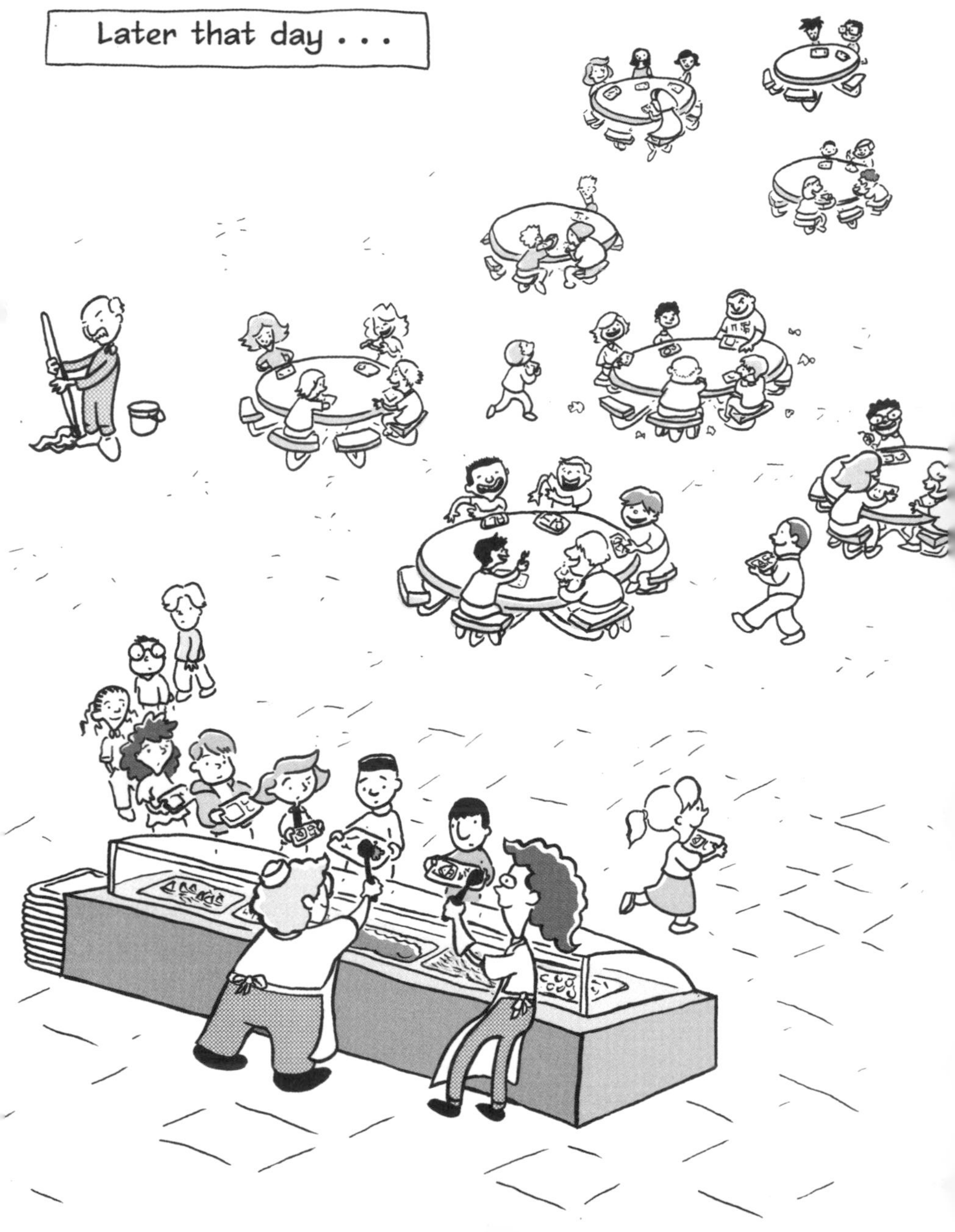
Later that day . . .

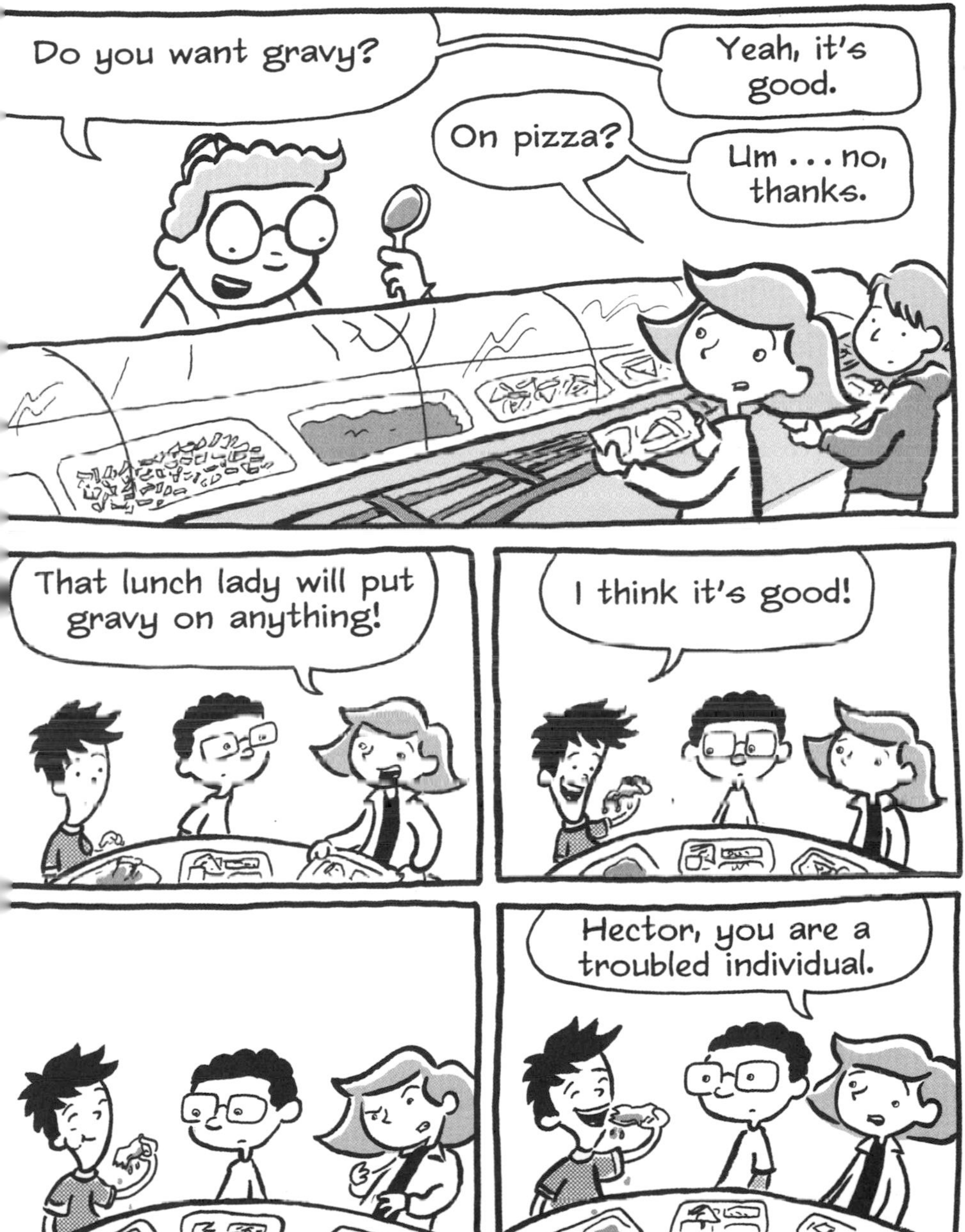
Do you want gravy?
Yeah, it's good.
On pizza?
Um . . . no, thanks.
That lunch lady will put gravy on anything!
I think it's good!
Hector, you are a troubled individual.

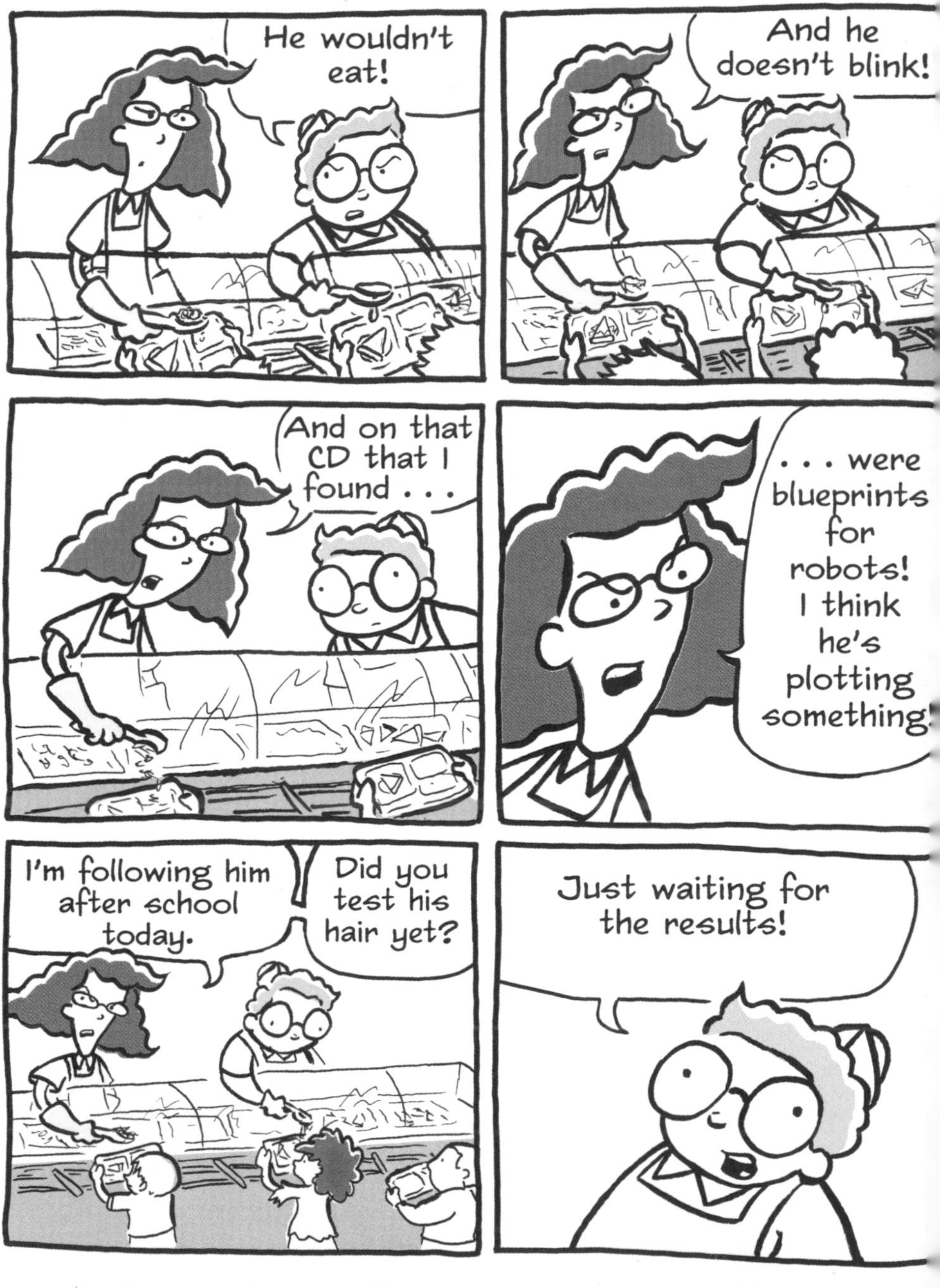
He wouldn't eat!
And he doesn't blink!
And on that CD that I found . . .
. . . were blueprints for robots! I think he's plotting something!
I'm following him after school today.
Did you test his hair yet?
Just waiting for the results!

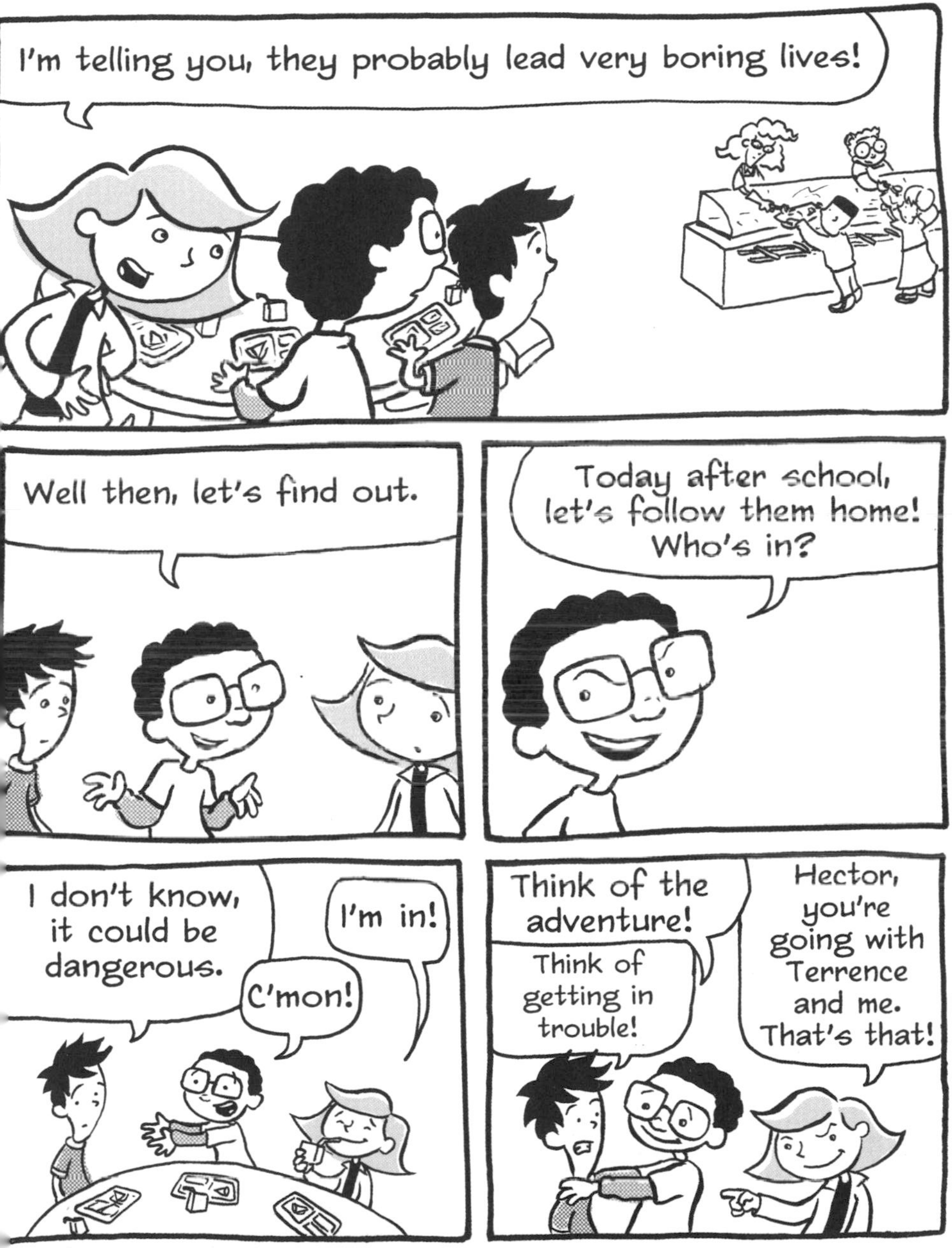
I'm telling you, they probably lead very boring lives!
Well then, let's find out.
Today after school, let's follow them home! Who's in?
I don't know, it could be dangerous.
I'm in!
C'mon!
Think of the adventure!
Think of getting in trouble!
Hector, you're going with Terrence and me. That's that!

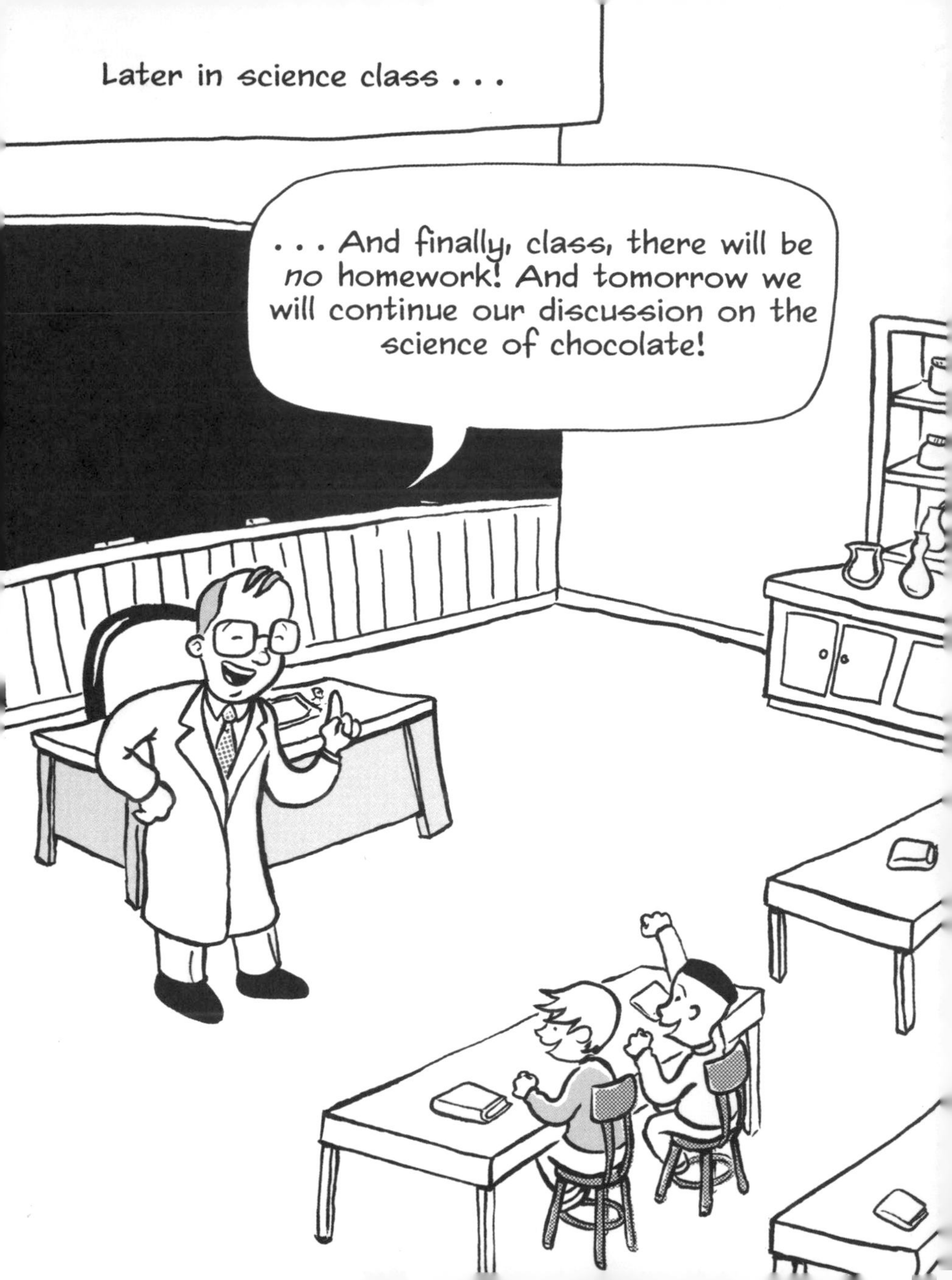
Later in science class . . .
. . . And finally, class, there will be *no* homework! And tomorrow we will continue our discussion on the science of chocolate!

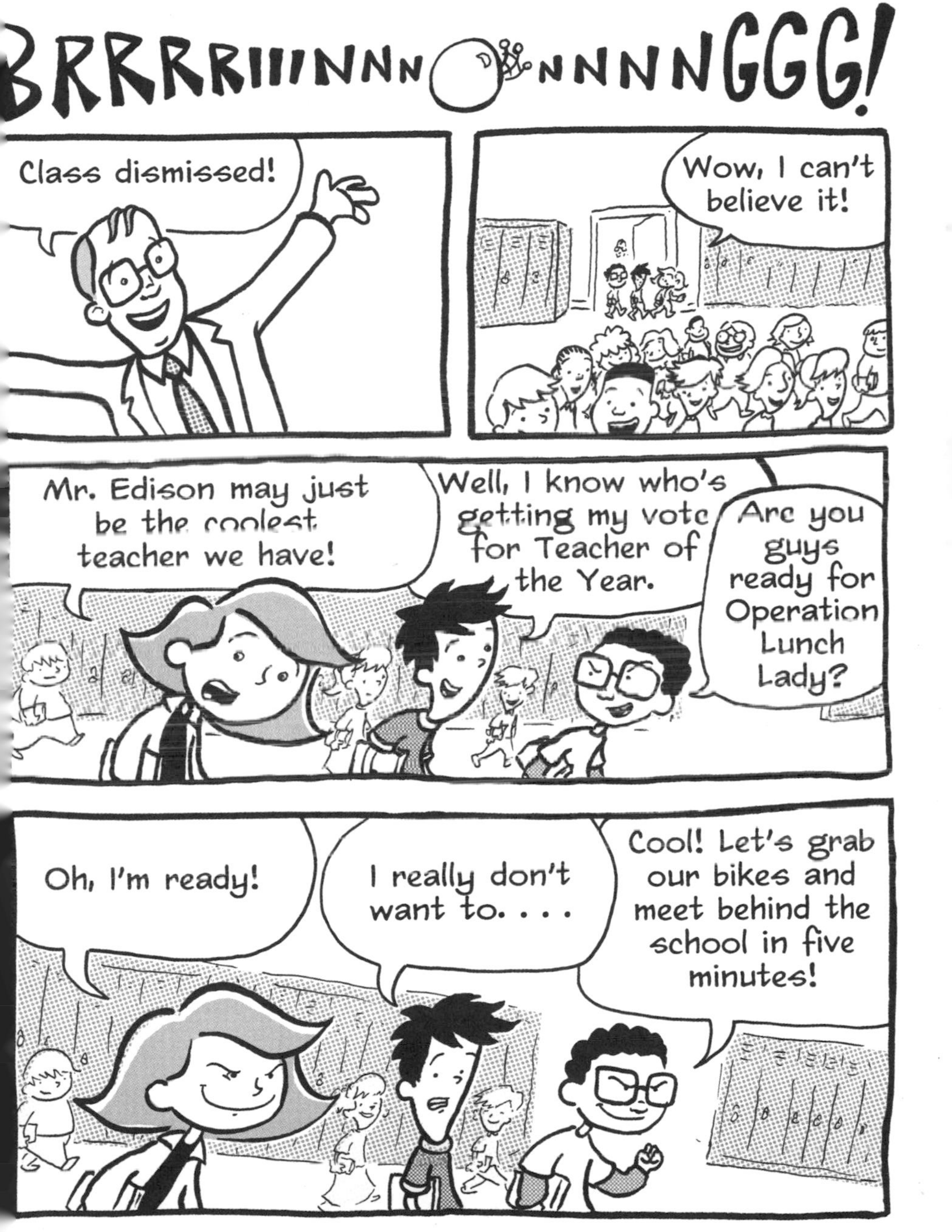
BRRRRIIIINNNNNNNNGGG!
Class dismissed!
Wow, I can't believe it!
Mr. Edison may just be the coolest teacher we have!
Well, I know who's getting my vote for Teacher of the Year.
Are you guys ready for Operation Lunch Lady?
Oh, I'm ready!
I really don't want to. . . .
Cool! Let's grab our bikes and meet behind the school in five minutes!

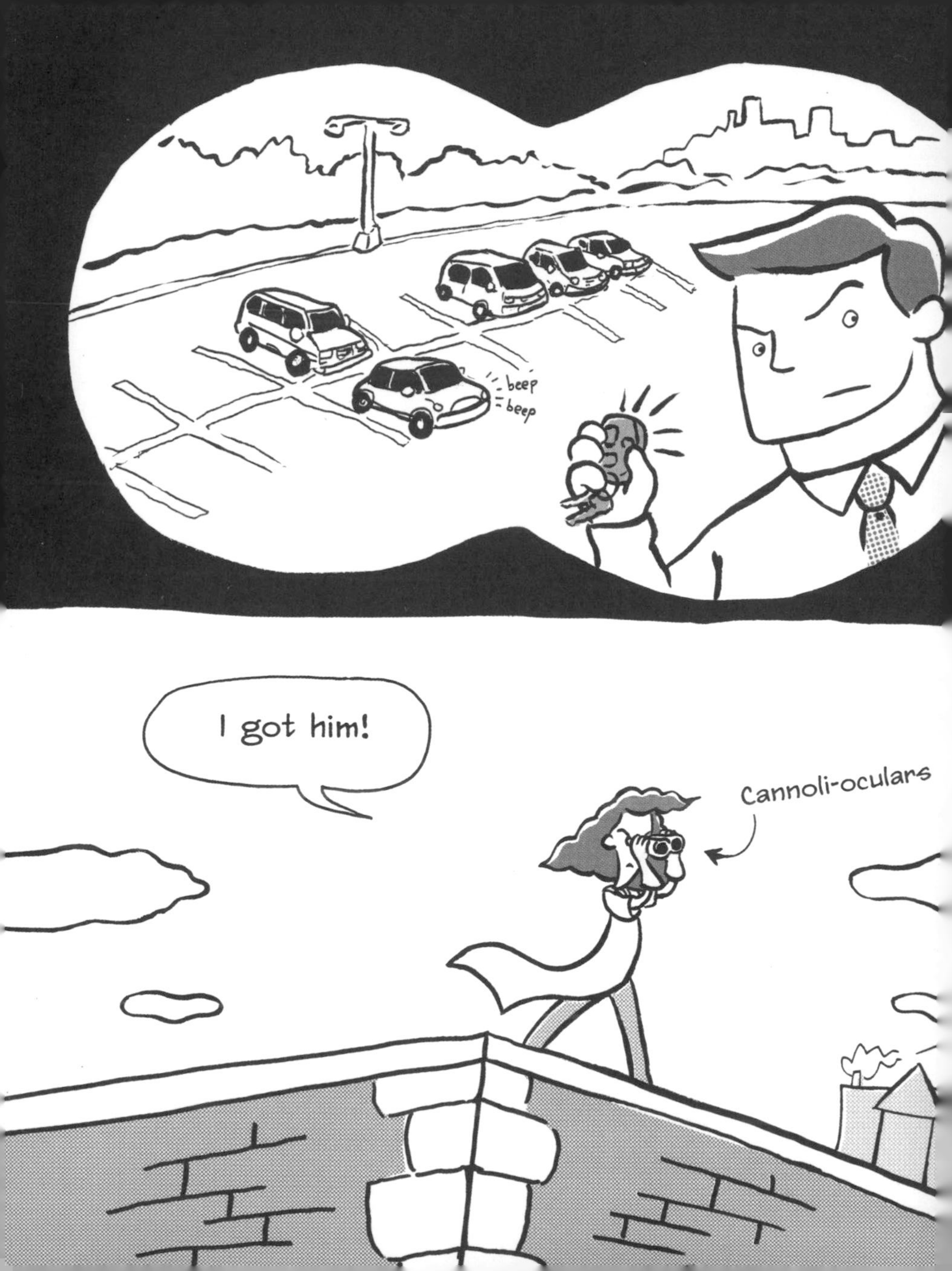
beep
beep
I got him!
Cannoli-oculars

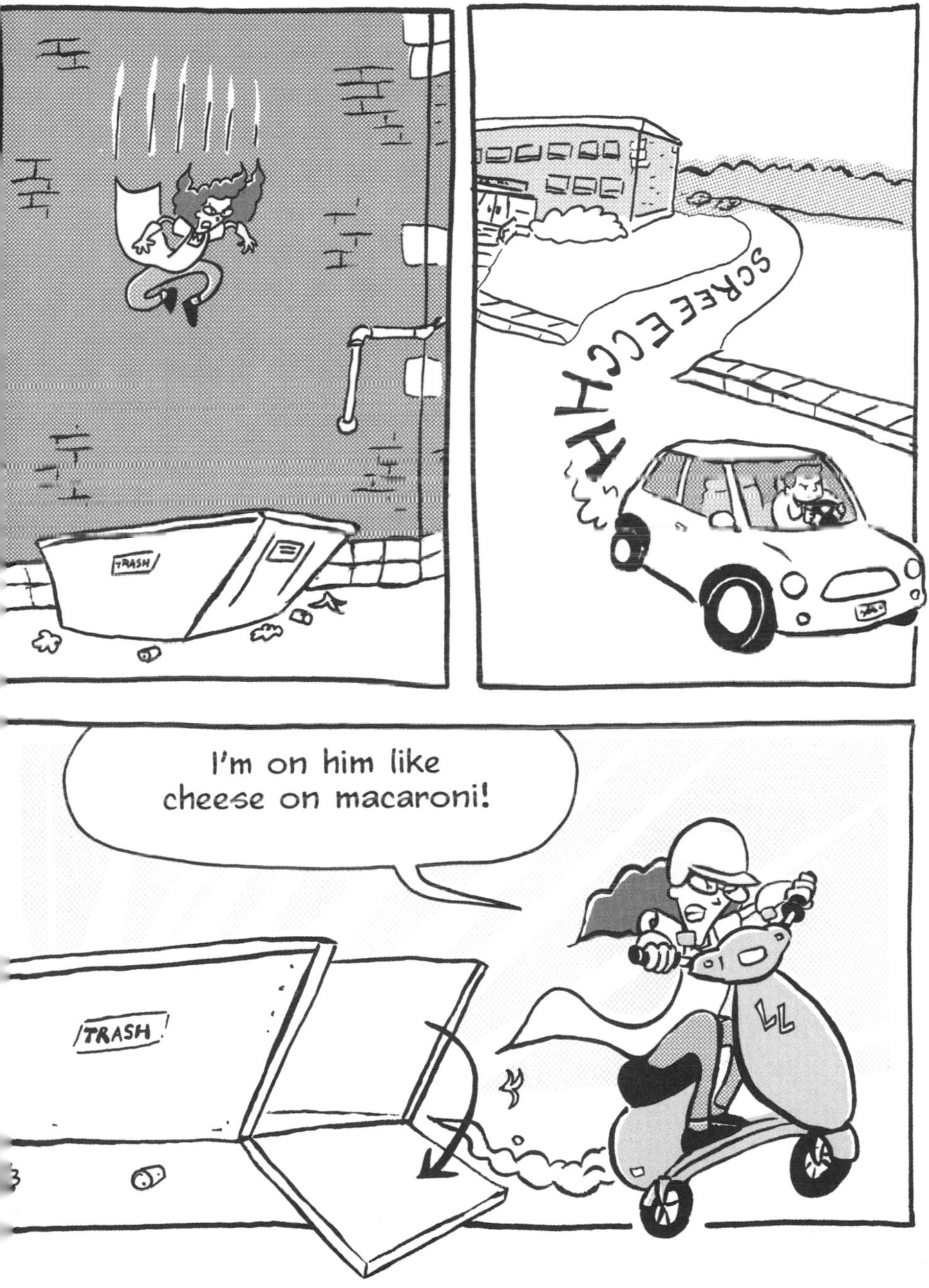
TRASH
SCREEECCHH
I'm on him like
cheese on macaroni!
TRASH

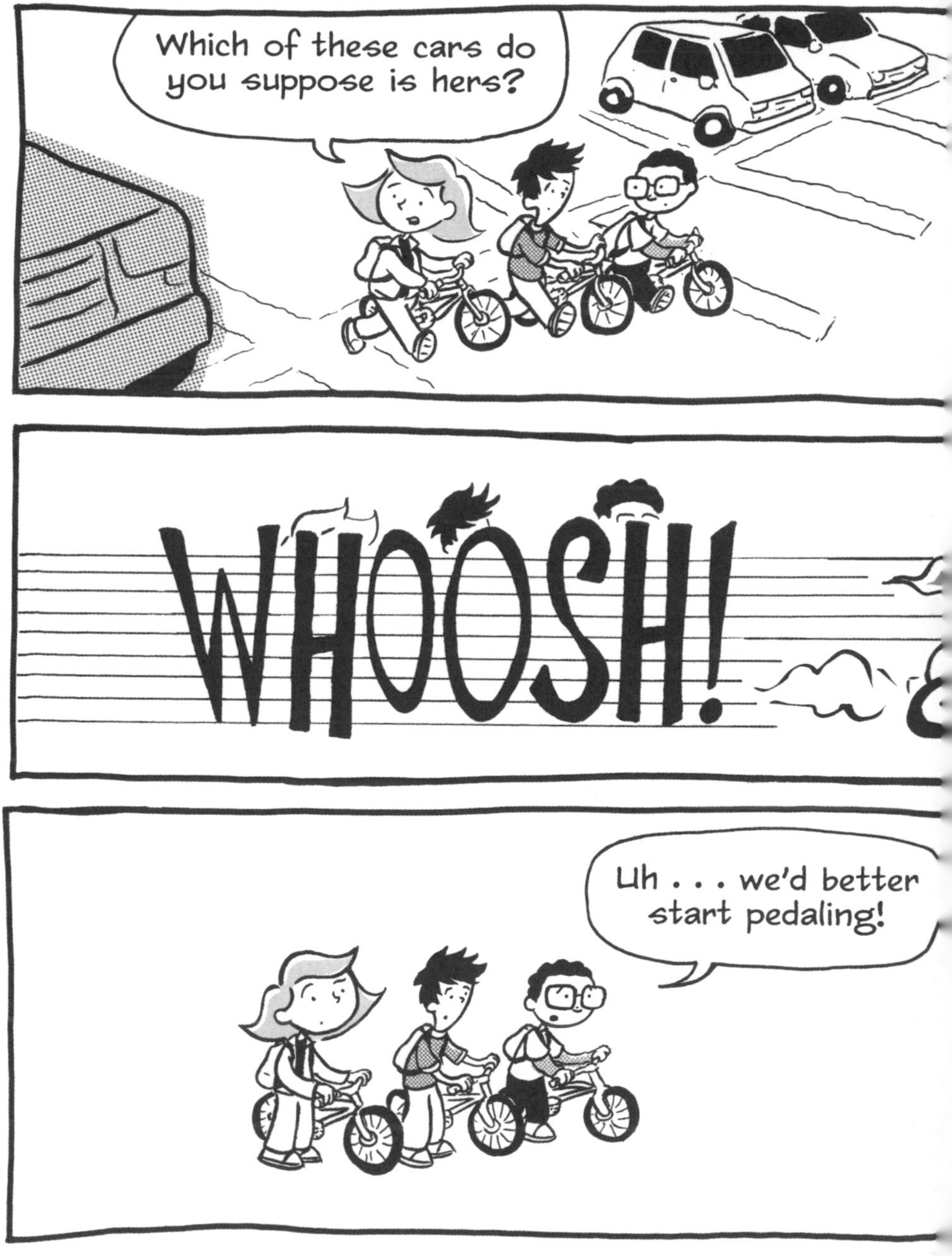
Which of these cars do you suppose is hers?
WHOOSH!
Uh . . . we'd better start pedaling!

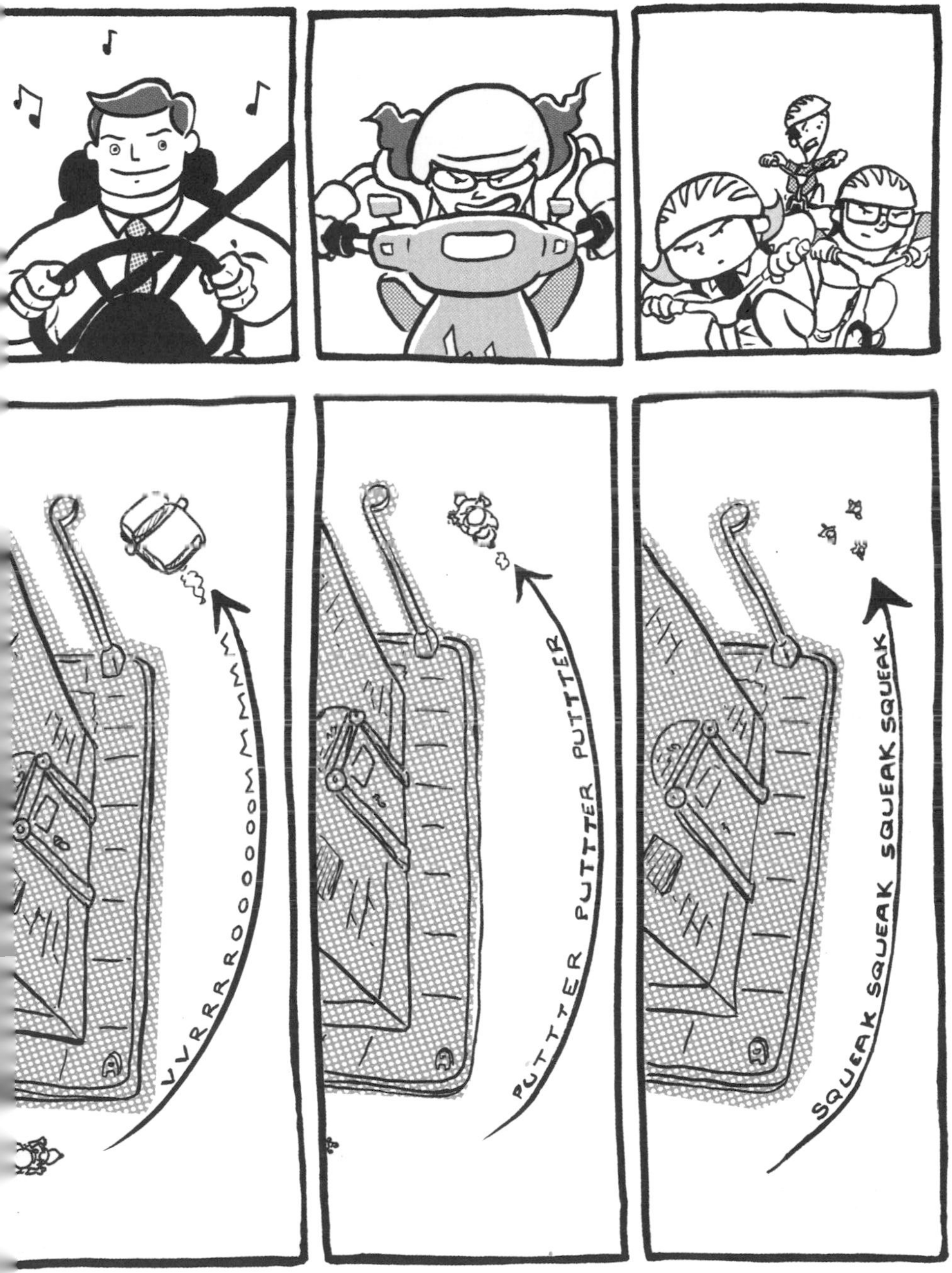
VVRRRROOOOOMMMMMM
PUTTTER PUTTTER
SQUEAK SQUEAK SQUEAK SQUEAK

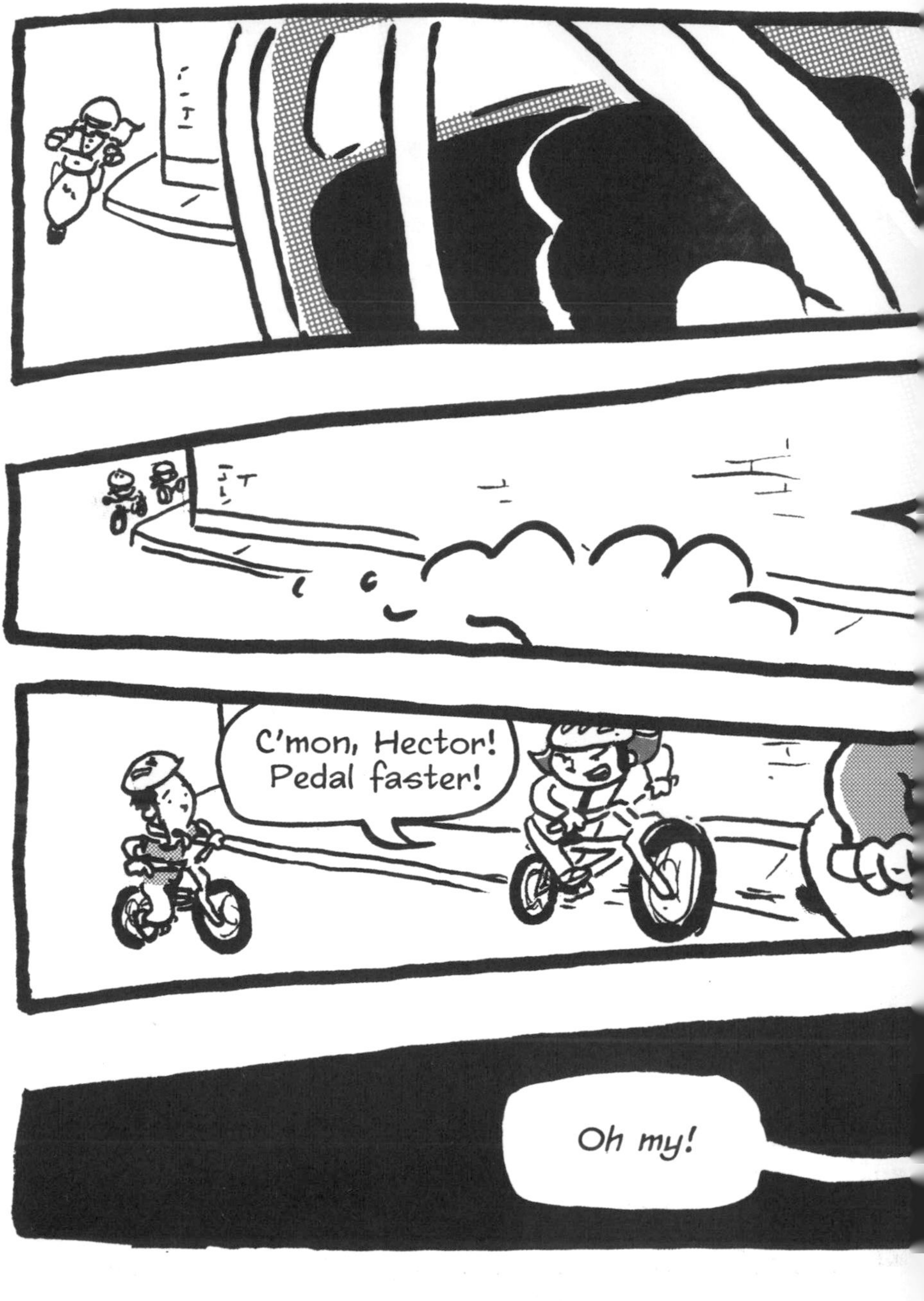
C'mon, Hector! Pedal faster!
Oh my!

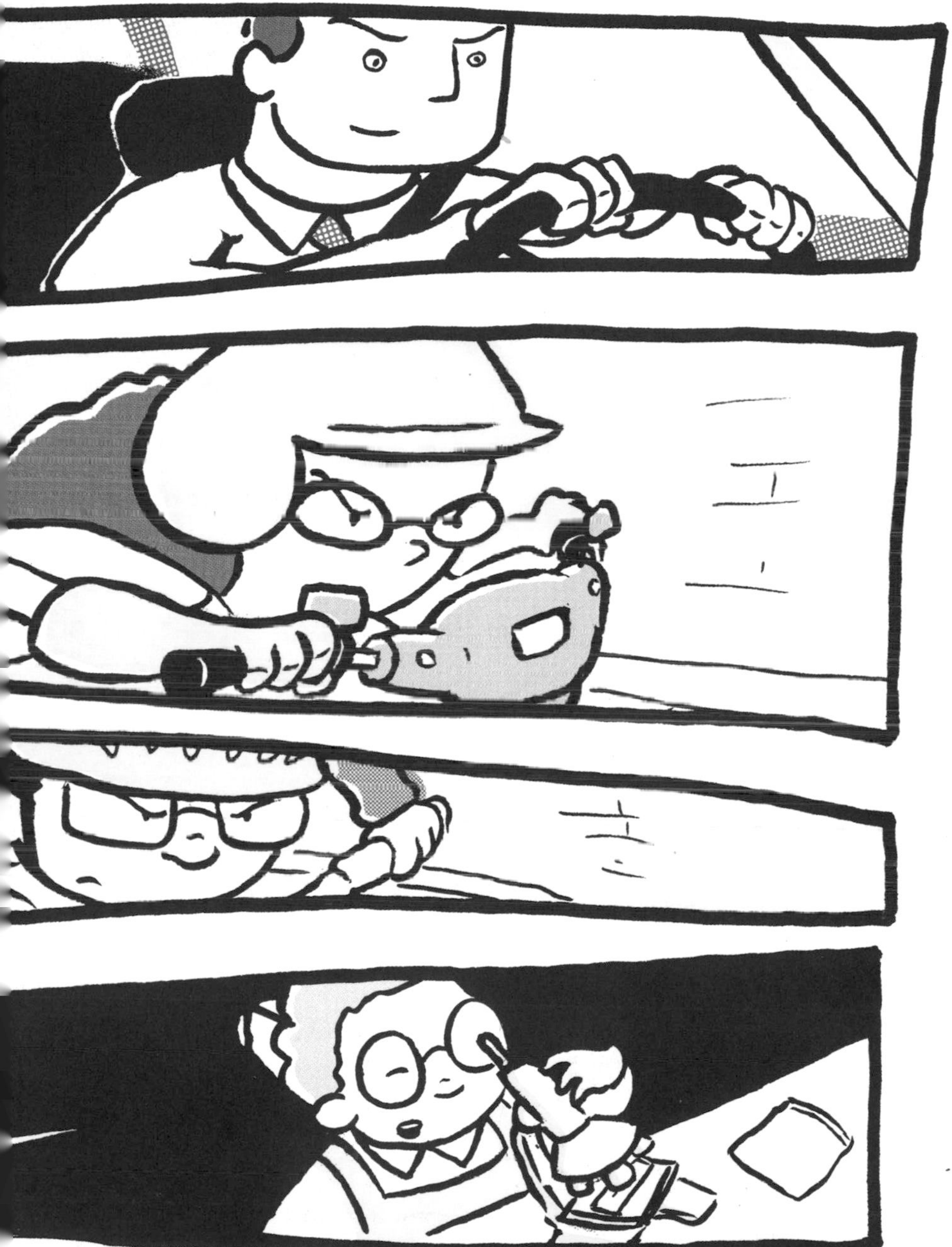

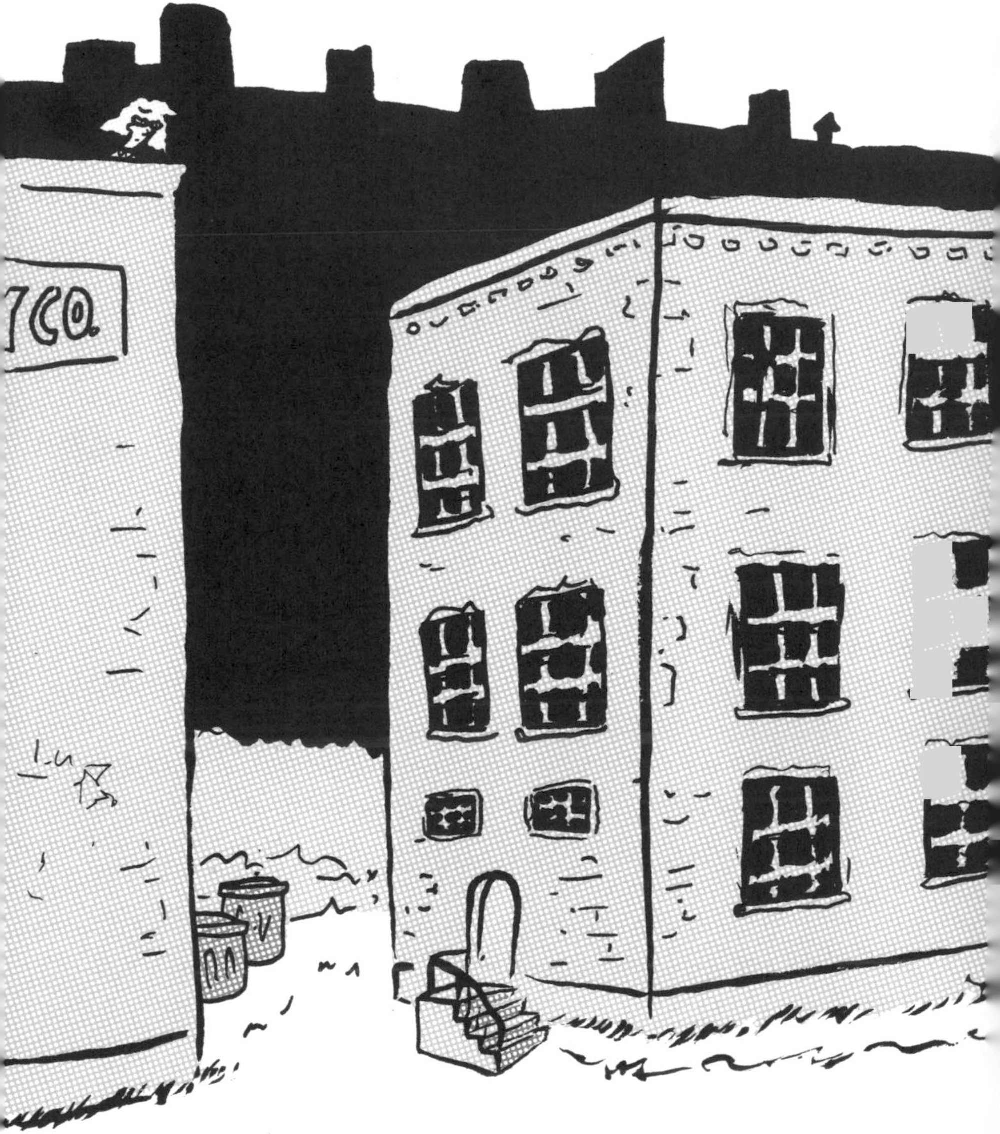
CO.

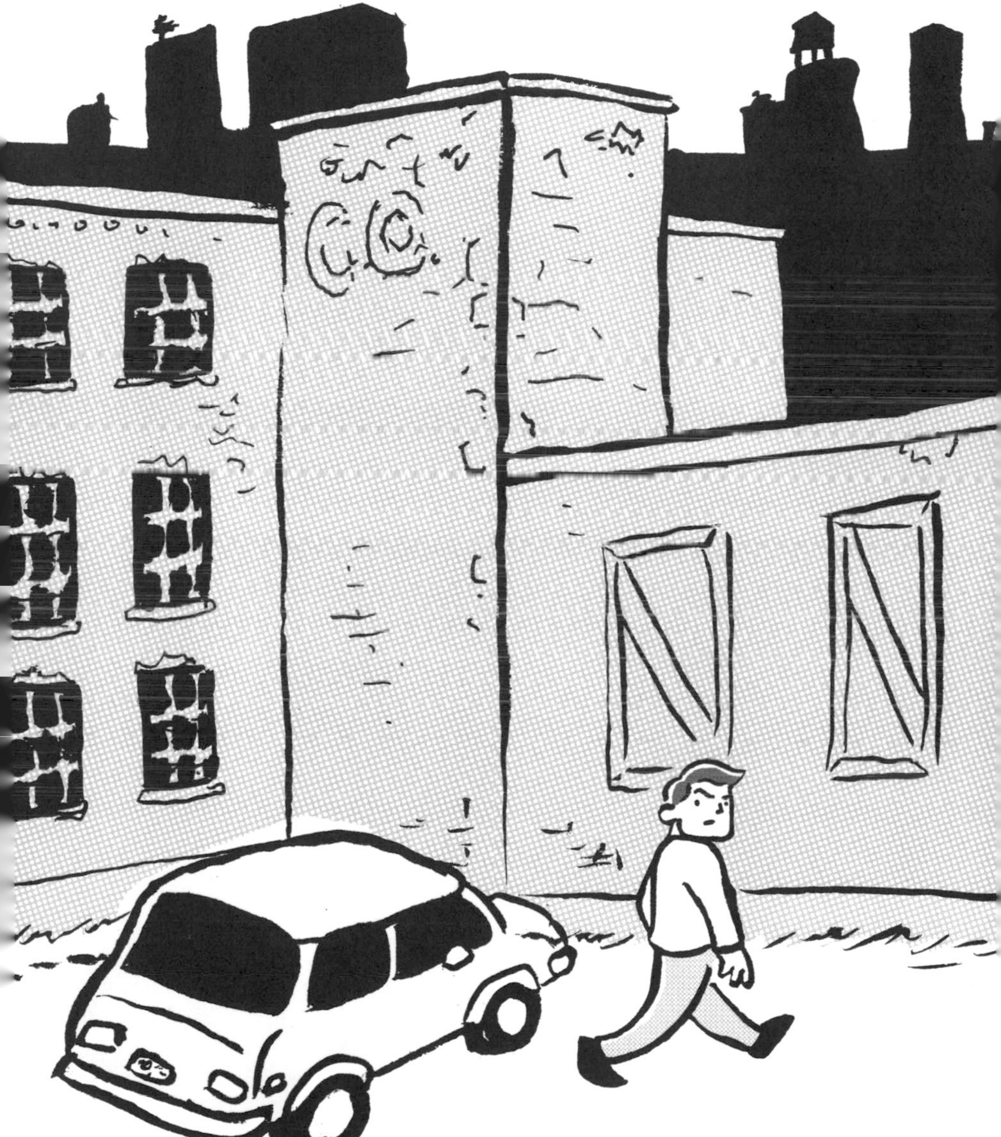

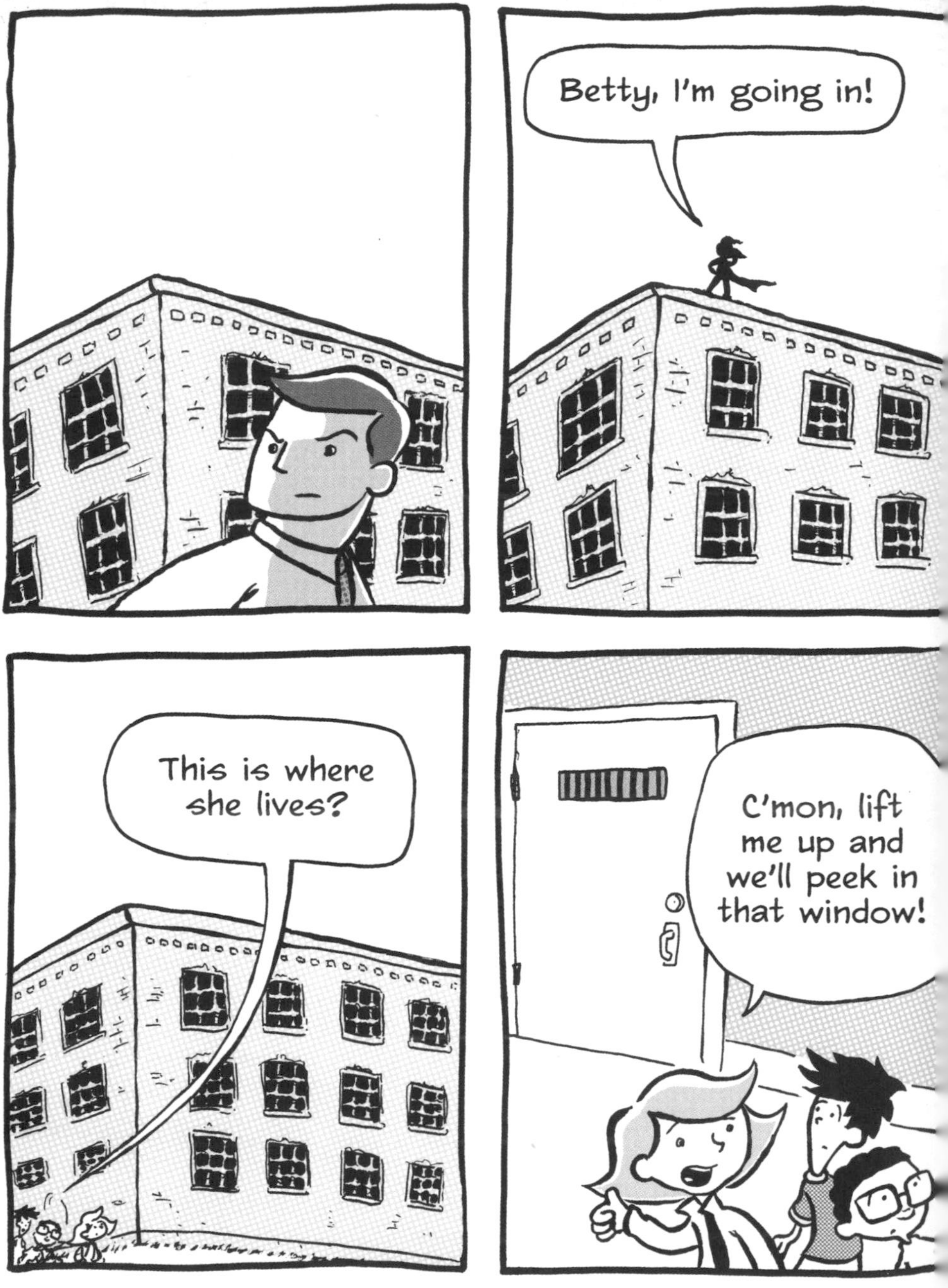

Betty, I'm going in!
This is where she lives?
C'mon, lift me up and we'll peek in that window!

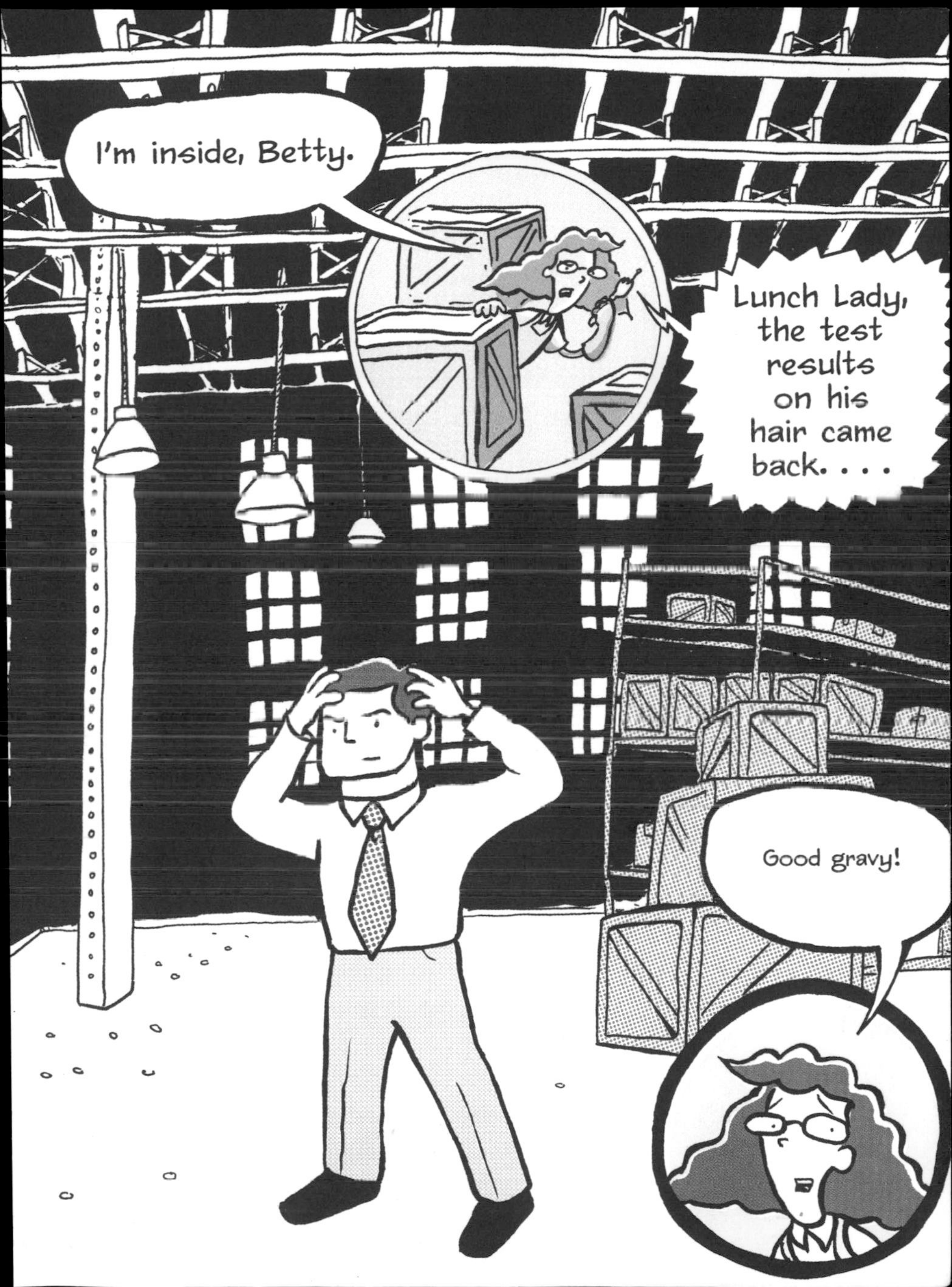
I'm inside, Betty.
Lunch Lady, the test results on his hair came back. . . .
Good gravy!

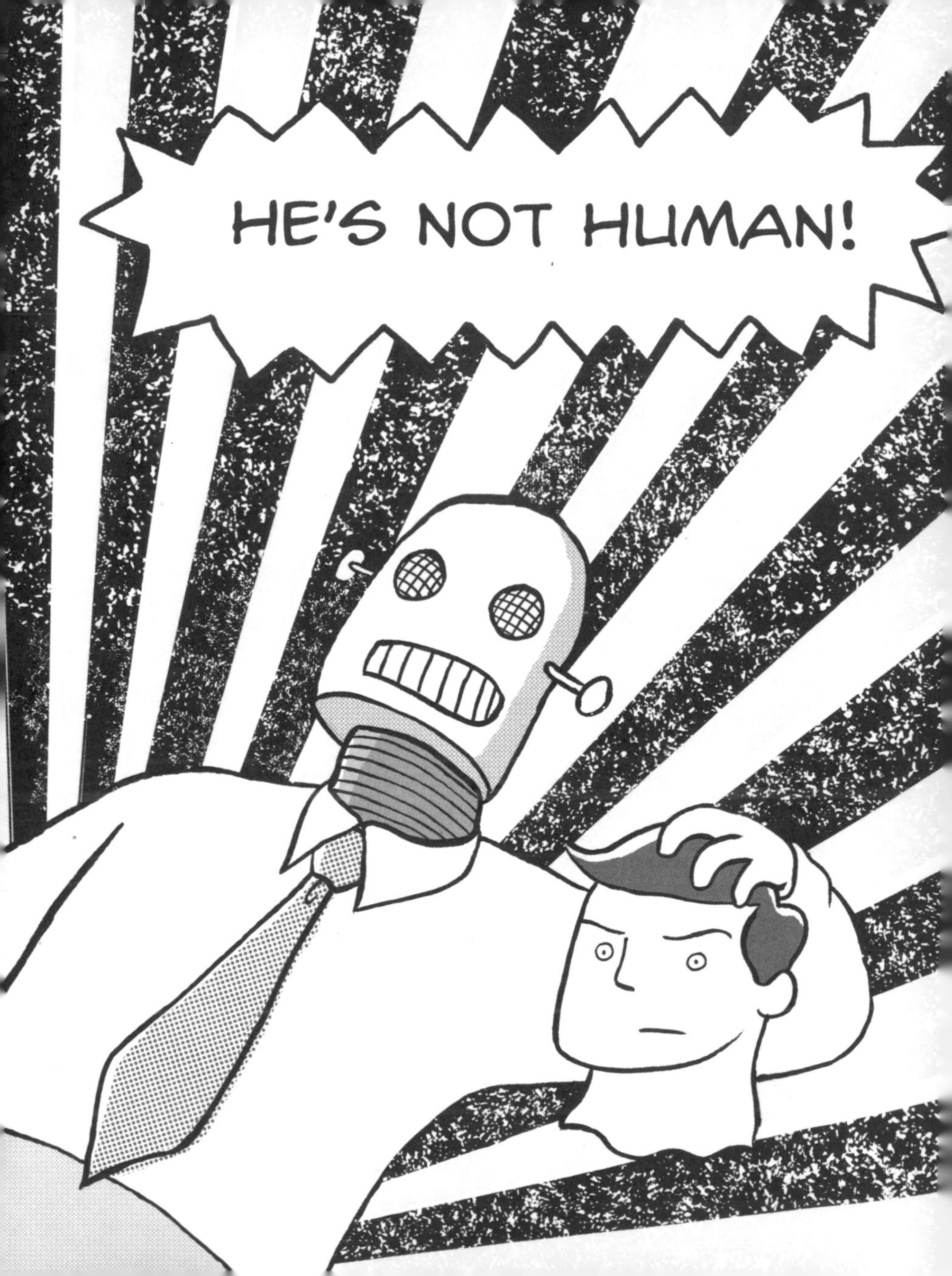
HE'S NOT HUMAN!

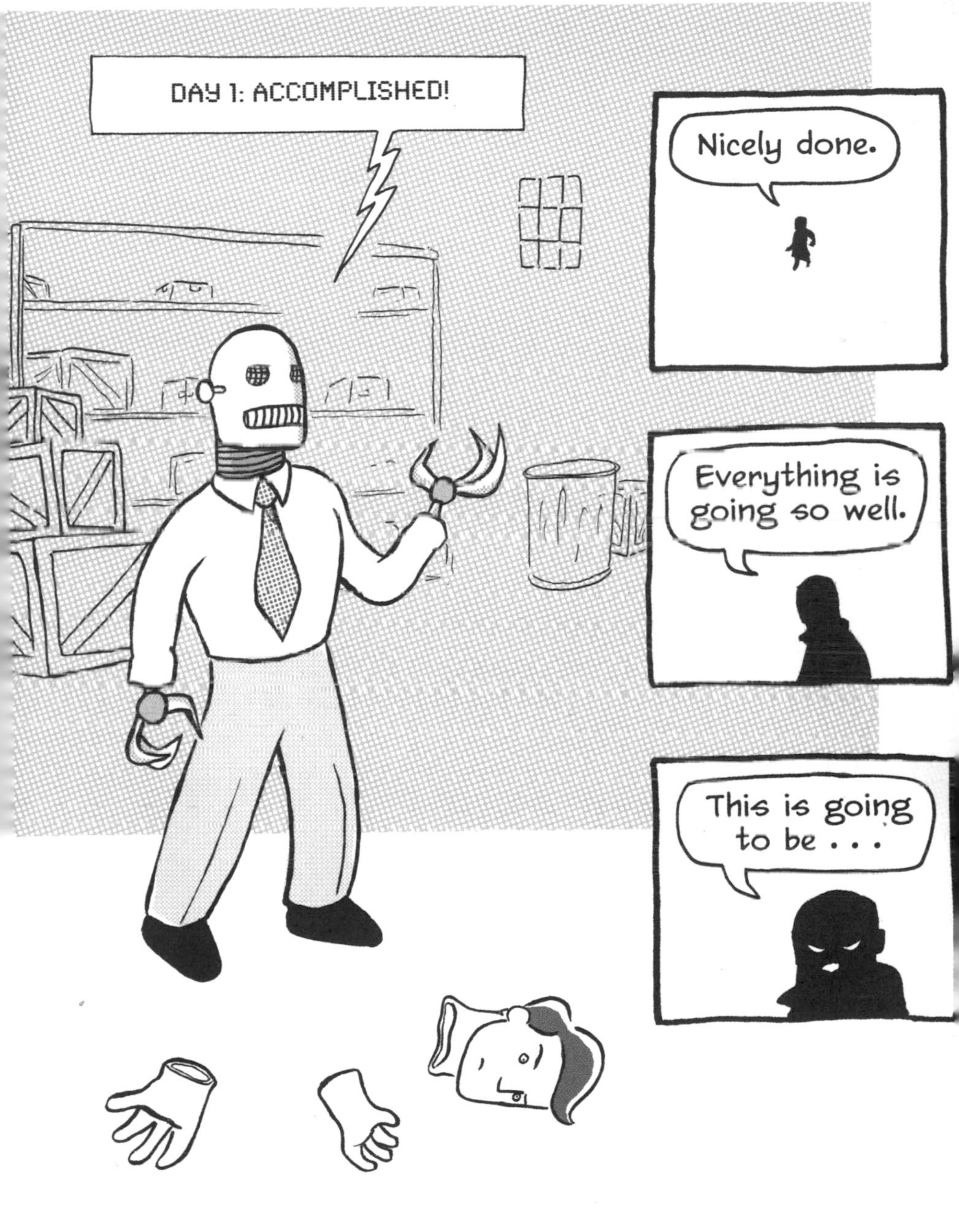
DAY 1: ACCOMPLISHED!
Nicely done.
Everything is going so well.
This is going to be . . .

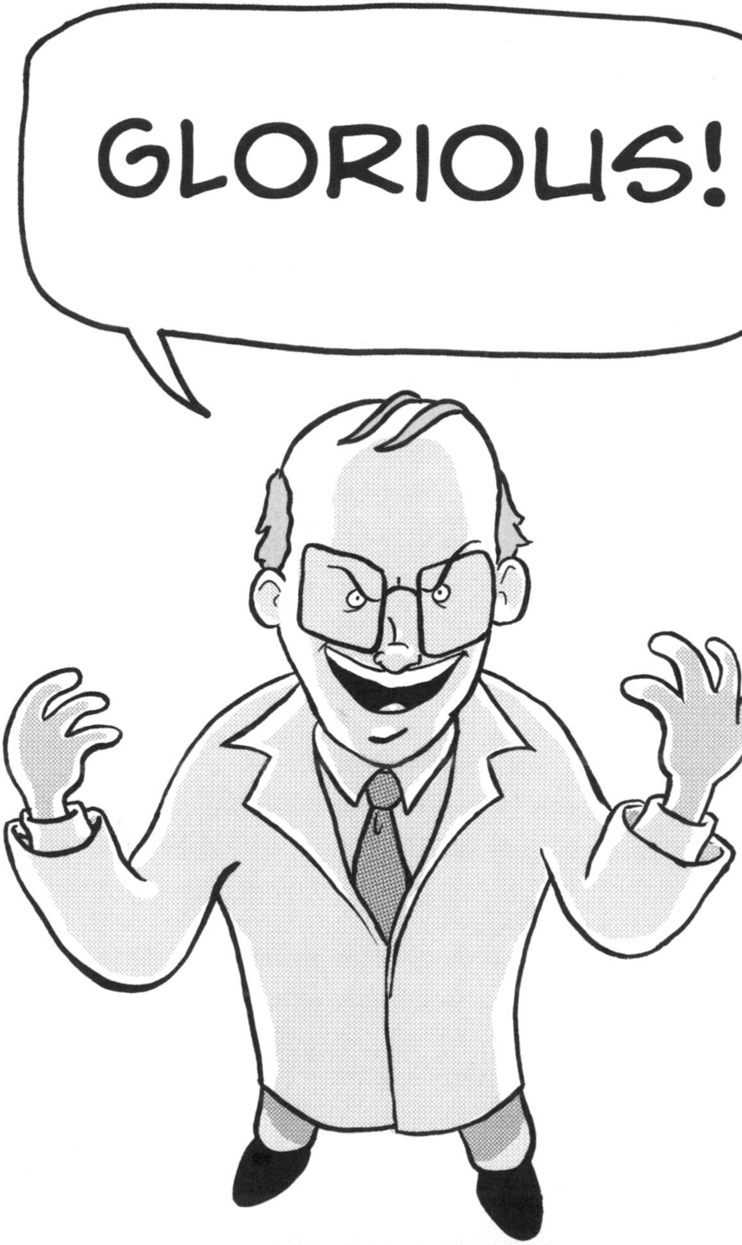
GLORIOUS!

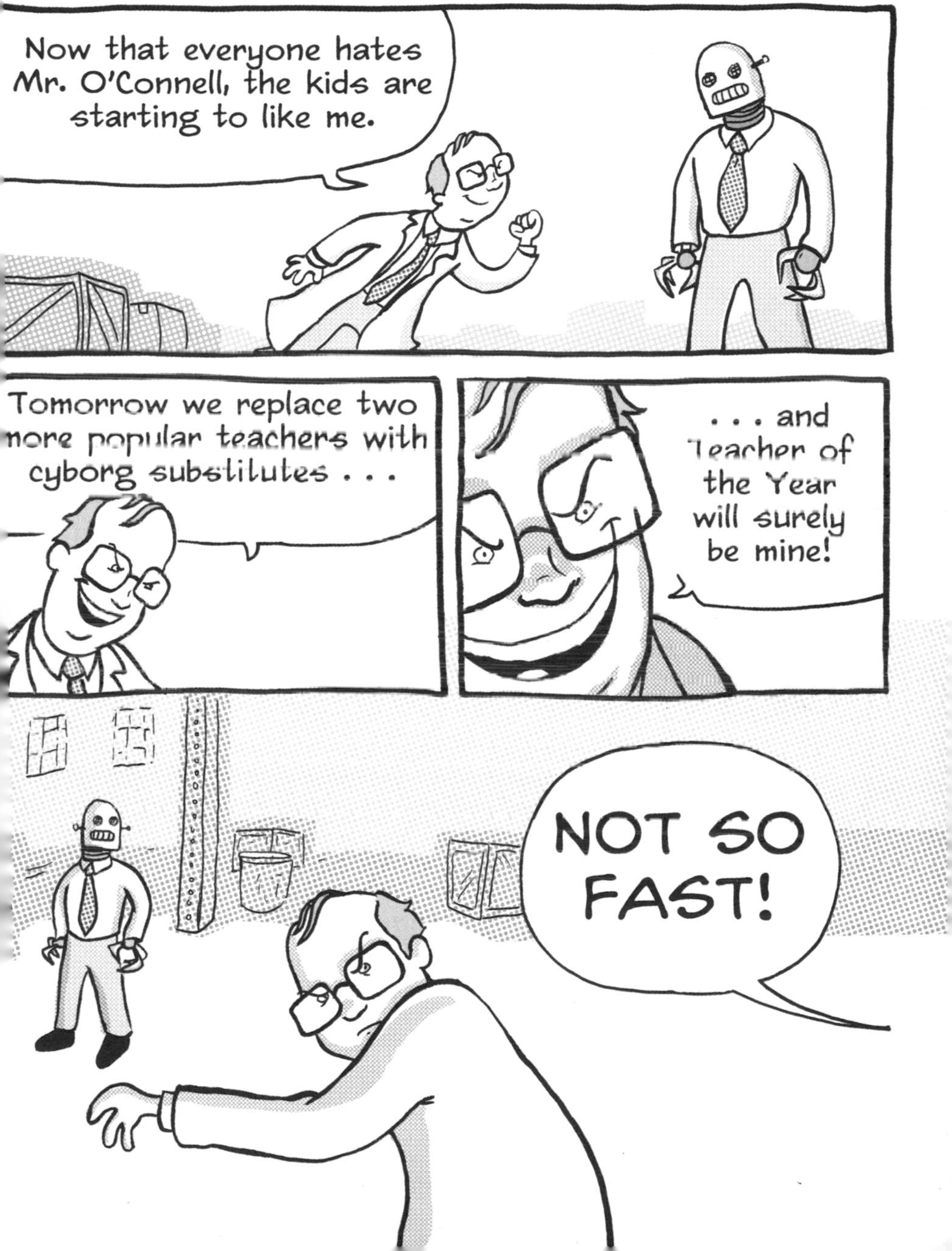
Now that everyone hates Mr. O'Connell, the kids are starting to like me.
Tomorrow we replace two more popular teachers with cyborg substitutes . . .
. . . and Teacher of the Year will surely be mine!
NOT SO FAST!

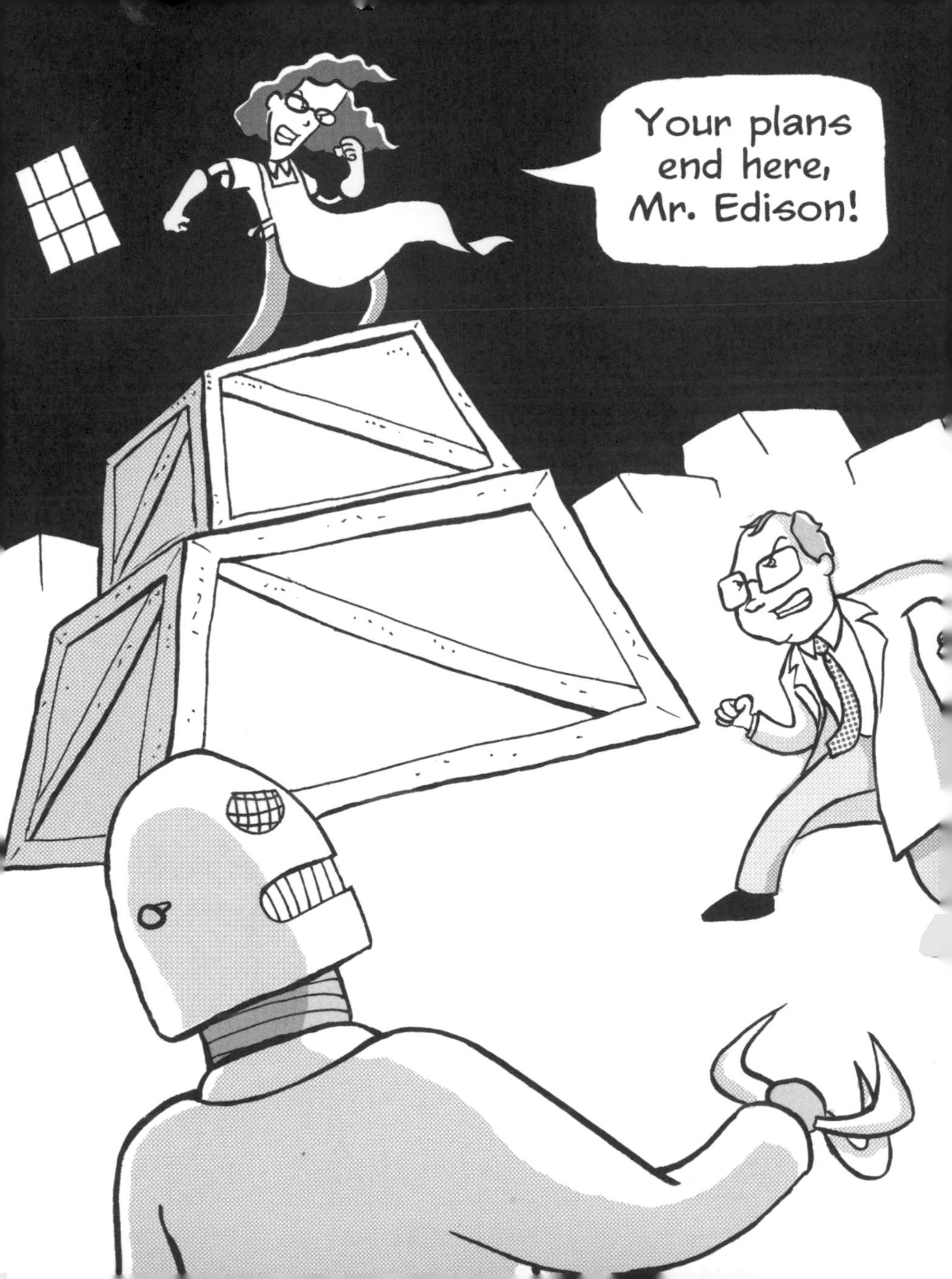
Your plans end here, Mr. Edison!

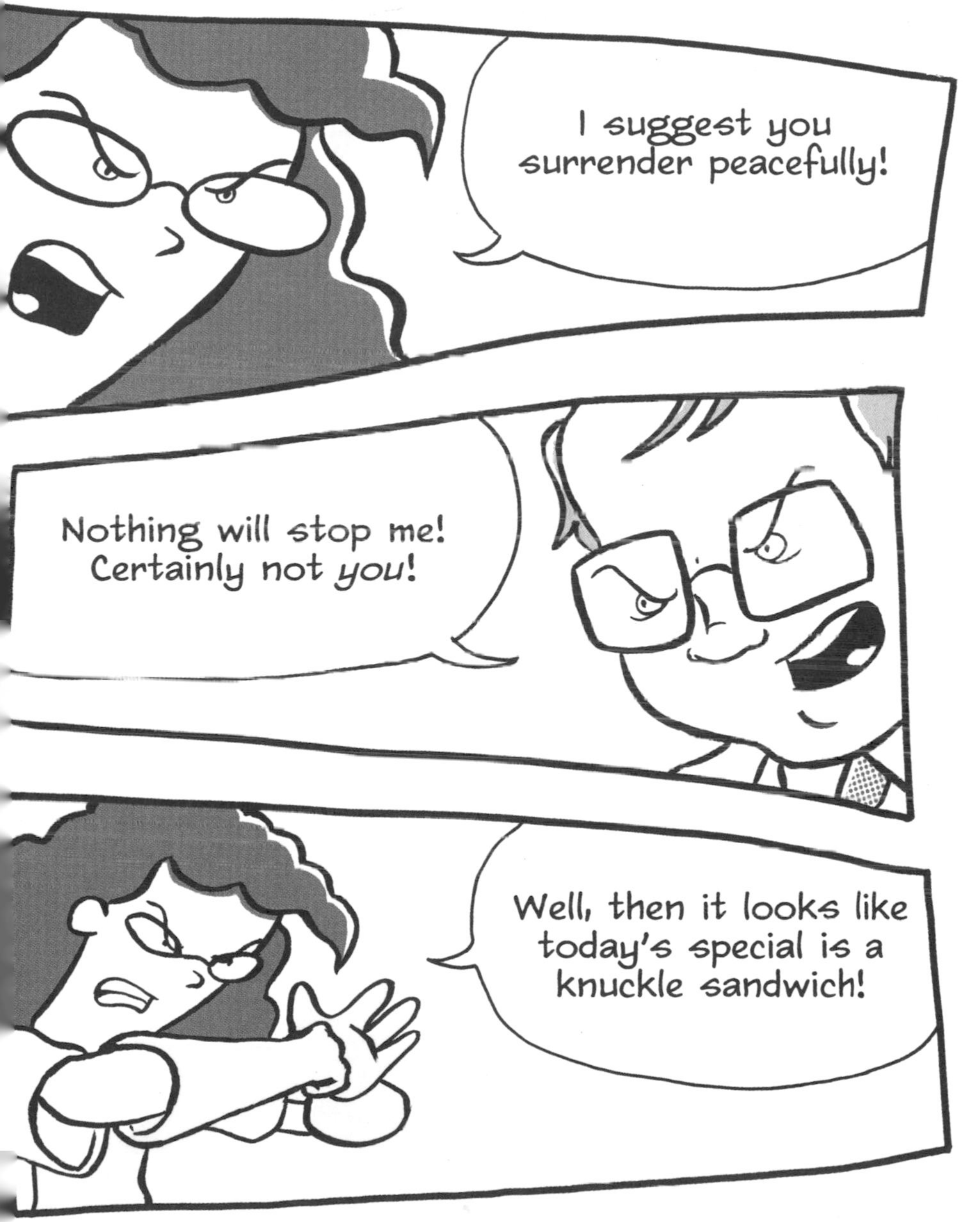
I suggest you surrender peacefully!
Nothing will stop me! Certainly not *you*!
Well, then it looks like today's special is a knuckle sandwich!

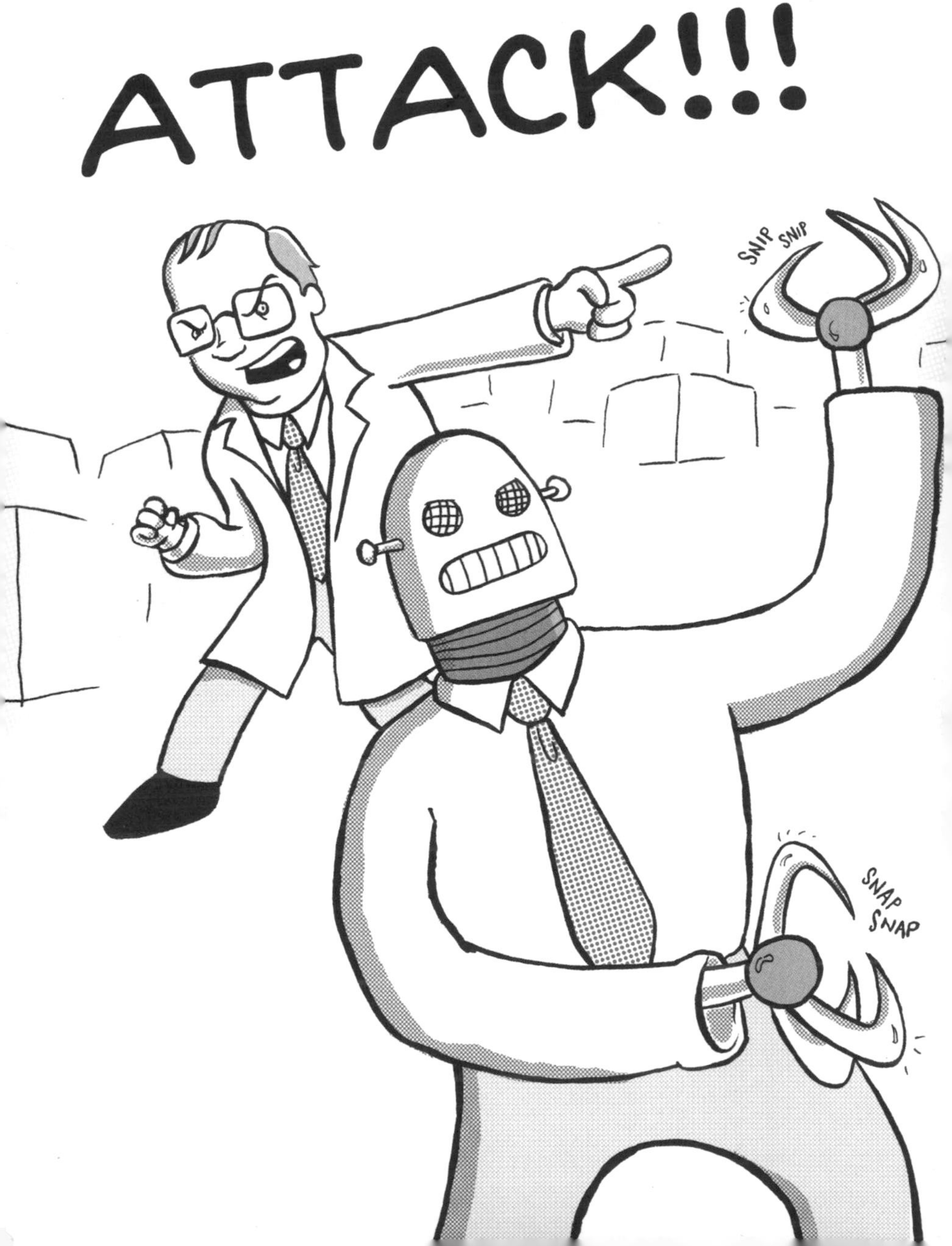
ATTACK!!!
SNIP SNIP
SNAP SNAP

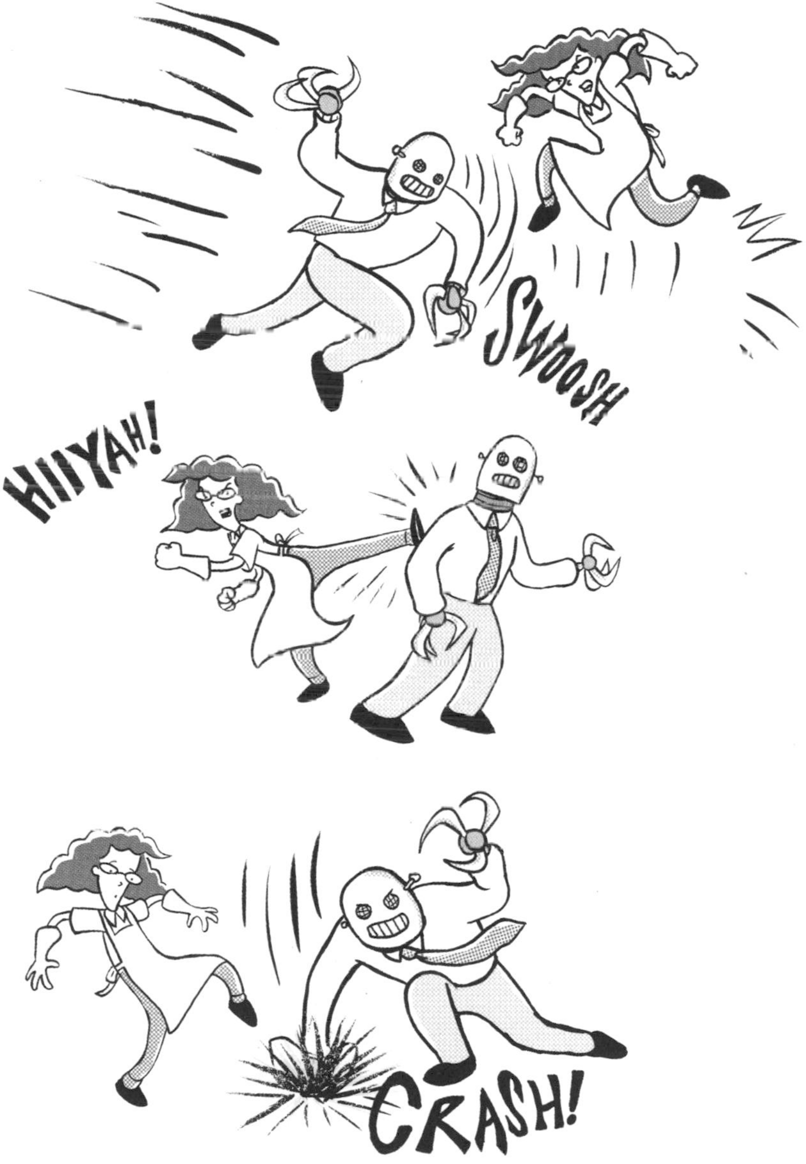
SWOOSH
HIIYAH!
CRASH!

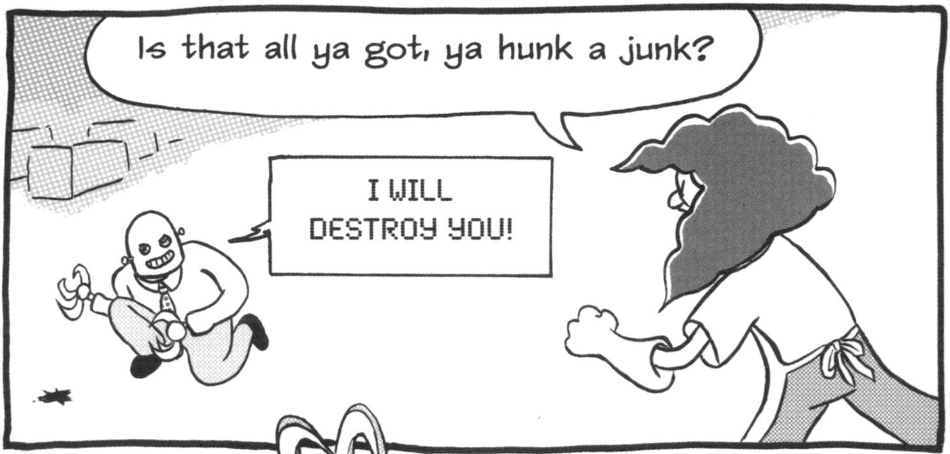
Is that all ya got, ya hunk a junk?
I WILL DESTROY YOU!

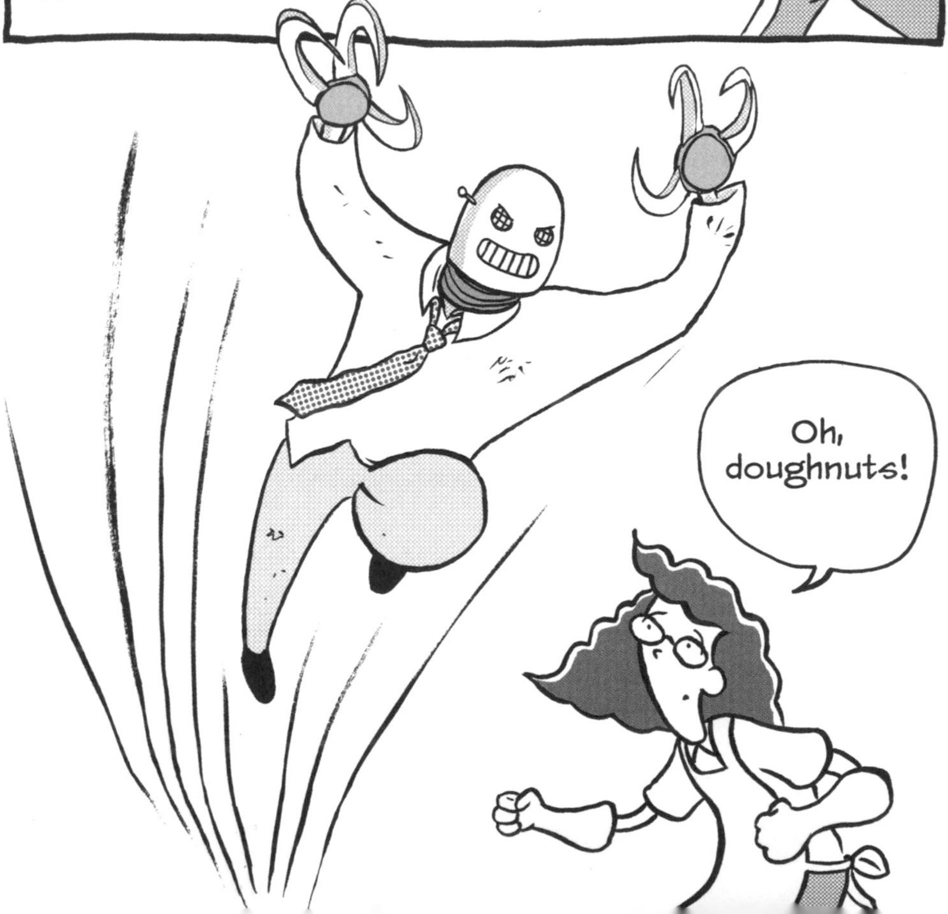
Oh, doughnuts!

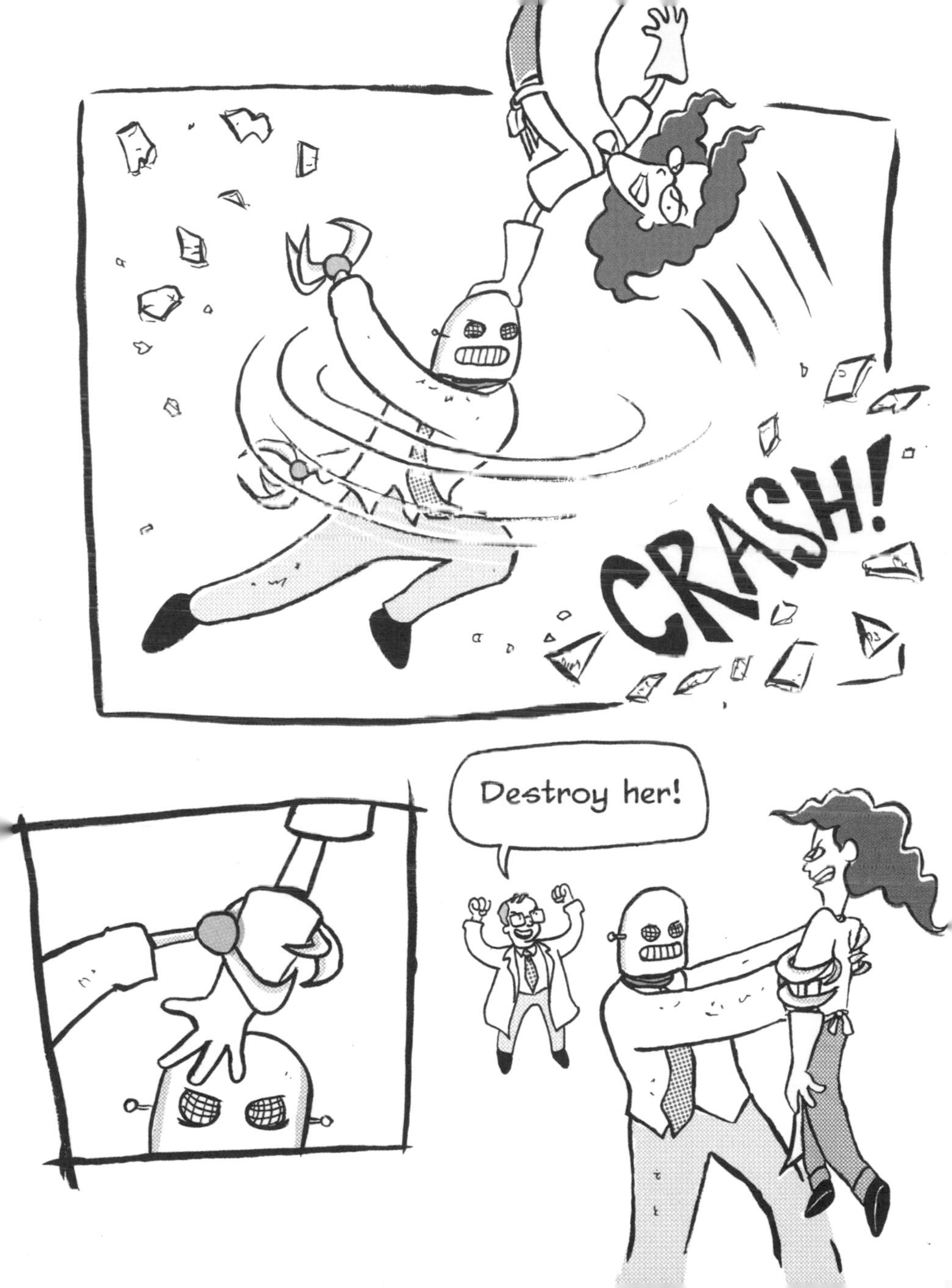
CRASH!
Destroy her!

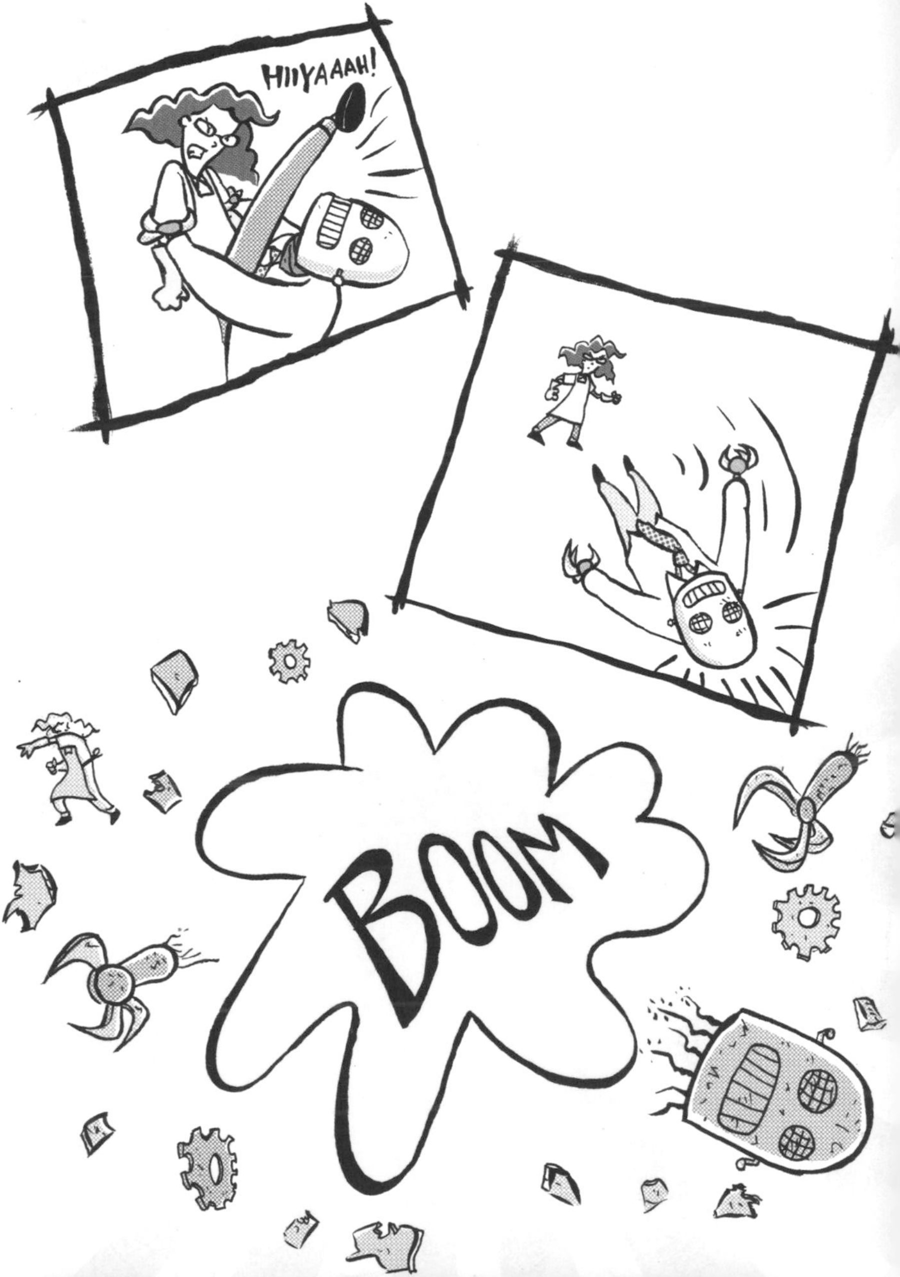

HIIIYAAAH!
BOOM

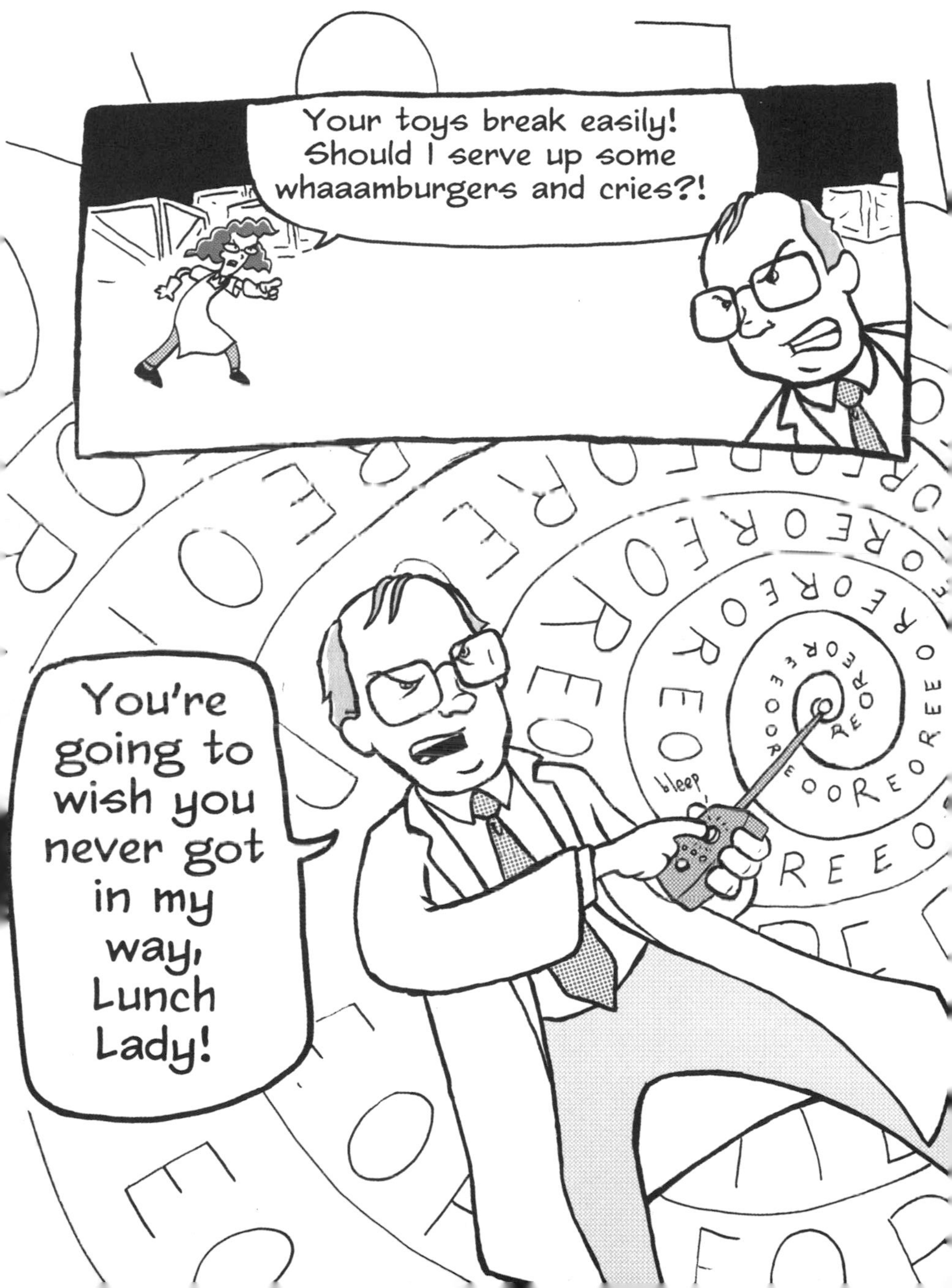
Your toys break easily! Should I serve up some whaaamburgers and cries?!
bleep
You're going to wish you never got in my way, Lunch Lady!

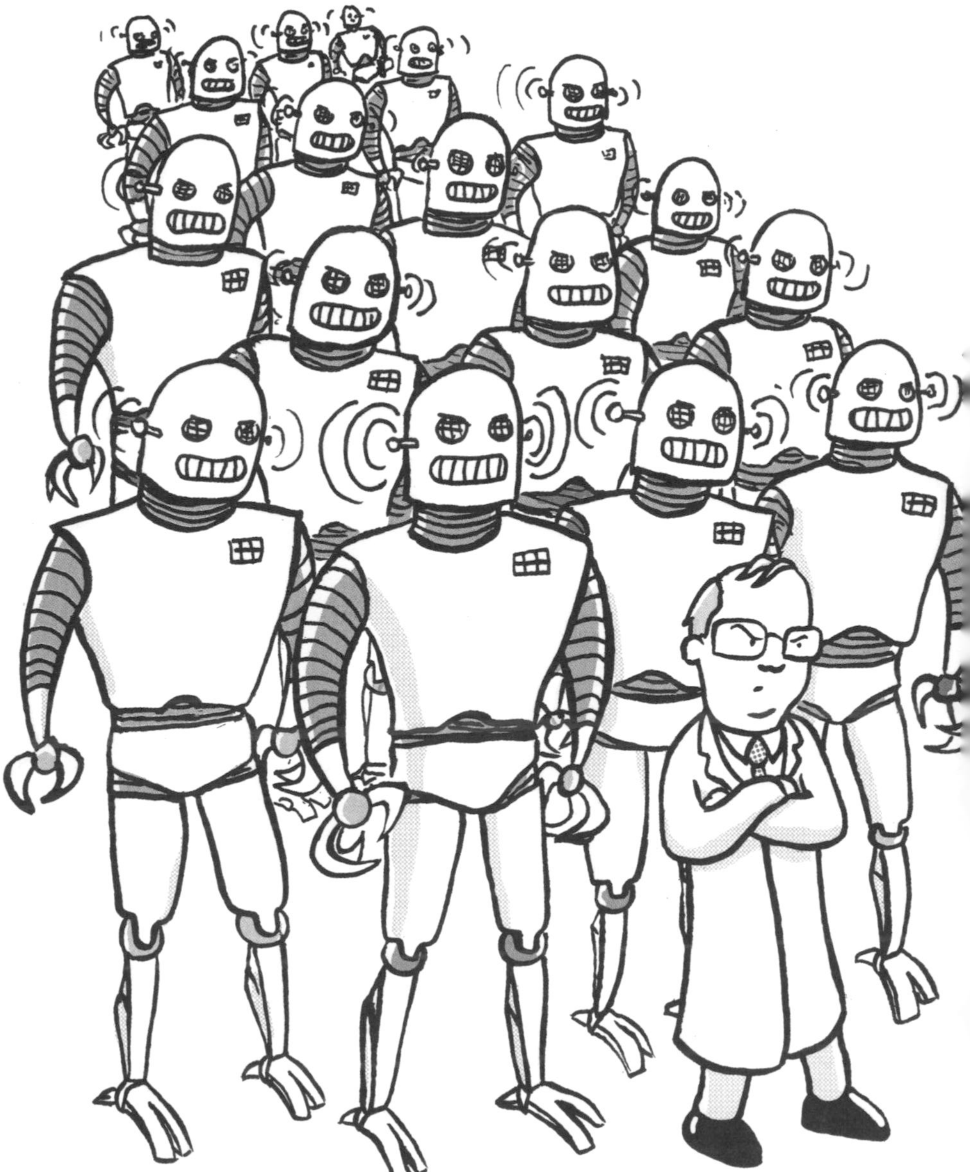

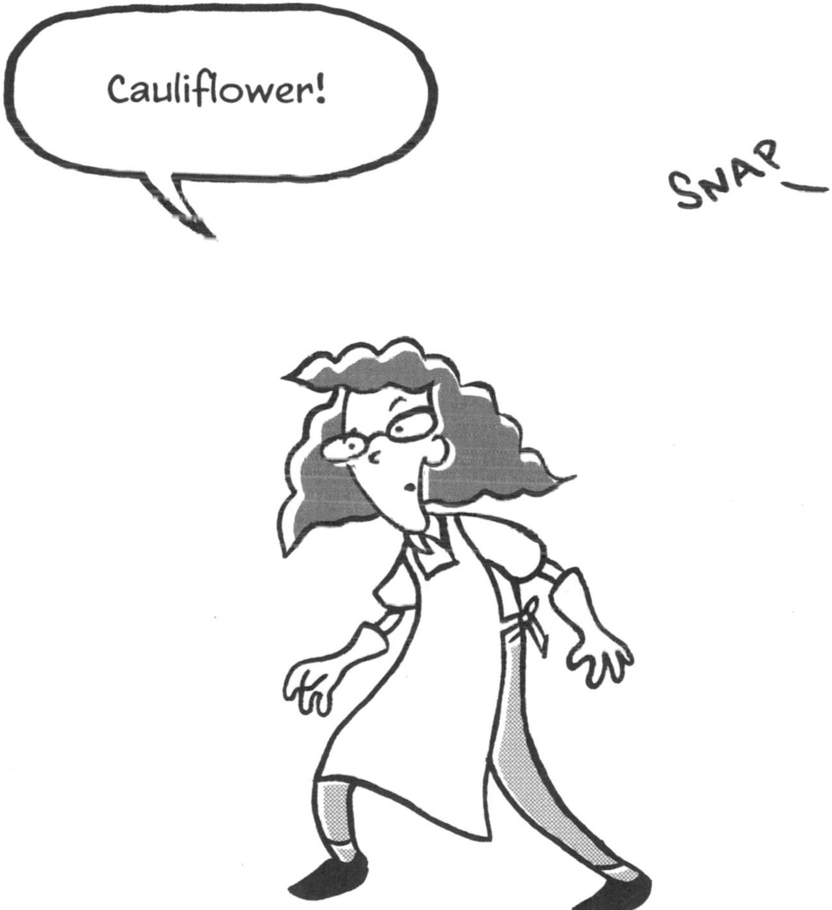
Cauliflower!
SNAP

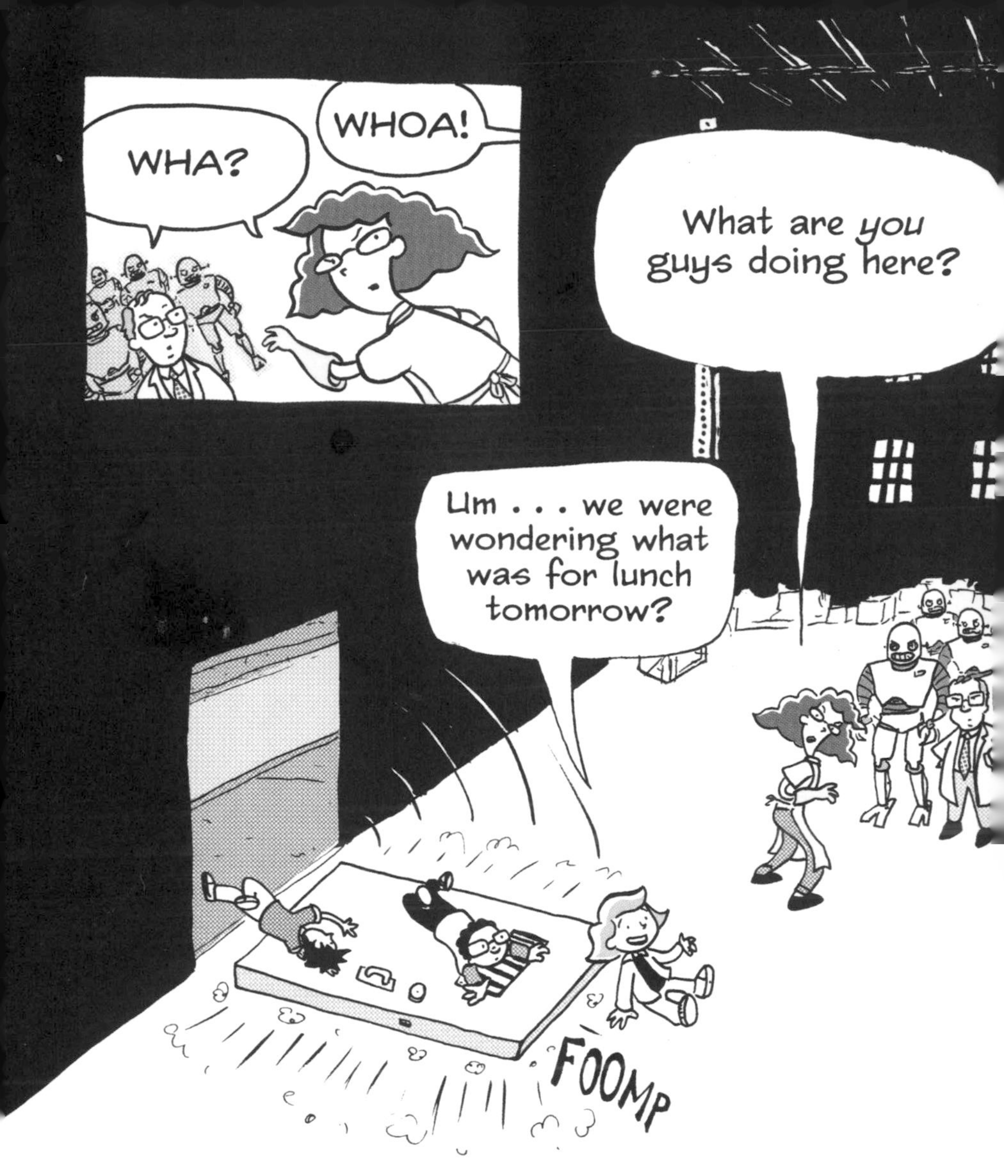
WHA?
WHOA!
What are *you* guys doing here?
Um . . . we were wondering what was for lunch tomorrow?
FOOMP

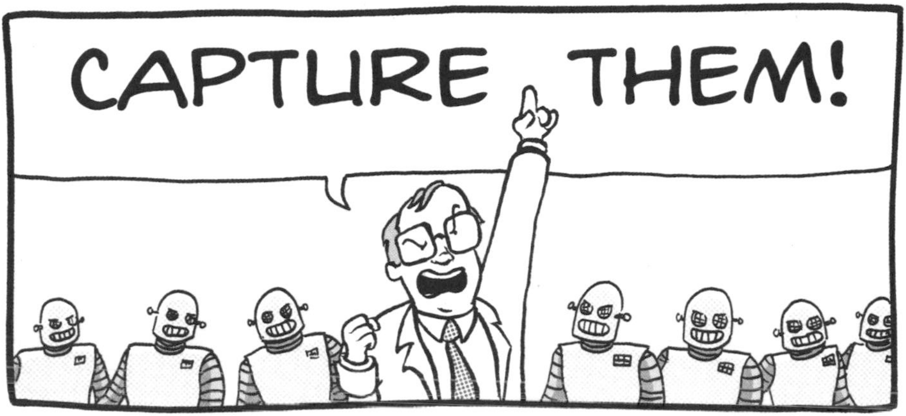
CAPTURE THEM!

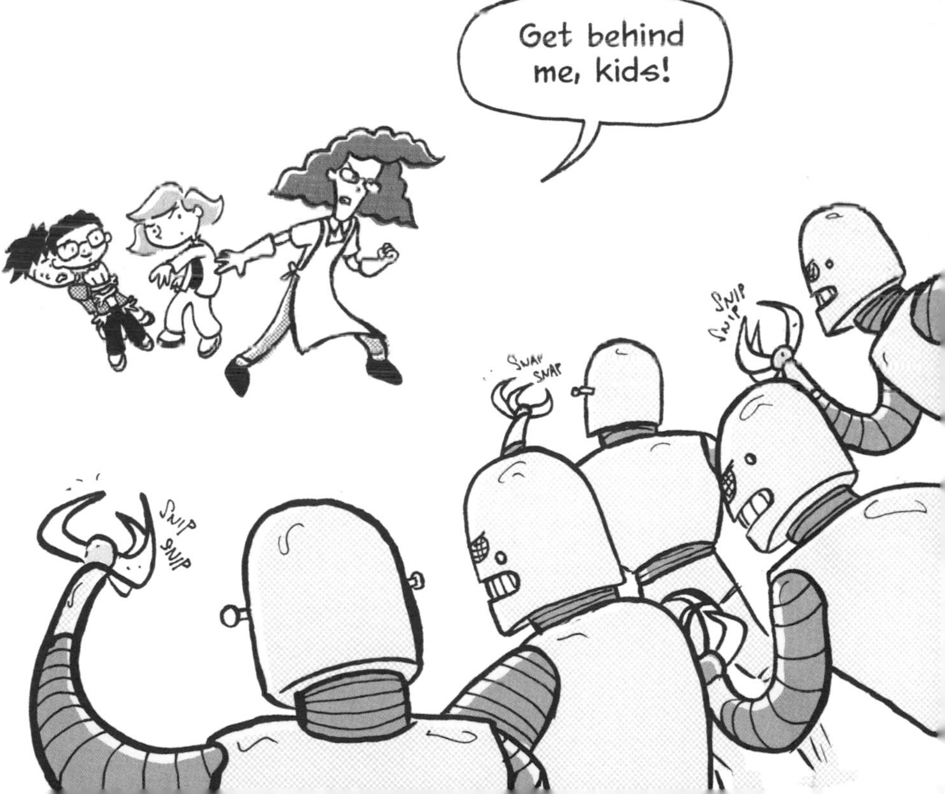
Get behind me, kids!
SNAP SNAP
SNIP SNIP
SNIP SNIP

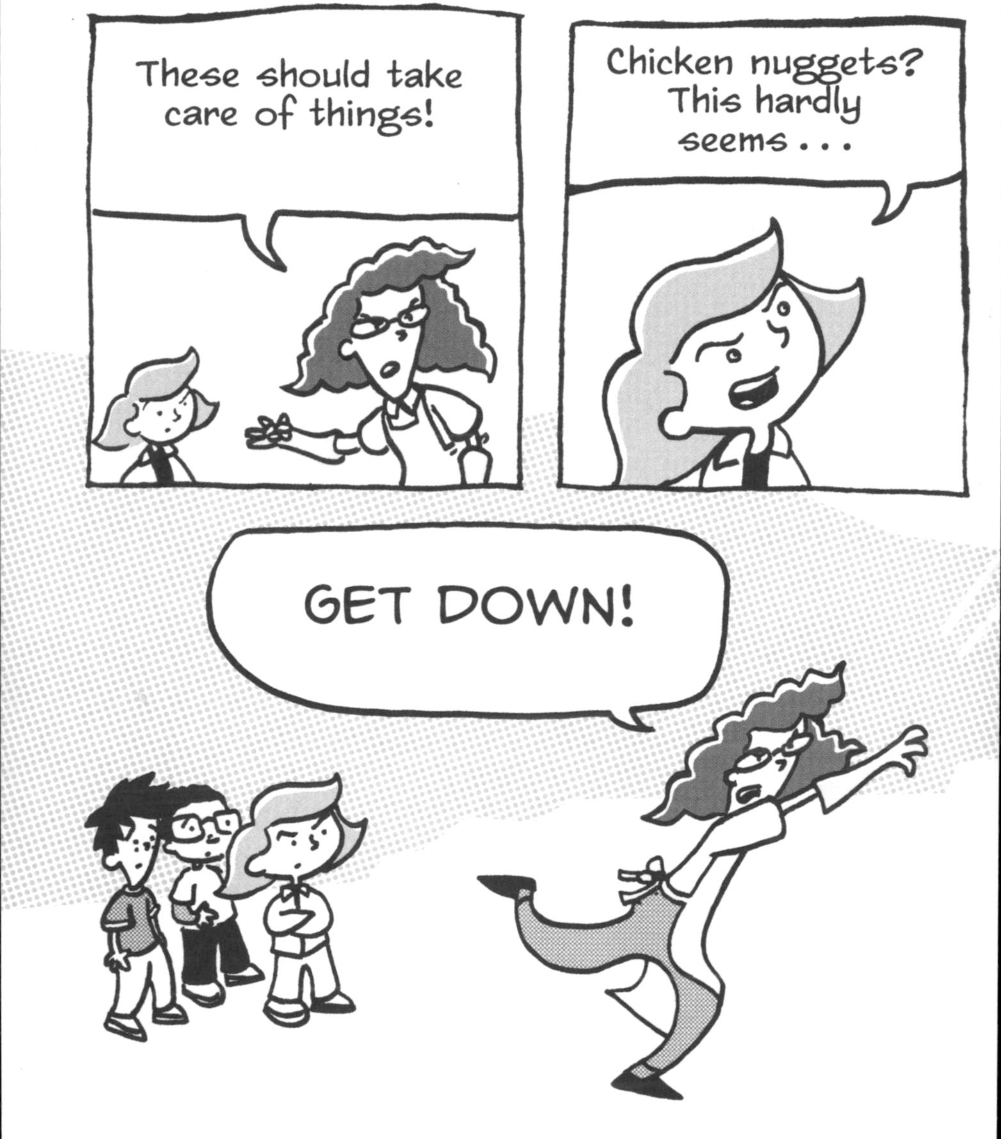
These should take care of things!
Chicken nuggets? This hardly seems . . .
GET DOWN!

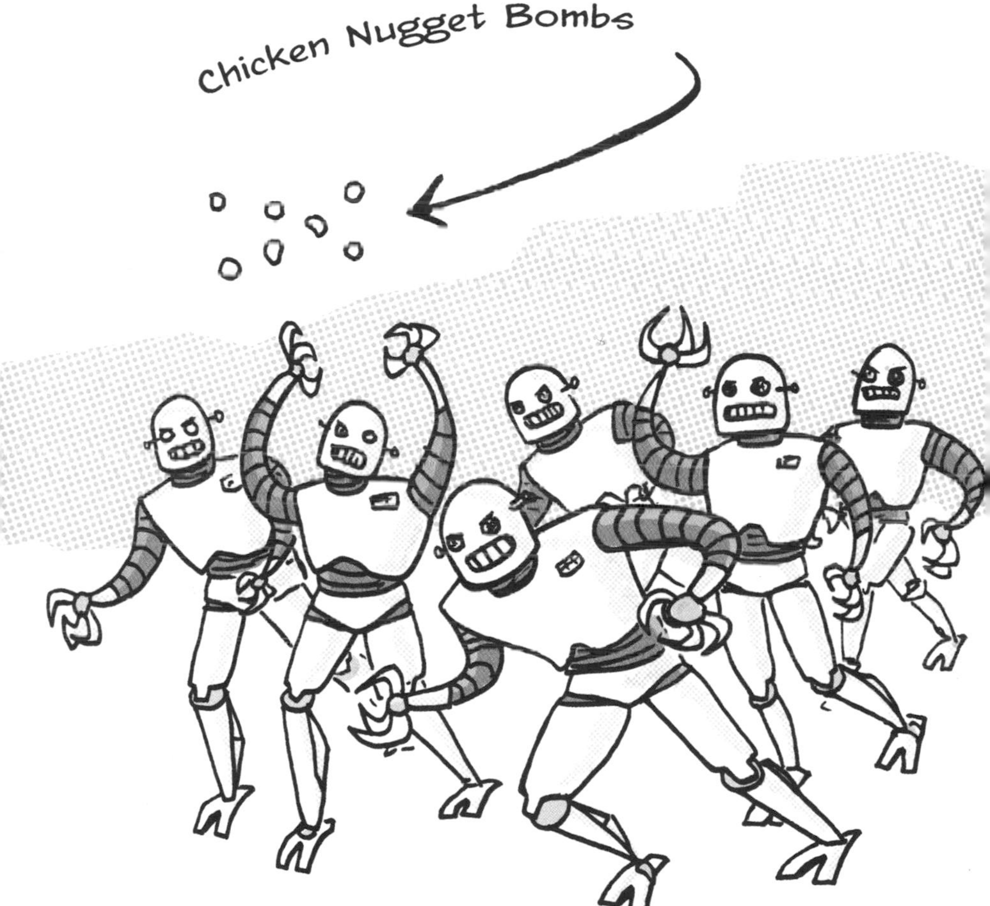
Chicken Nugget Bombs

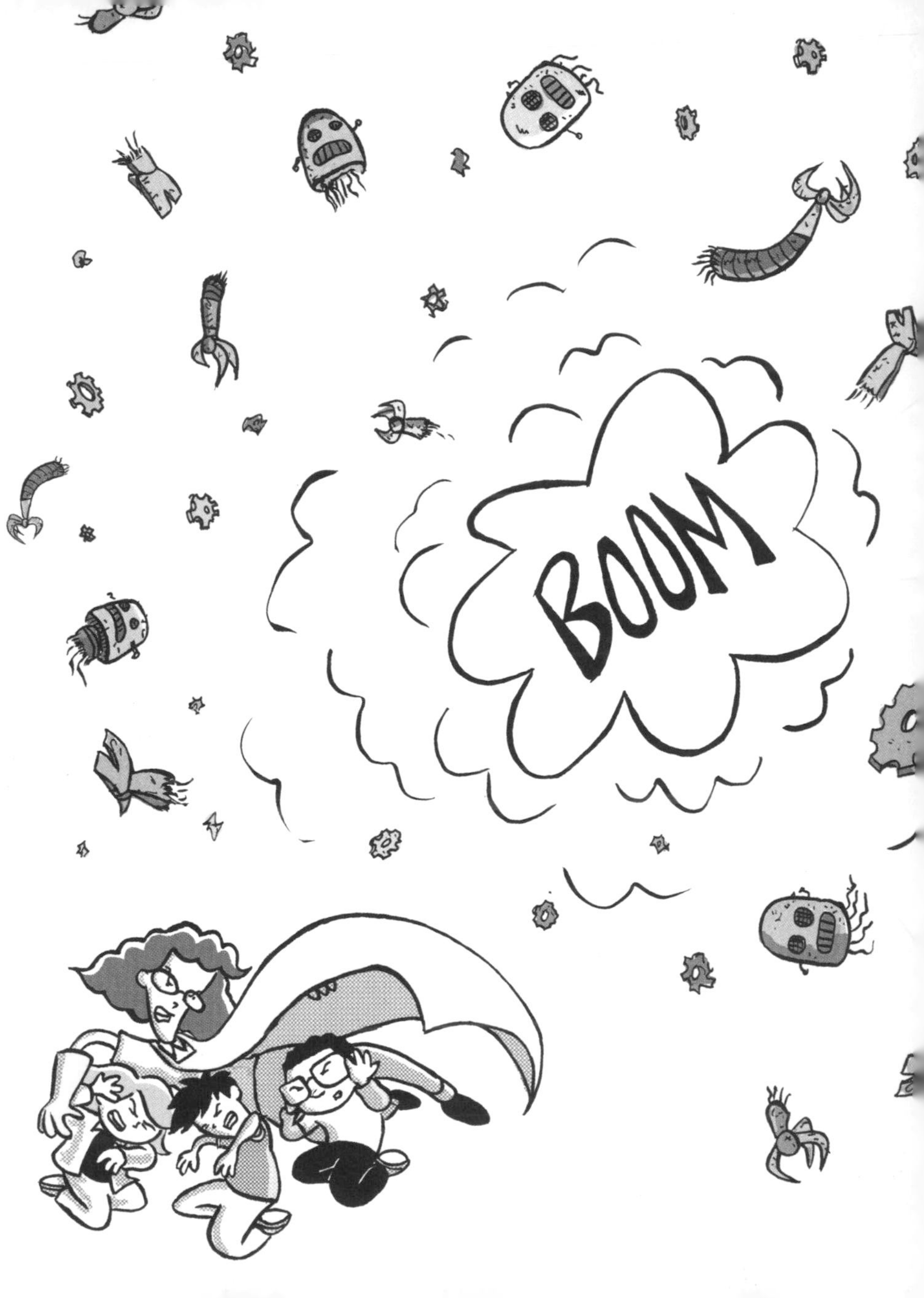
BOOM

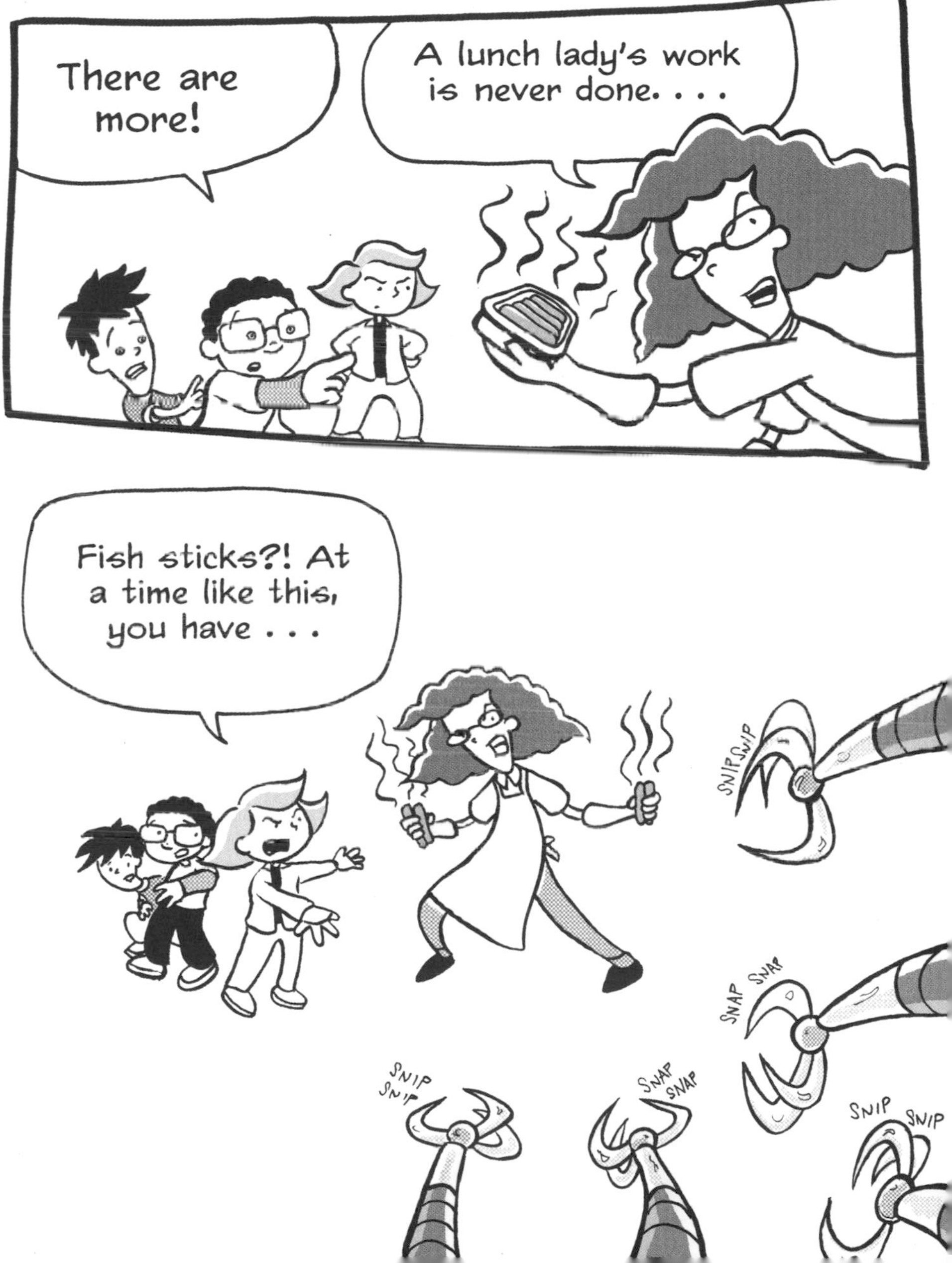
There are more!
A lunch lady's work is never done. . . .
Fish sticks?! At a time like this, you have . . .
SNIP SNIP
SNAP SNAP
SNIP SNIP
SNAP SNAP
SNIP SNIP

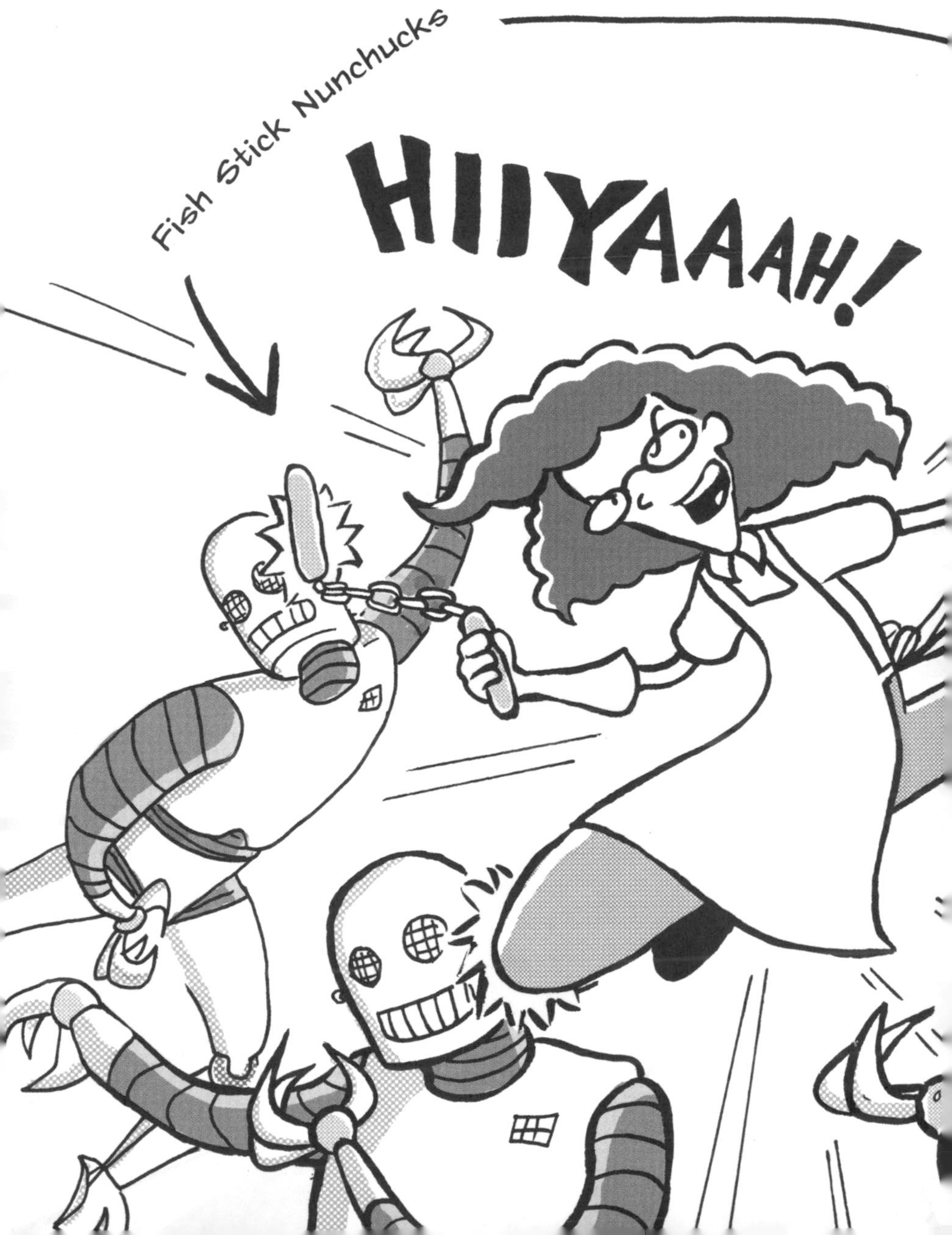
Fish Stick Nunchucks
HIIYAAAAH!

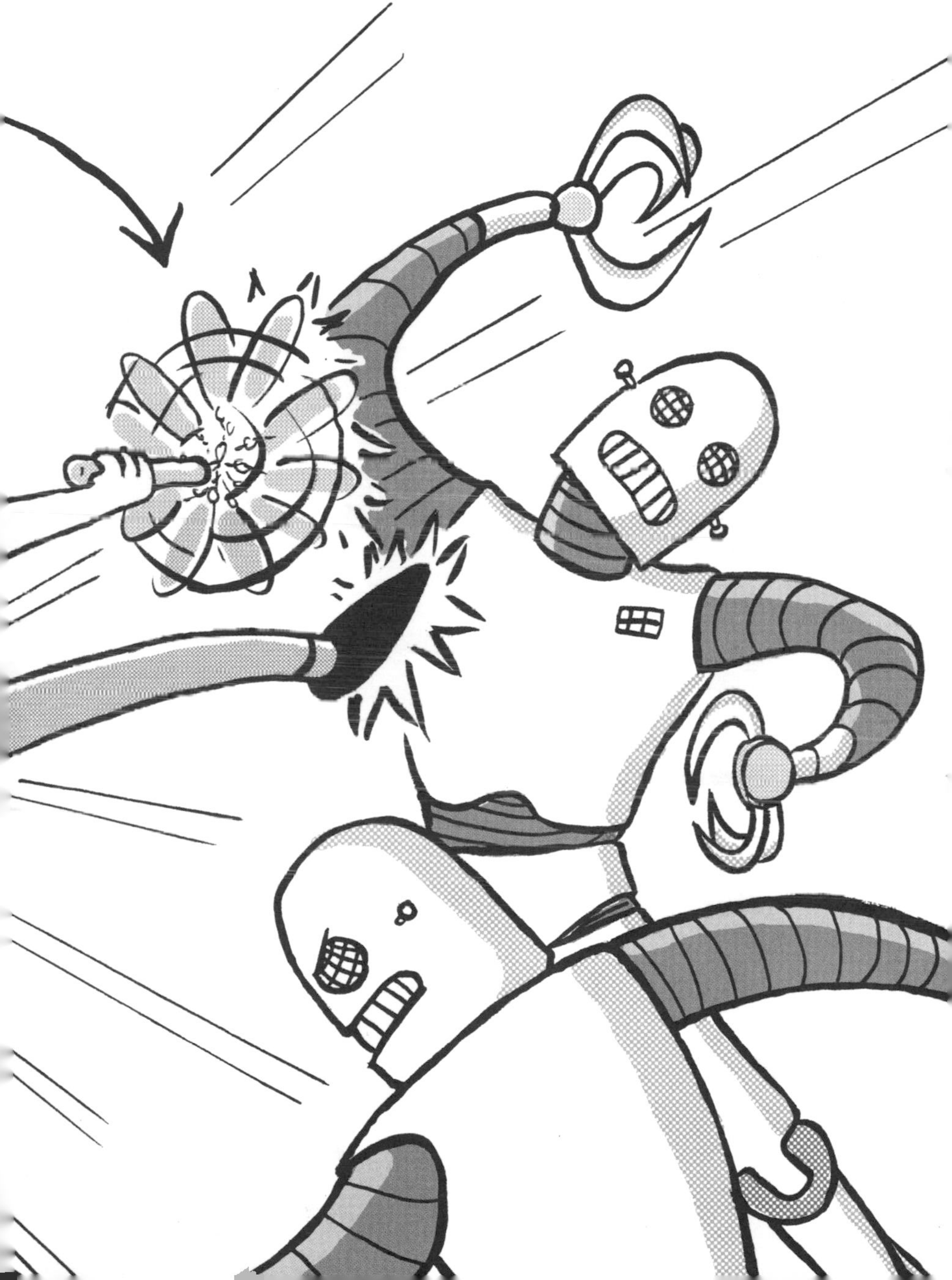

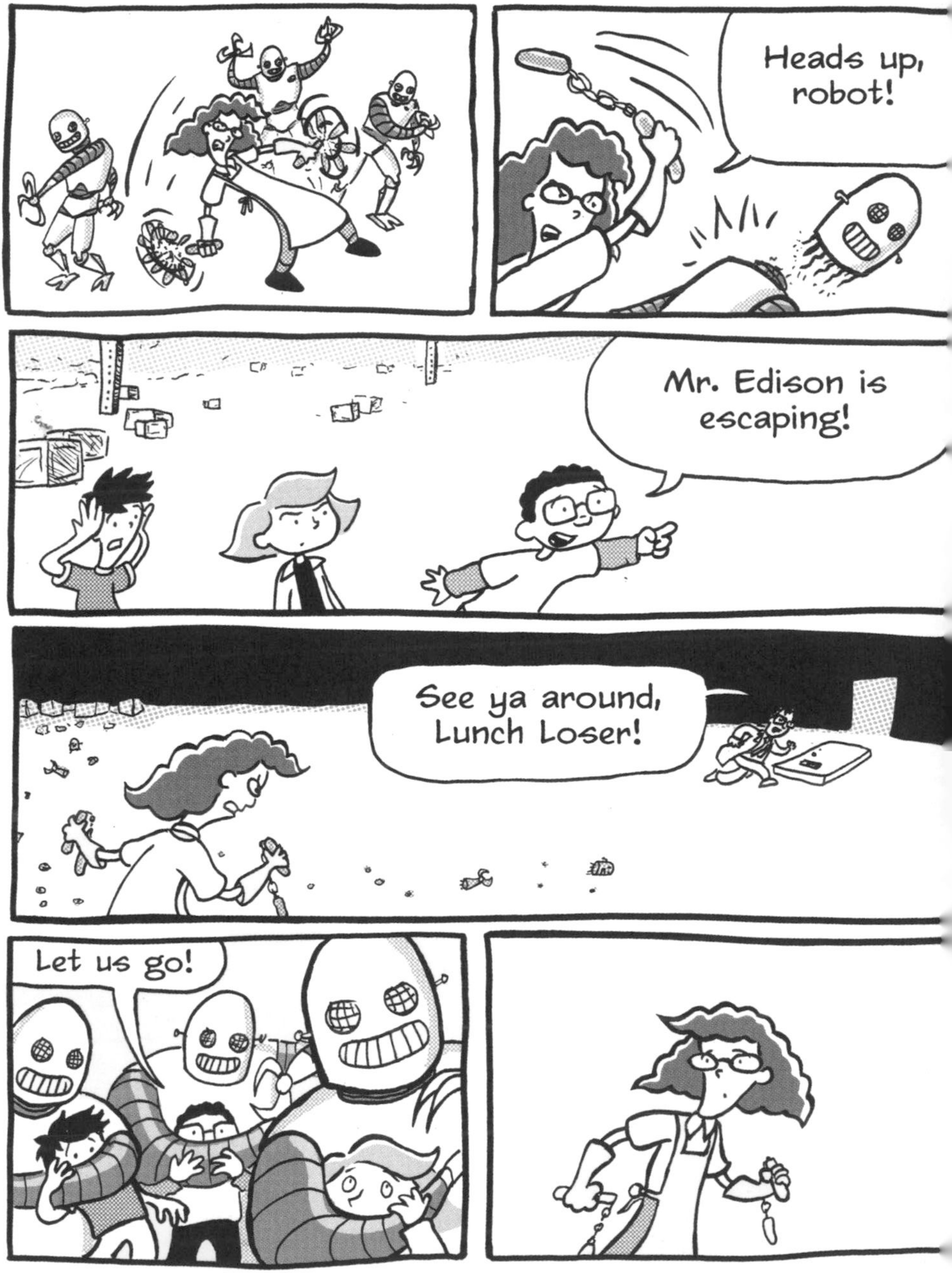
Heads up, robot!
Mr. Edison is escaping!
See ya around, Lunch Loser!
Let us go!

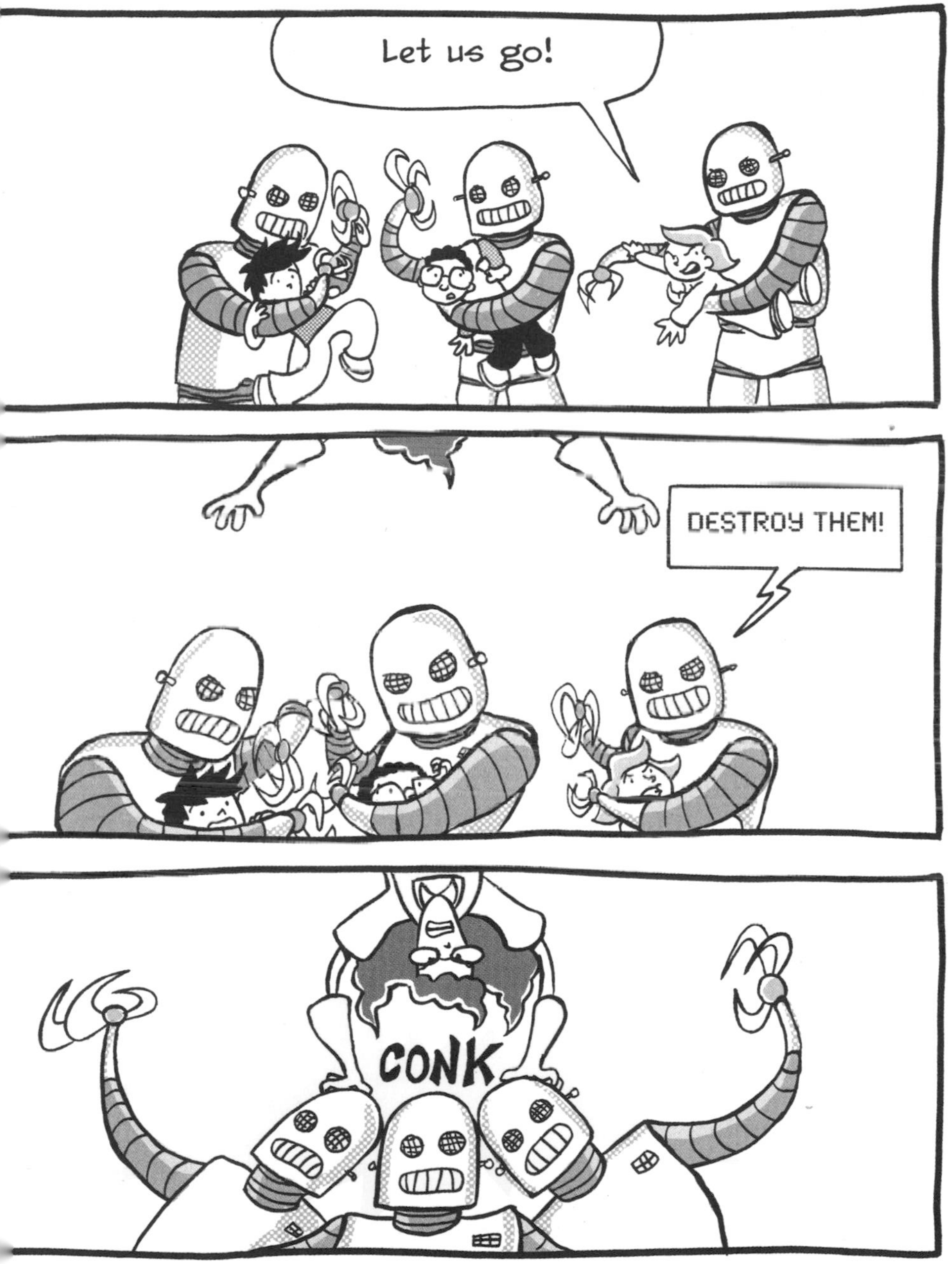
Let us go!
DESTROY THEM!
CONK

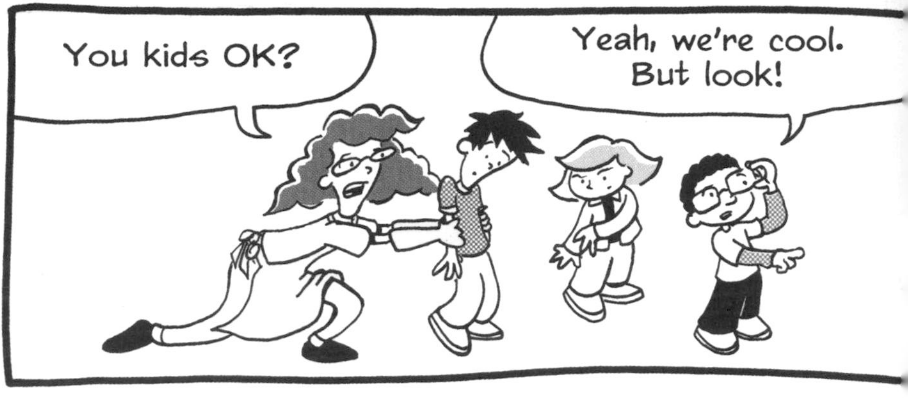
You kids OK?
Yeah, we're cool. But look!

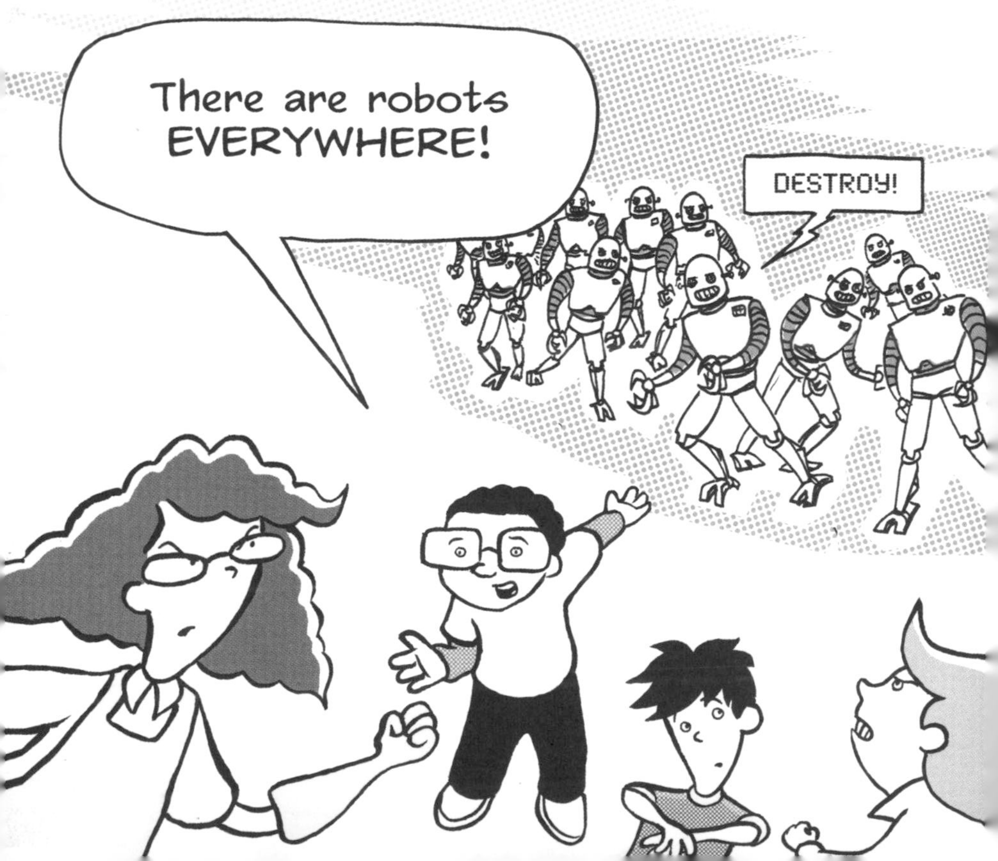
There are robots EVERYWHERE!
DESTROY!

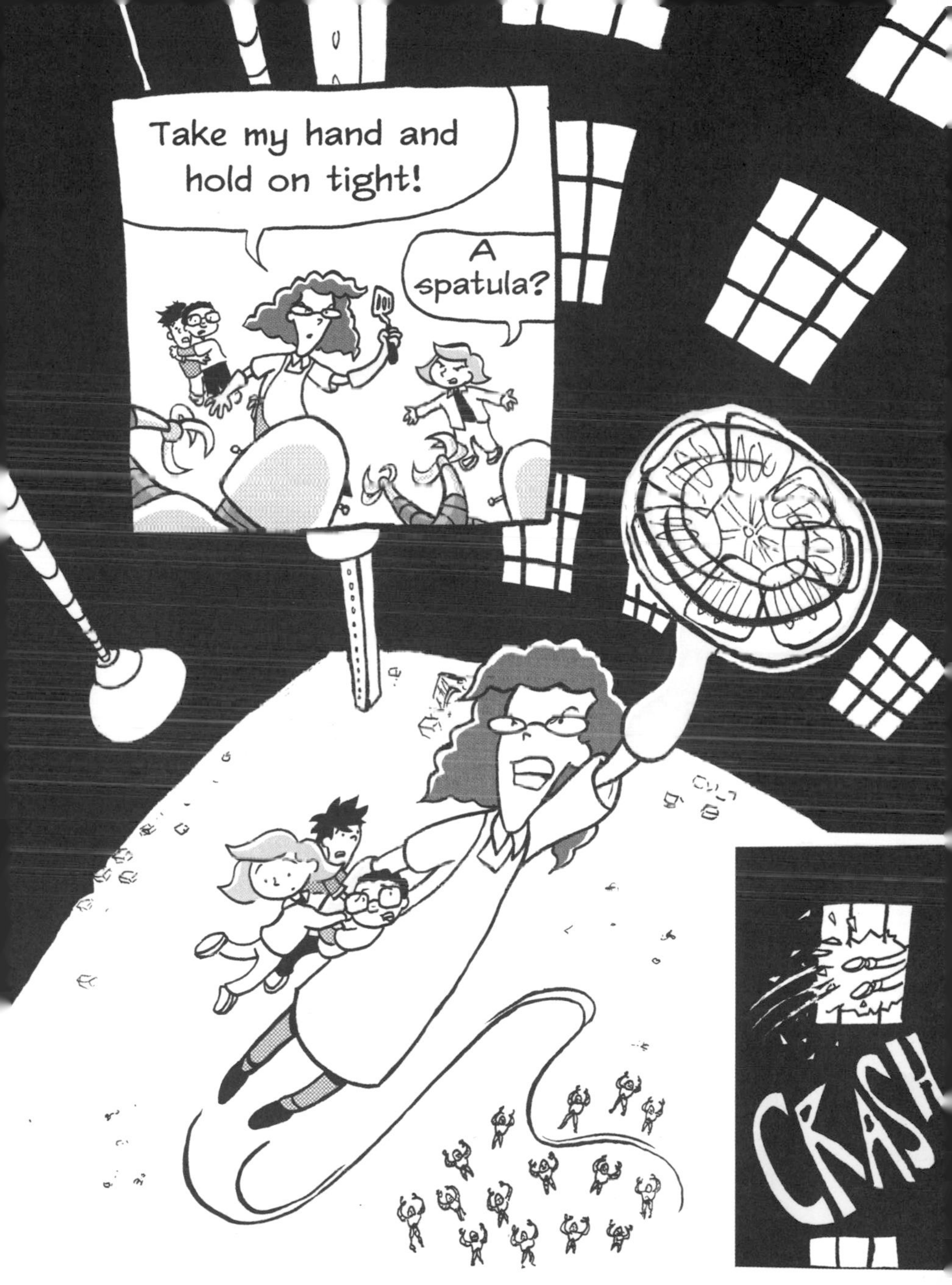
Take my hand and hold on tight!
A spatula?
CRASH

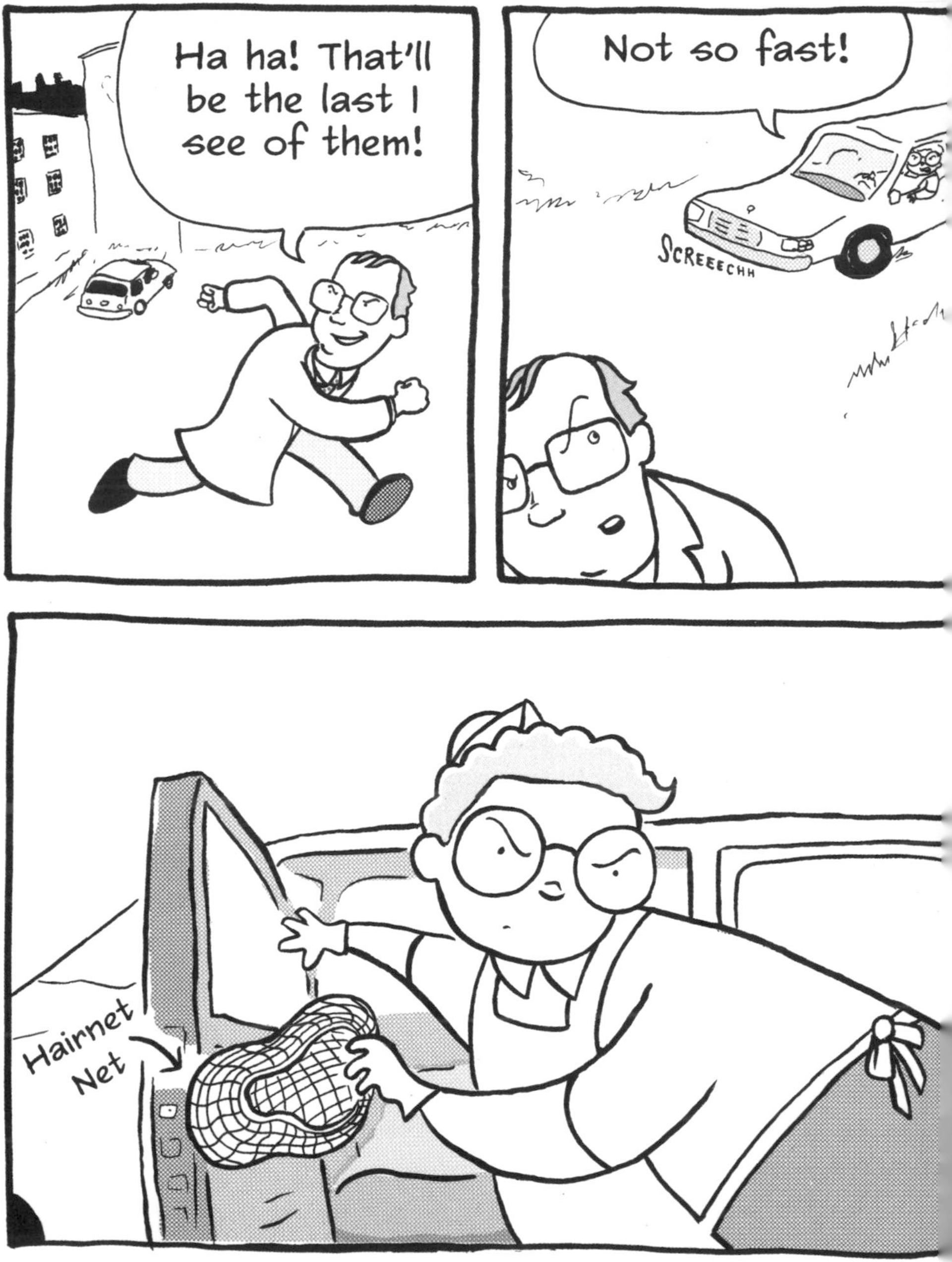

Ha ha! That'll be the last I see of them!
Not so fast!
SCREEECHH
Hairnet Net

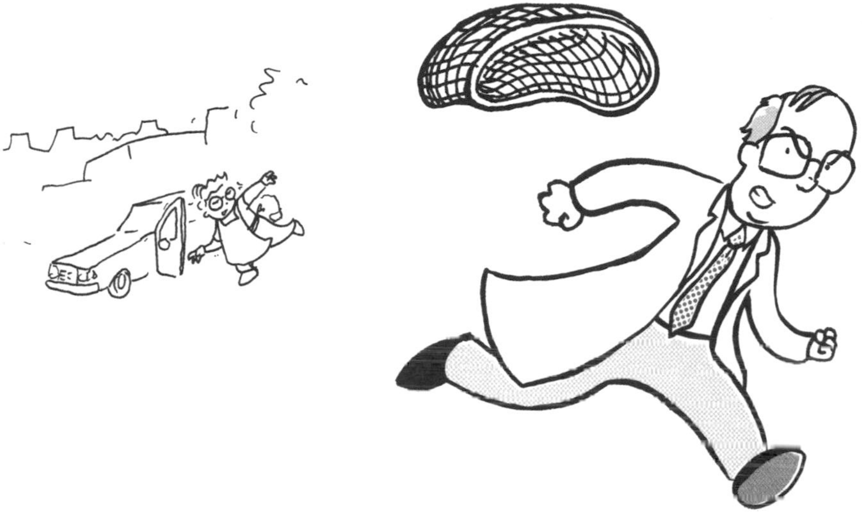

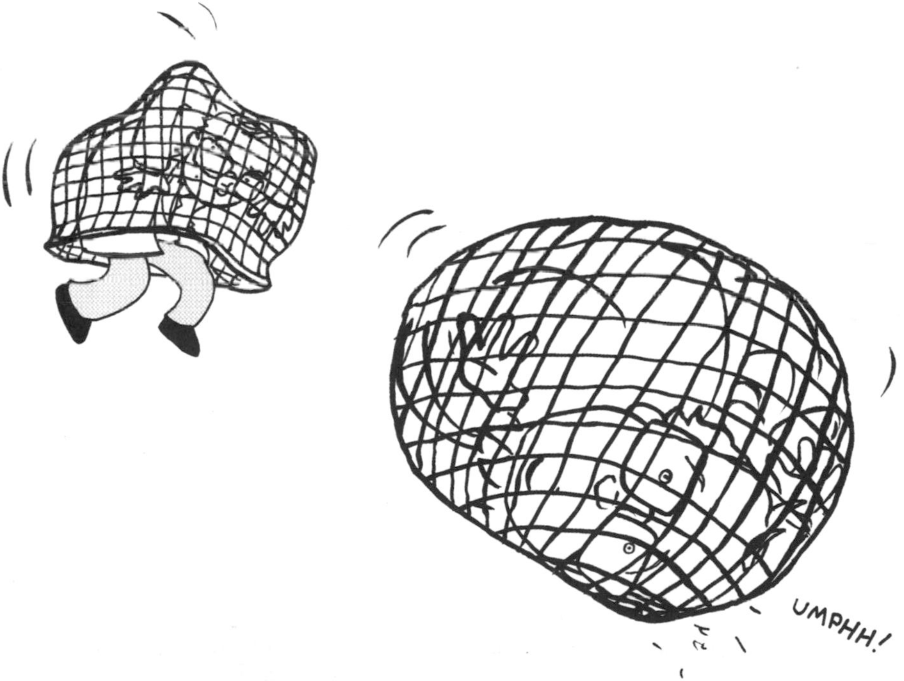
UMPHH!

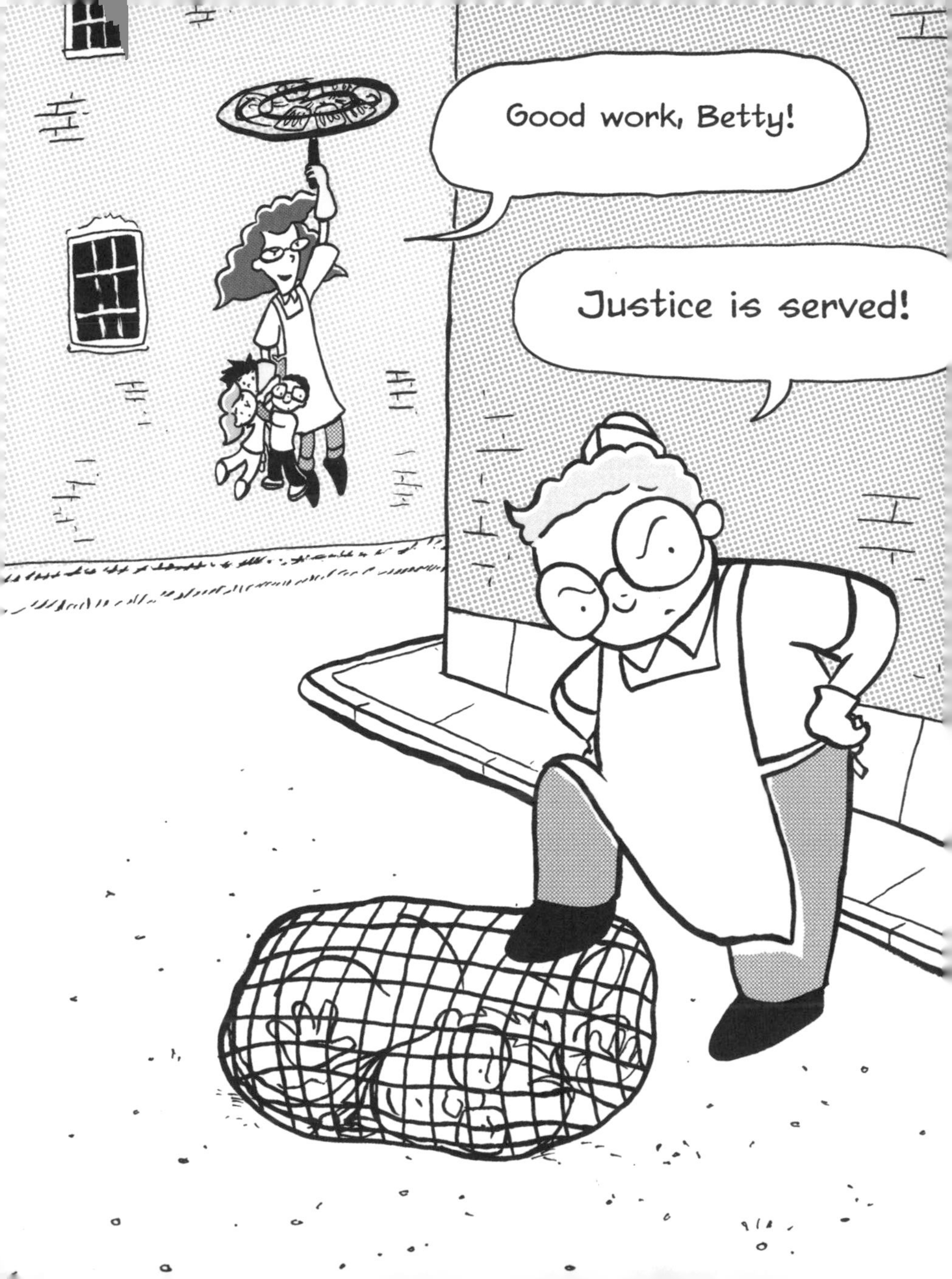
Good work, Betty!
Justice is served!

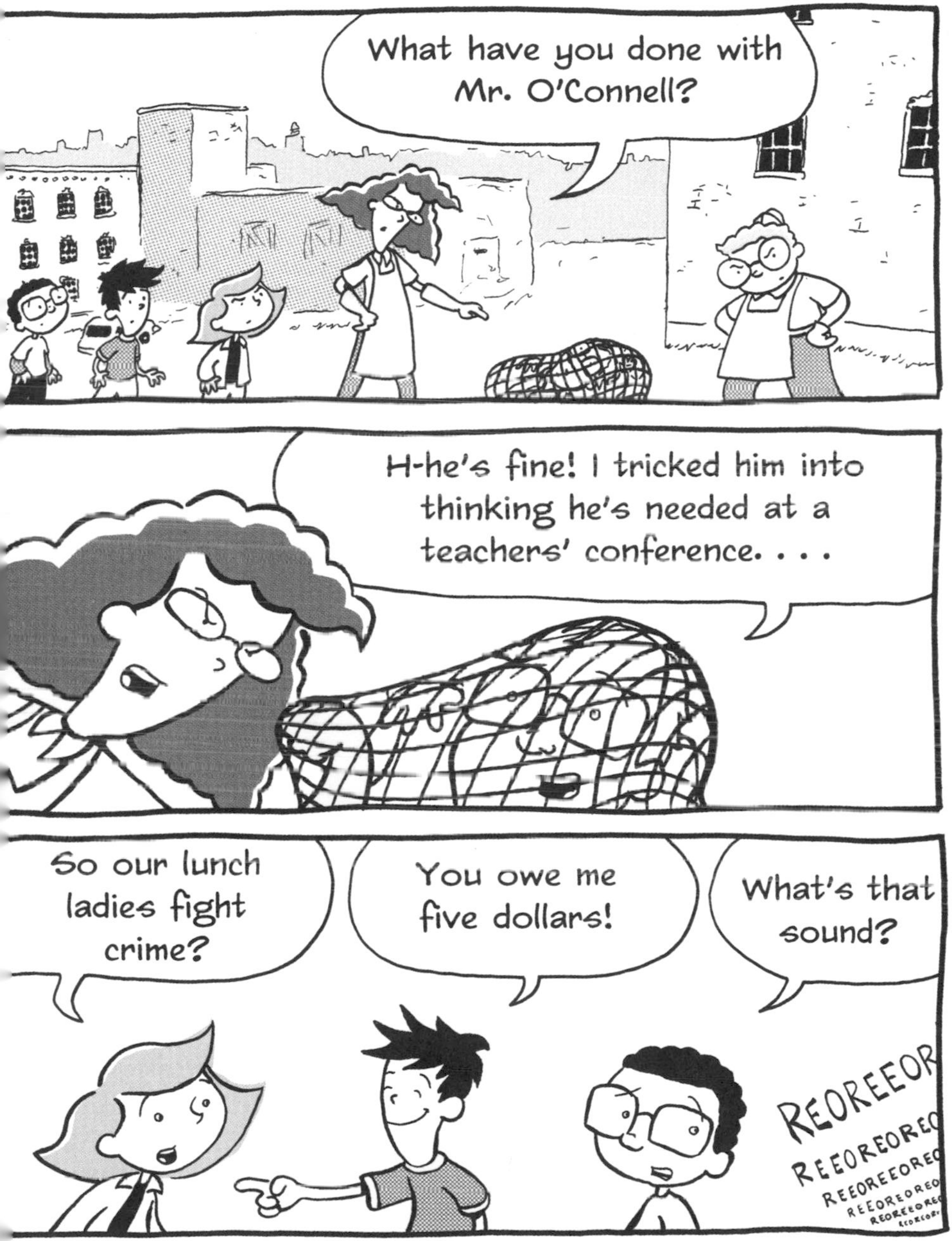
What have you done with Mr. O'Connell?
H-he's fine! I tricked him into thinking he's needed at a teachers' conference. . . .
So our lunch ladies fight crime?
You owe me five dollars!
What's that sound?
REOREEOR
REEOREOREO
REEOREEOREO
REEOREEOREO
REEOREEOREO

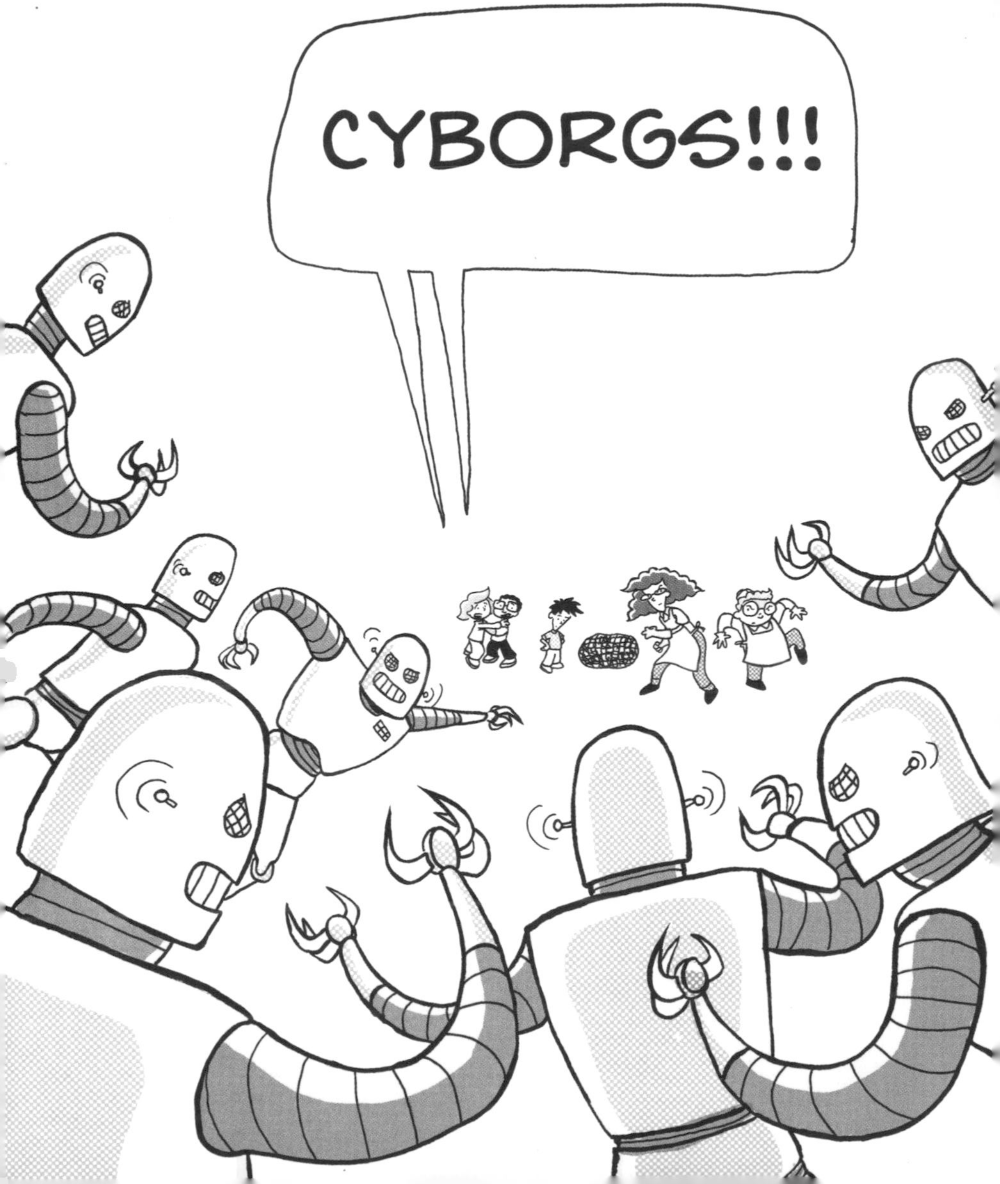
CYBORGS!!!

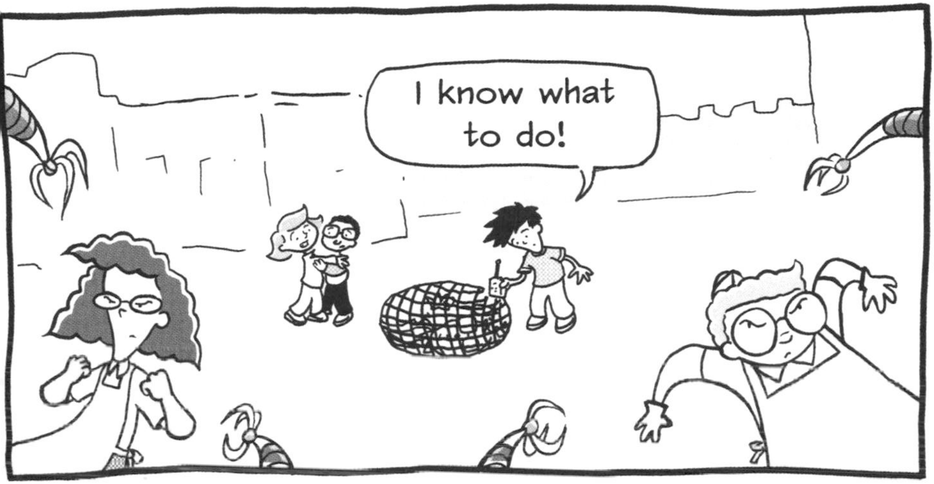
I know what to do!

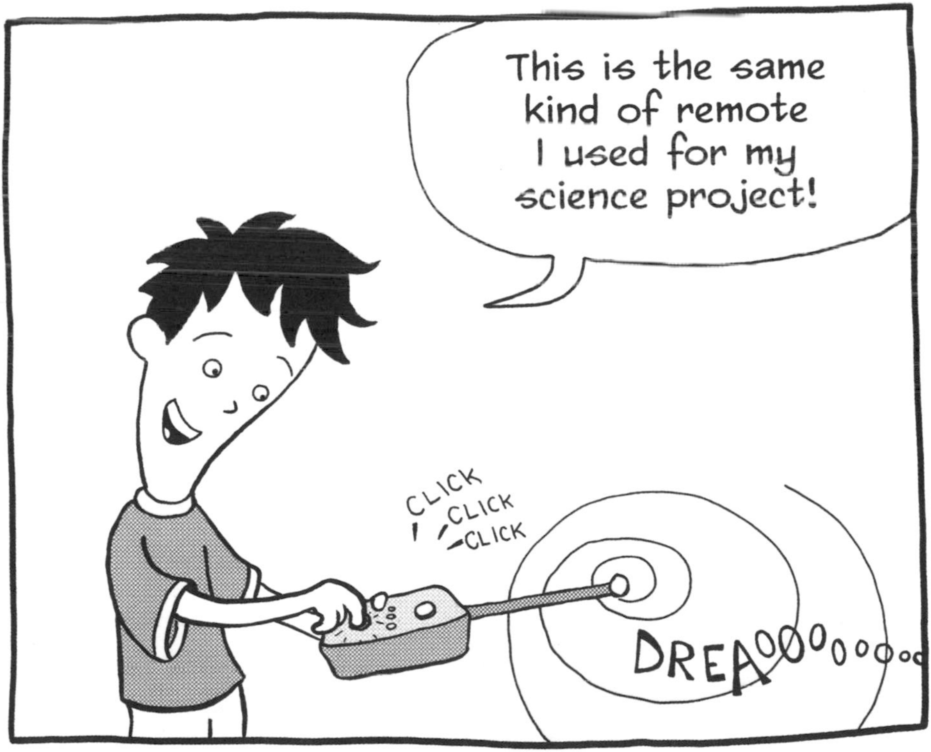
This is the same kind of remote I used for my science project!
CLICK CLICK CLICK
DREAOOOooo..

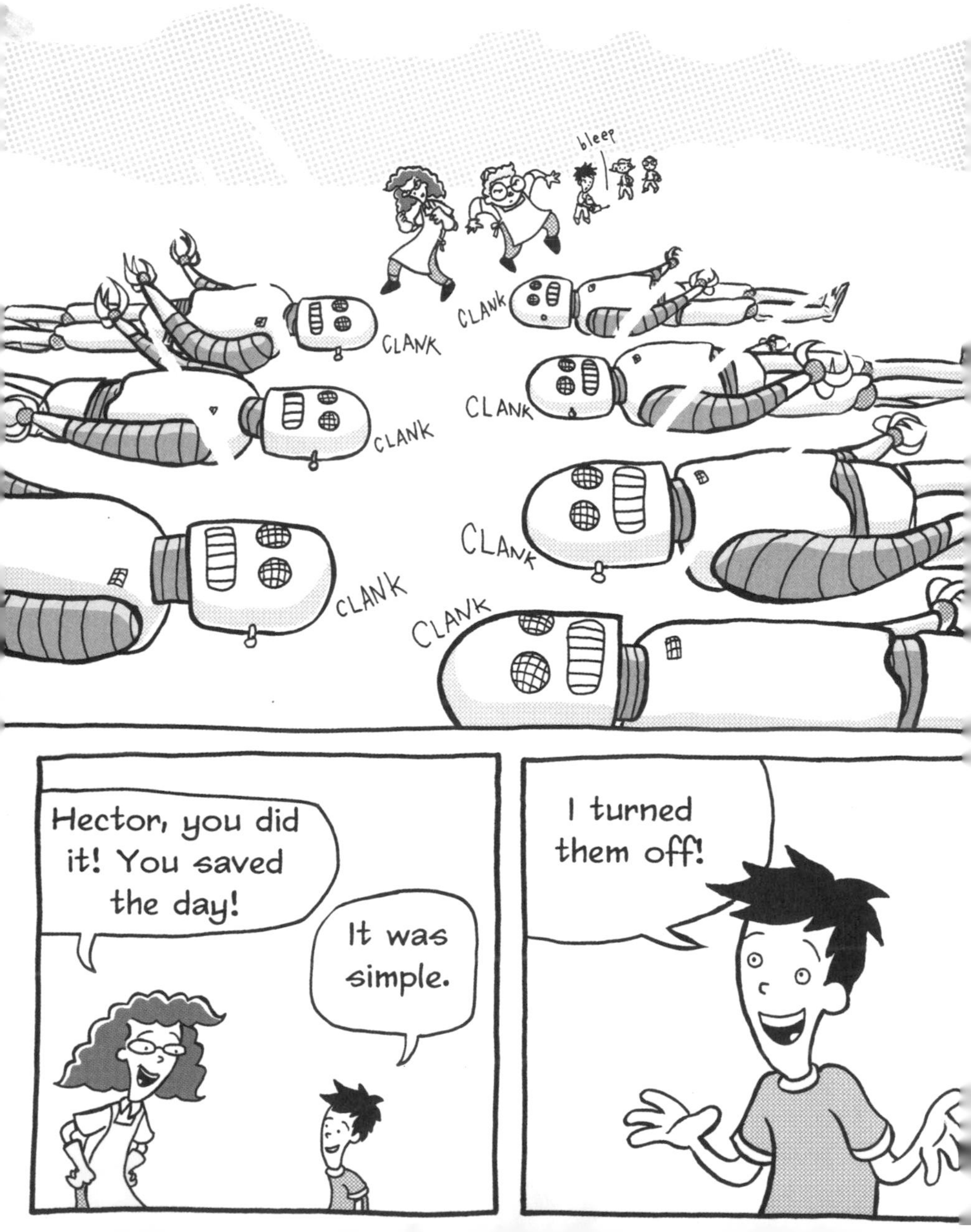
bleep
CLANK
CLANK
CLANK
CLANK
CLANK
CLANK
CLANK
Hector, you did it! You saved the day!
It was simple.
I turned them off!

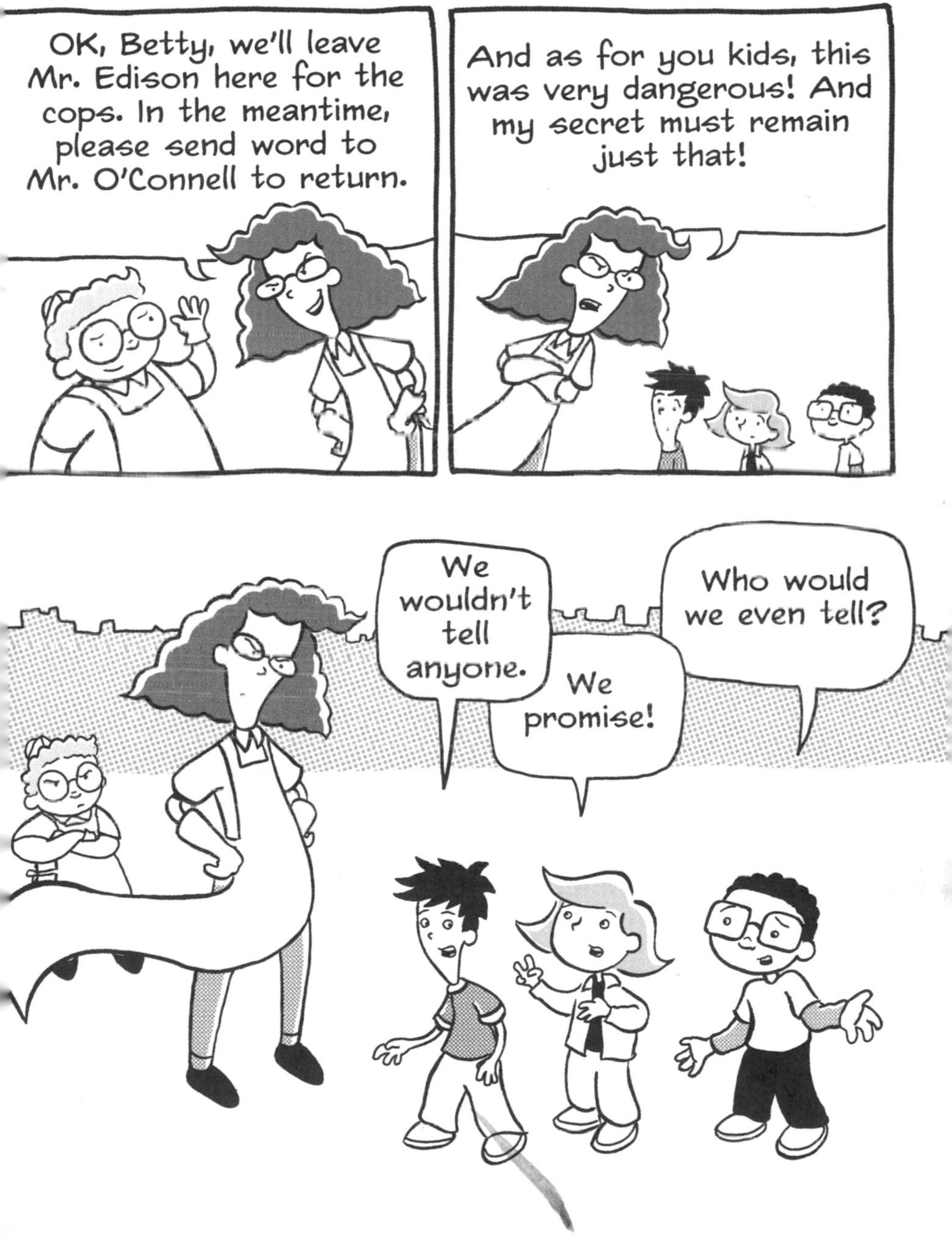
OK, Betty, we'll leave Mr. Edison here for the cops. In the meantime, please send word to Mr. O'Connell to return.
And as for you kids, this was very dangerous! And my secret must remain just that!
We wouldn't tell anyone.
We promise!
Who would we even tell?

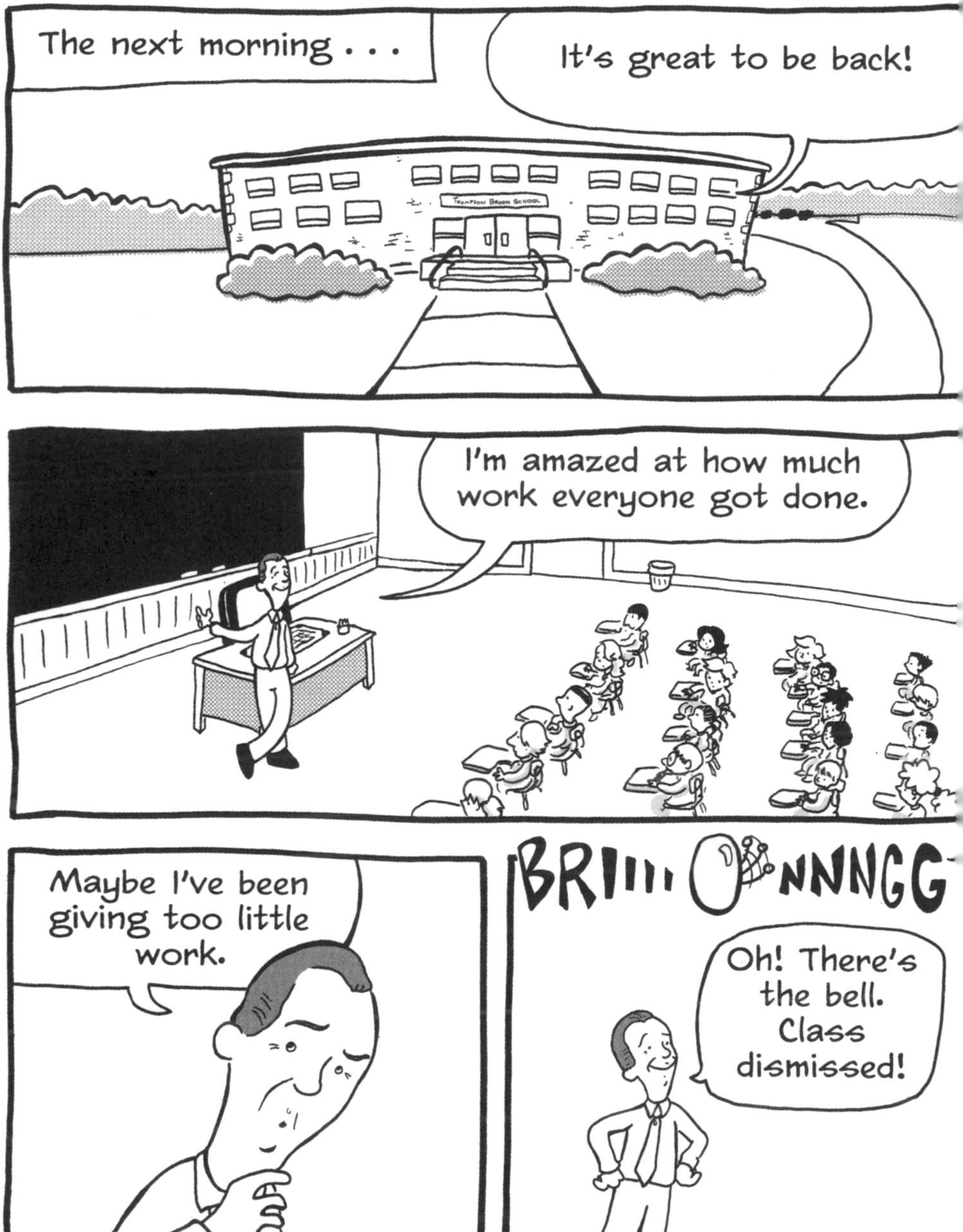
The next morning . . .
It's great to be back!
I'm amazed at how much work everyone got done.
Maybe I've been giving too little work.
BRIIII NNNGG
Oh! There's the bell. Class dismissed!

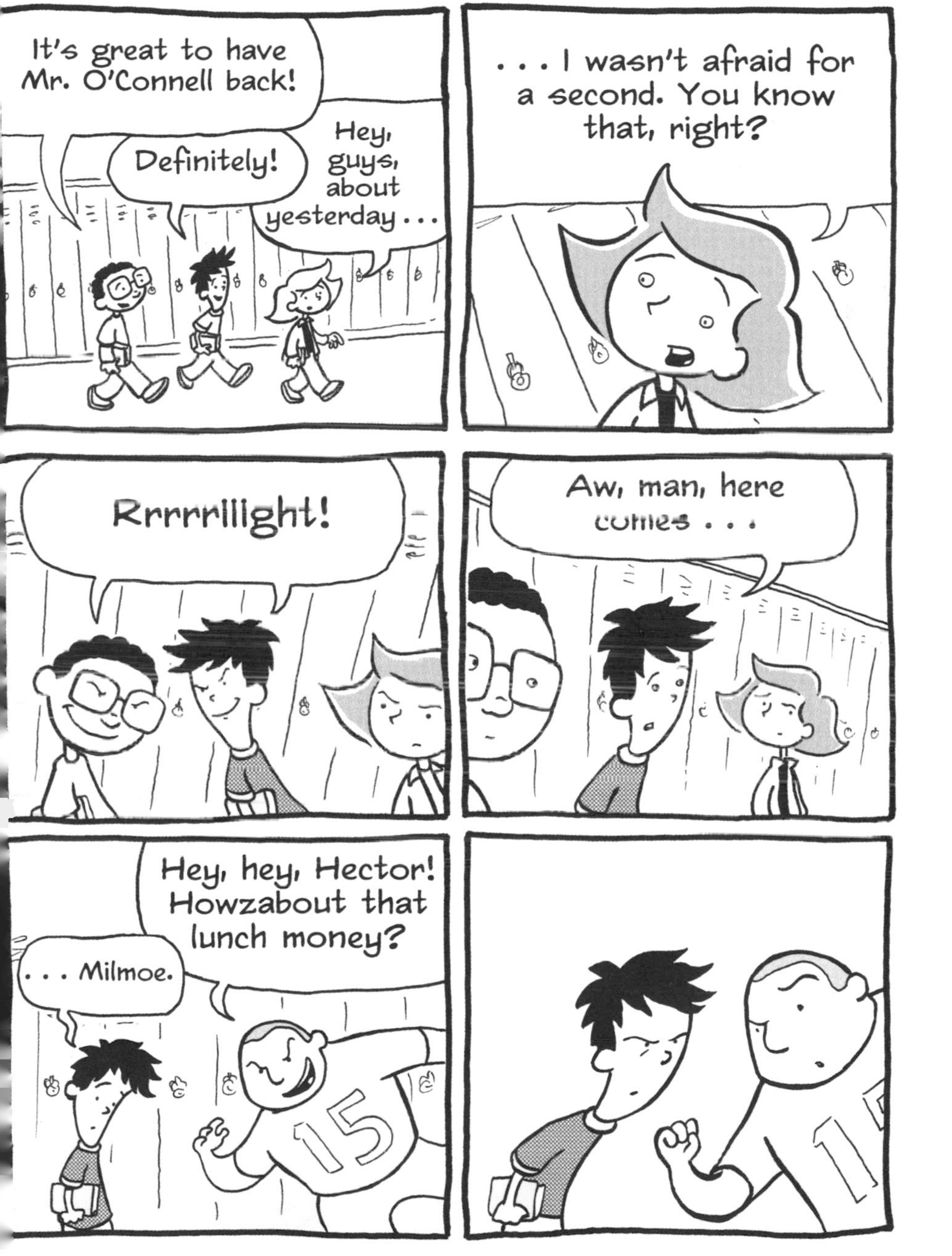
It's great to have Mr. O'Connell back!
Definitely!
Hey, guys, about yesterday . . .
. . . I wasn't afraid for a second. You know that, right?
Rrrrrlllght!
Aw, man, here comes . . .
. . . Milmoe.
Hey, hey, Hector! Howzabout that lunch money?

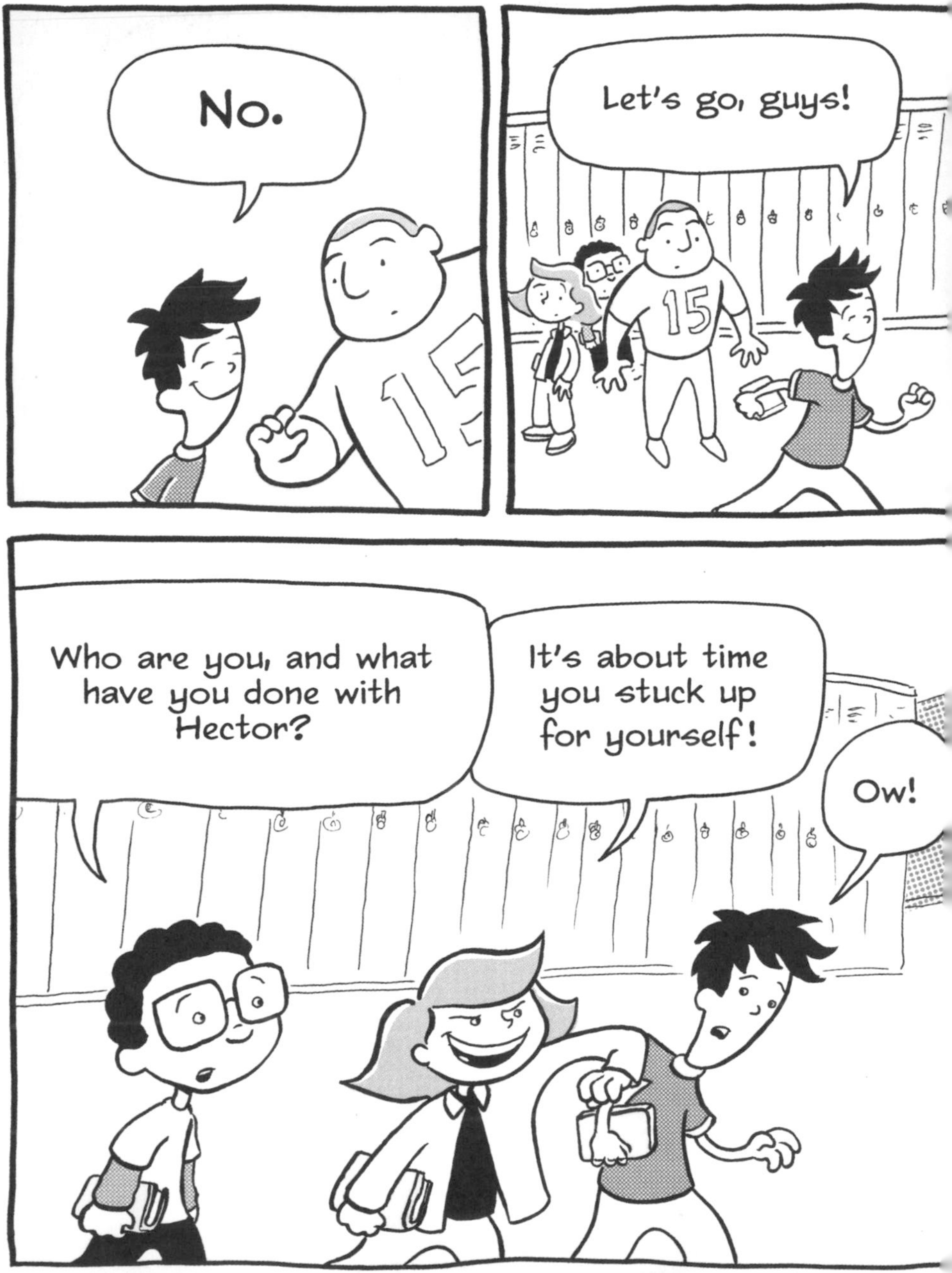
No.
Let's go, guys!
Who are you, and what have you done with Hector?
It's about time you stuck up for yourself!
Ow!

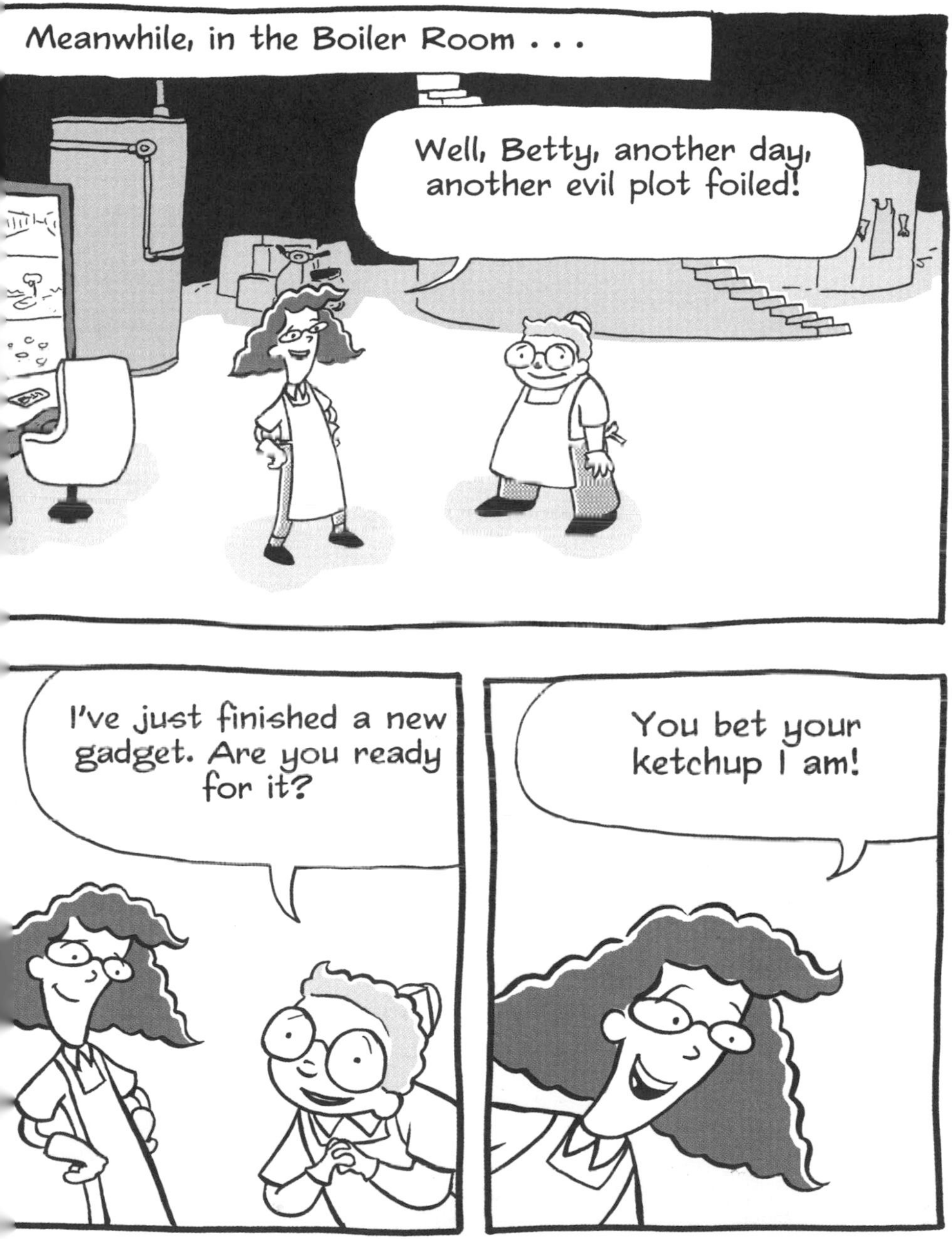
Meanwhile, in the Boiler Room . . .
Well, Betty, another day, another evil plot foiled!
I've just finished a new gadget. Are you ready for it?
You bet your ketchup I am!

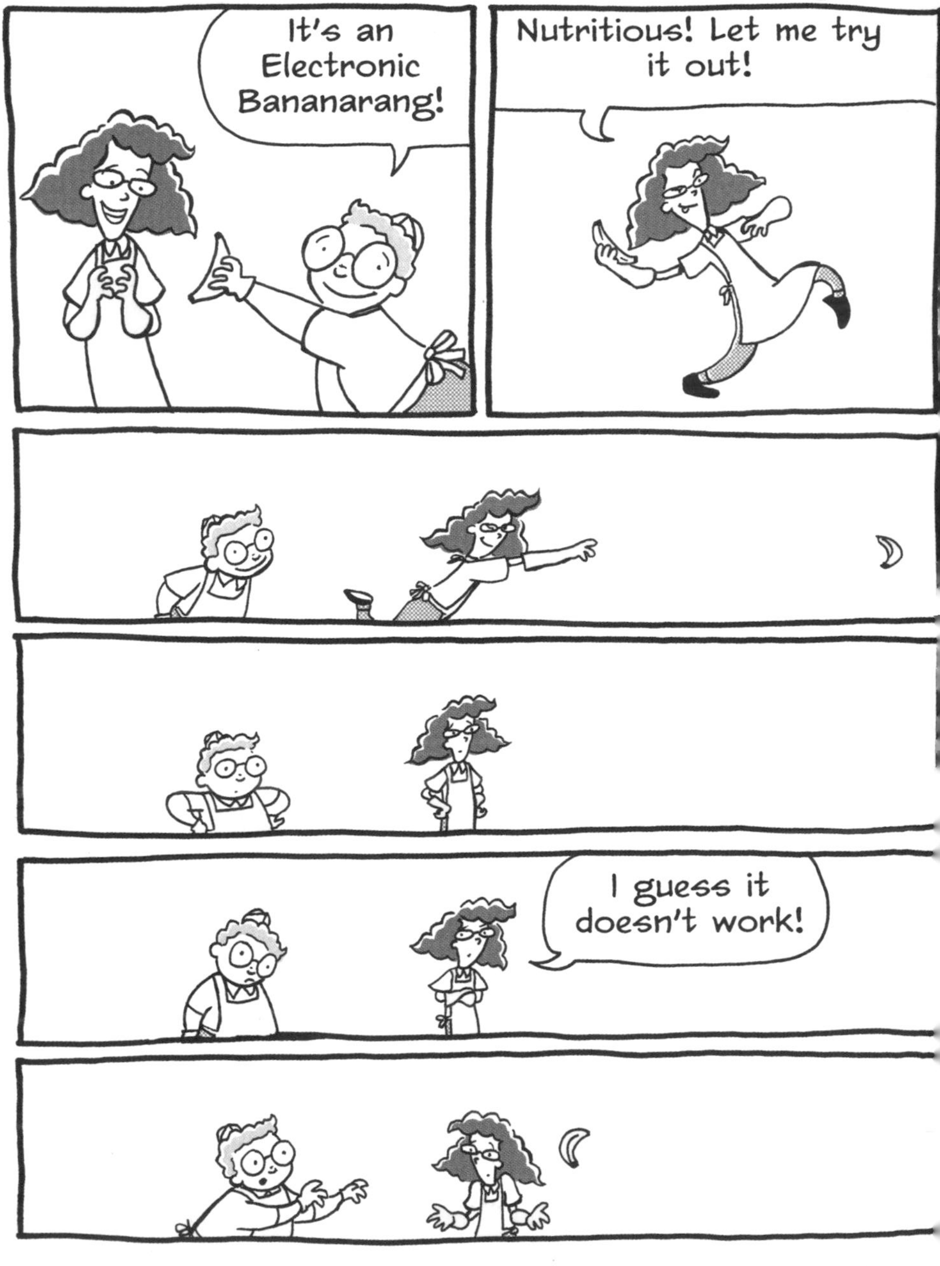
It's an Electronic Bananarang!
Nutritious! Let me try it out!
I guess it doesn't work!

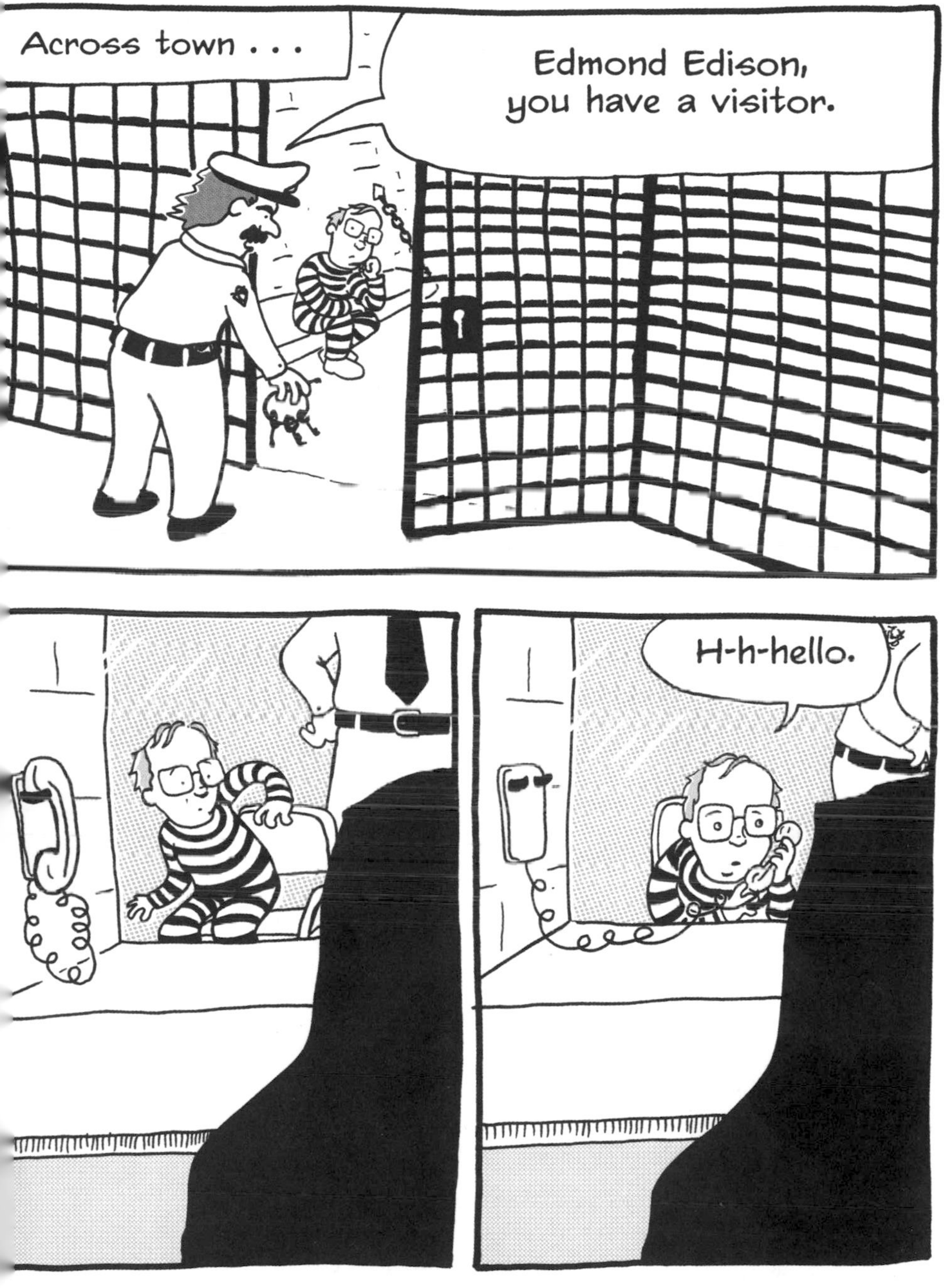
Across town . . .
Edmond Edison, you have a visitor.
H-h-hello.

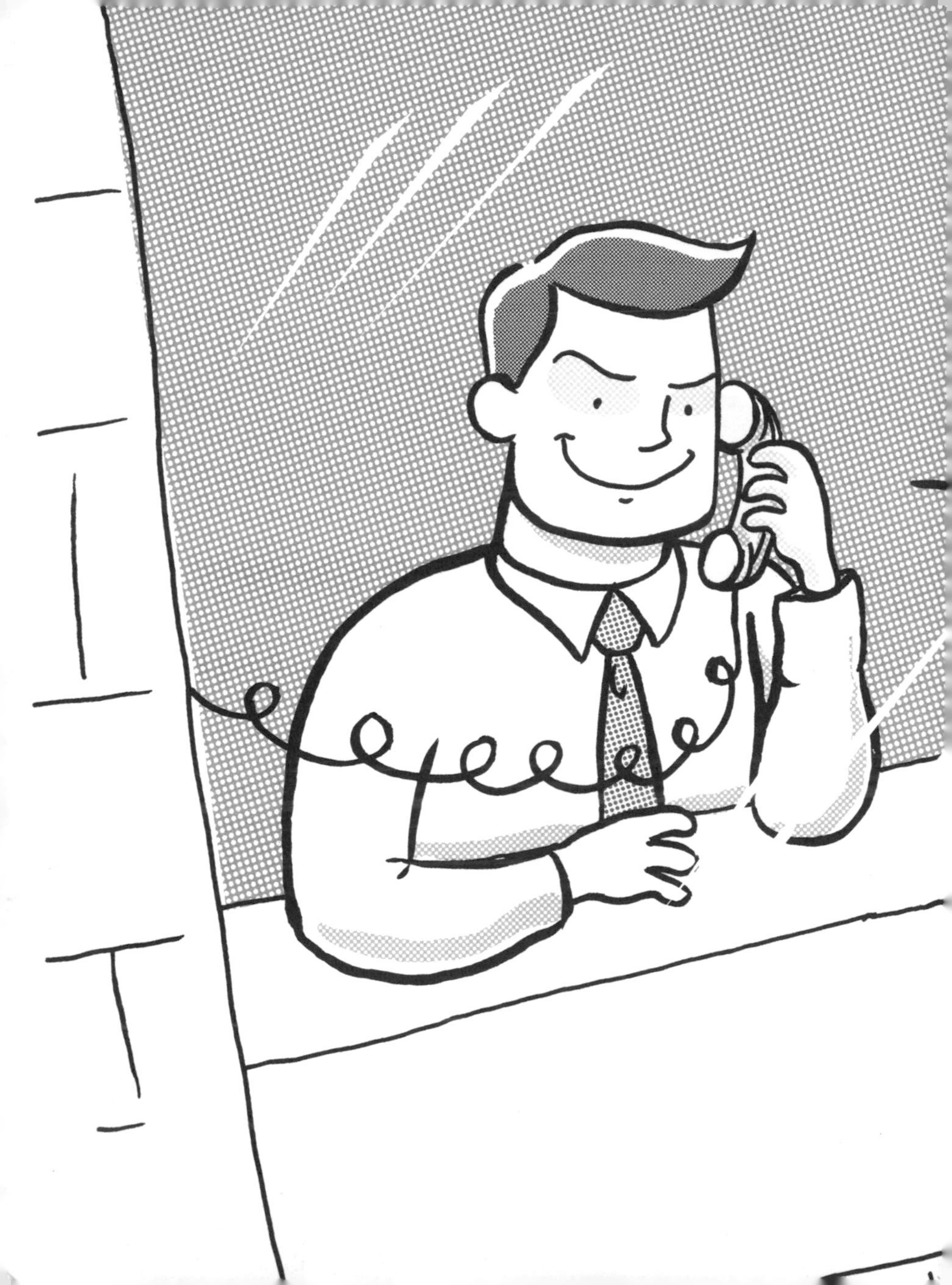

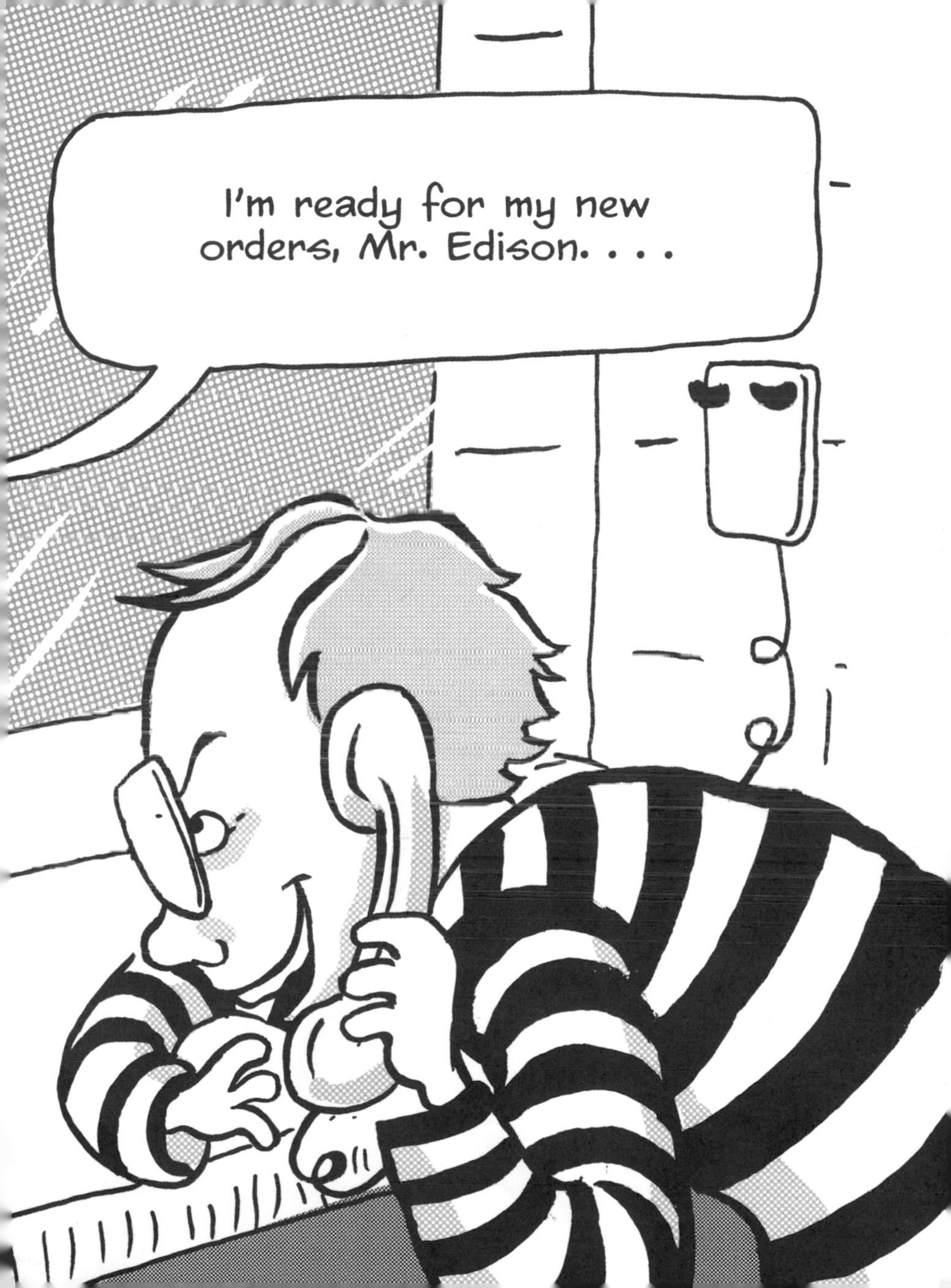
I'm ready for my new orders, Mr. Edison. . . .

FOR MY G
—J.J.K.

THIS IS A BORZOI BOOK PUBLISHED BY ALFRED A. KNOPF

All rights reserved. Published in the United States by Alfred A. Knopf, an imprint of Random House Children's Books, a division of Random House, Inc., New York.

Knopf, Borzoi Books, and the colophon are registered trademarks of Random House, Inc.

Visit us on the Web! www.randomhouse.com/kids

Educators and librarians, for a variety of teaching tools,
visit us at www.randomhouse.com/teachers

Library of Congress Cataloging-in-Publication Data
Krosoczka, Jarrett.
Lunch lady and the cyborg substitute / Jarrett J. Krosoczka. — 1st ed.
p. cm.
Summary: The school lunch lady is a secret crime fighter who uncovers an evil plot to replace all the popular teachers with robots.
ISBN 978-0-375-84683-0 (trade) — ISBN 978-0-375-94683-7 (lib. bdg.)
1. Graphic novels. [1. Graphic novels. 2. Robots—Fiction. 3. School lunchrooms, cafeterias, etc.—Fiction. 4. Schools—Fiction.] I. Title.
PZ7.7.K75Lu 2009
[Fic]—dc22
2008004709

The illustrations in this book were created using ink on paper and digital coloring.

MANUFACTURED IN MALAYSIA
July 2009
10 9 8 7 6 5 4 3

First Edition